ON SECOND
THOUGHT

Praise for C. Spencer

"*Truth or Dare* is an entirely fun read. When *Truth or Dare* reaches into the realm of the erotic, it excels. Such scenes are sexy and palpable; they're striking and tense…and there's much solace to be found in the book's snowed-in, relaxed atmosphere and pleasing plot. This book is a must for fans of multiple-character structures and shows like *The L Word*. *Truth or Dare* is charming with its stories of queer women falling in and out of love. It is smart, funny, and romantic—the perfect read for a snowy night in."—*Foreword Reviews*

"*Truth or Dare* is a thoughtful, intimate, slice-of-life story that delves into relationships and the intertwining of lives. It's a must read for those who enjoy unique and well-done character work and a multiple-character structure that allows for a more expansive look at our humanity. Because of its depth and many layers woven into this work, I know it's one of those books that will offer something new with each read, so it's a story I'll revisit many times."—*The Lesbian Review*

"This is a great story for a debut novel. One that quite honestly, I wasn't expecting. This is more than a romance novel. I think it's a Lesbian Romance and Drama novel. Great debut novel and I can't wait for what's next from C. Spencer."—*Les Reveur*

By the Author

Truth or Dare

On Second Thought

Visit us at www.boldstrokesbooks.com

ON SECOND THOUGHT

by

C. Spencer

2020

ON SECOND THOUGHT

ISBN 13: 978-1-63555-415-1

THIS TRADE PAPERBACK ORIGINAL IS PUBLISHED BY
BOLD STROKES BOOKS, INC.
P.O. BOX 249
VALLEY FALLS, NY 12185

FIRST EDITION: FEBRUARY 2020

CREDITS
EDITOR: RUTH STERNGLANTZ
PRODUCTION DESIGN: STACIA SEAMAN
COVER DESIGN BY TAMMY SEIDICK

Acknowledgments

I enjoy writing. But quite honestly, there's little reason to put as much effort into it as I have without a reader on the other side of the page. On most days, I like to think of writing as a conversation I might be having with an old friend. So thank you for picking up this book and for making that conversation possible.

I'm eternally grateful to my editor, Ruth Sternglantz, for her brilliant (and that's no exaggeration) critique and guidance, for steering me in the right direction—and for brainstorming me through the areas I simply could not have navigated on my own.

To the entire team at Bold Strokes Books.

To Radclyffe for her humility, vision, and leadership. Thank you for backing this book.

To my aunt Debbie, who taught me the meaning of loyalty, friendship, and family.

To my daughter Tera, who is my everything.

And with immense love and gratitude to my wife, who makes the best daiquiris, reads drafts, braves to offer suggestions (even if it's mostly "add more sex scenes"), and encourages me—not an easy feat. This would not have happened without you.

To every girl who has stayed home alone on a Friday night
listening to love songs or watching rom-coms
in hopes of finding true love.

CHAPTER ONE

How to Raise a Tomboy

Madisen

It isn't every day that your wife says she's walking out on you, taking the kid, leaving your twenty-one-year-old cat (who was yours to begin with), and good luck paying the mortgage on your own. Let's break out the bubbly. Where have I been for the past ten years because I thought I was sitting pretty.

But I only have myself to blame for not catching those warning signs. Not just the arguments but the fact that neither of us could compromise, let alone see the other side, certainly not in the way we used to.

And maybe I didn't want to see her side. Maybe I had stopped listening. Maybe I wanted to talk—talk over her, talk louder, talk before I even listened to a word she said. And she stopped understanding me. She stopped looking at me that way. And I stopped wanting her to. Until we eventually stepped back to marvel at all of those subtle cracks that had ruptured into a gaping Grand Canyon between the two of us.

But who actually realizes how emotionally unstable you've become until you're standing in front of some small-town county courthouse, face-to-face with the family court judge, hashing out some mutually beneficial visitation schedule complete with child support payments and split assets and 401(k)s? Signing it all away as if this really was just a legal contract.

All because of those two little words: *It's over.*

To me it was a question mark. To her, an exclamation.

And anyway, that's how parenting became constrained into our court-ordered biweekly schedule—with my weekend commencing on

Friday, as in last night, and our daughter Jordan camping out on my living room floor watching Netflix as I dealt with emails well into the night.

In fact, I think it was well after midnight before I crawled into bed, which explains why I'm flat-out exhausted notwithstanding three cups of the strongest of all brewed coffee. Blissfully spent, mind you, given the outset of my day wasn't marked in panic as it had been just a year ago, when our new arrangement officially commenced.

Such a difference a year makes. In some ways, at least.

Still, my weekends haven't changed all that much.

Which brings us to today and our current midday distraction, watching Andi, my BFF, in cleats obliterating her opponents while immersed in her field of soccer dykes, all sporting low ponytails or cropped frosted tips. Add my chilled bottle of Snapple unsweetened straight-up tea. Coconut sunscreen. And a pack of Post-it flags prepped to study this year's *International Building Code*.

Thinking to myself, if we all just could be as athletically inclined as she, if only for that hero's reception.

Unlike me up here, yanking the corner of my blanket back into the shade, a shadow that keeps shifting with the sun. On one of those rare but welcome days when it's not pouring down rain across New England.

Until eventually I've settled comfortably into my book, and my gaze drifts over the edge of the page where I catch Andi ducking through the crowd as she heads through the team in my direction, cleats tugging turf, shirt hiked across flushed cheeks in that *oh my* way, before she's collapsing beside me on the blanket, palms tucked under her head as she gazes up at a Tiffany-blue sky.

"Did you win," I say, "or is this another inning?"

"There are no innings in soccer," she tells me with such a glare. "I scored the winning goal. Weren't you even watching?"

"So that's what that was," I say, scanning the field to find my kid's now kicking the ball around.

And who knows, maybe I do have this parenting thing down after all. If only I could say the same about *single*.

Because why is it two gay parents at a park shout *Modern Family*, while solo lesbian me—even right here beside Andi—gets labeled *straight girl* instead? Every single time.

Andi, on the other hand, enjoys her constant relationship turnstile.

The good news being, for a fleeting moment last weekend, as we stepped into the only gay bar left in town, drinks in hand, cracking up about who remembers what, I was almost gay by association.

And that would be where I met Rae.

Chapter Two

Racked

Rae

"Look, I have too many deadlines," I tell Avery.

Not helping matters is a terse email I mistakenly read from a client, leading me to Command+Q him away since I have little patience for this new tier of mansplaining. Particularly on a Saturday night, when my response should not be par for the course.

And still Avery's insisting I join her as opposed to spending another night hunched over my keyboard amid the glow of task lighting with a chilled bottle of Dogfish Head as I click through thousands of photos, cataloging each.

"You're tempted," she says, only to bribe me with a drink.

"Deadlines, dear."

"But I'm usually so convincing," she tells me.

"You need to up your game," I say.

"Why isn't this working?"

"I didn't say it wasn't."

Because I admit, Avery's beginning to wear me down. Or maybe I just need to get out.

Even still, the thought of becoming her captive audience as she mourns the loss of true love number…whatever we're up to now—the biologist. And that's this thing she does—conjuring up this and that, all of her goings on, in short hoping to convince me that 1) either I stay home and sit on the phone with her like this indefinitely, or 2) I hang up, give up, and join her. It's pretty obvious where this is going.

And music does tend to drown the worst of it, right?

Which means, predictably, by the time the sun's setting into a pretty sweet Coca-Cola red on the best excuse to pull out my leather racing coat sort of a night, I'm making my way toward the bartender in his hipster hat to order a beer on tap.

Afterward, I survey the Jack Daniel's, the Captain Morgan, the Vieux Pontarlier and Jose Cuervo lining shelves just beyond his shoulder. Edison bulbs dangling like pendants. And of course Avery's arrived—her thick nondescript curls let down for a night of I can only imagine, paired with that appreciative gaze.

And I'm enjoying the muffled beat spilling over from the dance floor when she shouts, "They're so perfect together," only to drop more of her sarcasm as I chalk my cue.

"They're not perfect," I say.

"*She* was perfect," Avery says.

"And you could literally care less about her before she walked out," I add as I break the balls. Thinking it's warm enough to prop a window.

But I peel off my coat instead. And I'm hitching it on the back of an empty chair when I hear, "I met this firefighter."

"Where?" I say.

"Panera during lunch," she tells me, "Friday. In steel-toed boots and full uniform."

"And did you swoon?" I say.

"I did, but—"

"There's a *but*?" Aghast, knowing her.

"She's not a top."

"Don't tell me she's a bottom."

"Not exactly," she says.

"Nobody can help you there," I say.

"I know," she says. "I'm far too selective."

"Or something like that," I say, now fixed on her. "It's your turn."

As she draws back her cue with, "Dreamy, though," bending across the table just so—those wide pendants casting shadows until her face is only half lit.

"Which means you're heading into your next Shakespearean tragedy," I say.

Afterward, she leans back against me, and we're peering at the dance floor where a few've stepped in, boisterous, making their rounds. "So what if I am?"

A mood that shifts when I catch this caramel blonde with her hair let down after what could've easily been a careless stroll along the shore. Disheveled in that surrendered sort of way. To which I would imagine, noting our glances, the sizing up, that she's convinced herself it might be less conspicuous to be apart from that crowded crowd out there. Her gaze catching mine.

Really, though, I need to quit staring.

"And who's this?" Avery says, startling me.

"How would I know?"

"And yet you can't take your eyes off her," she says.

Gesturing as if to say *It's your turn*. And I flatten a palm on the pool table, lifting my gaze, somehow managing the shot. Then afterward trying not to notice—but noticing—she's no longer alone. Which figures.

"Want me to handle that for you?" Avery's saying.

"As if I need help."

"I'll go distract her friend," she adds, bottoming her drink.

"So you're forfeiting the game?" I say. "Come on." As she hands me the cue then wanders off with the nonchalance of someone who has played this game a million times before.

Leaving me with little time to think it through, let alone hide the obvious.

As I make my way over and take a seat—admittedly nervous as hell.

To the tune of running palms down the length of my jeans as I shrug out a *hi*. Because that was a brilliant line. And, yeah, this girl's too much. But I'm pretty sure she's on to me. "I seem to have lost my opponent," I say.

"I've noticed."

"You wouldn't want to take her place?"

Next, she's mouthing something like, "Sure."

And I brush her thigh unintentionally, drown too deep in this, in her immediacy and the scent of something light, layered, her gaze clearly going to my head.

But what a commotion they're making in the next room. That's what she's thinking about, isn't she? That's what she's focused on.

As I get up, glance back, and offer a hand. "Are you in?" And, yeah, that she is.

Introducing herself. "Madisen," I hear.

So now I'm wondering everything. "Rae." Like that look and what it means. How half-witted and useless I feel. Because why is it the simplest thing, like a game of pool, can feel so much more complicated with a girl like this against my hips?

Her, bending over the table as I trace the muscles along her arm. Her gaze intent on the length of a cue before turning—as if her eyes are searching mine, and right, I'm to make the next move, eh? And this is where I could say something reasonably intelligent. But why haven't I? *Like this*, I say, hair trickling along my arm. *You want that ball in the side pocket.*

But what am I doing?

I'm stepping aside to find my empty drink at the table, admiring her build, her chest pressed against red felt. That beat pounding in time with my pulse.

And it's after that play, the slow anticipation, her studied stroke, which leads to my next three in a row, that I win.

I win and grab my coat and why not. "Could I buy you a drink?"

"Shouldn't I?" she says.

"Hey, follow me," I say and reach back and feel her hand.

Even still there's something in the way she orders, squeezing between stools, her gaze trailing the stretch of the bar as if she was expecting someone to step up. Me, transfixed by strands now winding along the front of everything unbuttoned, and I'm sorry, I'm thinking I'm too into this girl. She's just my kind of incredible, that's all.

Which is why I hardly notice when she turns to me with, "Confession—"

So I ask.

And she says, "I've never played in my life. I mean, not the actual game. I don't count racking a few balls as a kid, matching colors mostly. At that age, it's more like a puzzle."

"Which means you're not into the game but only played to appease me," I say, "or perhaps you're oddly into puzzles."

"I don't mind the game," she says. "And I wouldn't do anything to appease."

Next I sense her hand at my back as I lean against the bar. "You're not that bad," I say. "I can tell. So I'm thinking this might've been your plan all along."

"What's that?"

"Throwing the game deliberately," I say, "so I might buy you a drink?"

And she laughs. "Is that what you think. That I'm interested in…a drink?" As we settle into this look that doesn't want to stop. At least, I don't want it to. But her drink arrives and mine. And next, we're shouldering past the crowd, grabbing a seat as she draws a straw to her lips before leaning in. "You wouldn't be okay if I won the game, would you?"

"Is it that obvious?" I say.

"You must not lose often," she says.

"That I don't."

As light shifts and shadows cross her features.

Then I catch Avery's gaze from across the way. But this knee is brushing mine. And, yeah, it's warm in here again. "You're good," she says.

"I can be."

But with each opening, each *tell me about yourself*, each response cut short or unheard aside from her gaze fixed, which makes me lose all cool, I take a drink. As we play our conversation out nonverbally. As if we knew too much. While I enjoy the legendary taste of this drink.

And her.

"Can I ask you something?" she says.

"And what's that?" I say.

As she grips my thigh—"Why are we still here?"—her voice breathy.

It was the last thing I heard before I stopped listening. At least until I'm glancing across at the clock and it's four a.m. and she's flushed against a pillow and so am I. Even those rumors just outside our window have settled into still. Her gaze, indecipherable. Moonlit.

But this is where I roll over, slip on jeans, get her number, drive her back.

And shouldn't I be exhausted? But that hasn't happened yet, either.

Instead she's tucked in the crook of my shoulder, heavy. Rising as I breathe. Hair clinging to my chest.

"I should head back," I hear. But they're the most unconvincing words I've heard all night.

"You should," I say.

Weaving her fingers through mine.

So why is this so unsettling? It's not as if I expected her to stay, share coffee, break bread. This is not that. It's a night. And yet, as she slides knees off the edge of my bed and makes her way across the length of open space in silhouette, it doesn't feel like good-bye.

I find her, sensing hips first, then breasts, skin chilled as her shirt slips down around her abdomen. Her lips brushing mine. Her scent lingering as I dress, reluctantly. My soul sinking.

Outside, just whispers under the hum of crickets as I open the door to the car and she slips in and so do I. As I watch a knee lift, those streaks of light shading across her face. Her hair, the most beautiful mess the entire way.

And we exchange too many glances. Yet so few words.

"I'll call you," I say as I shift the car into Park. And it's not a friendly kiss before she opens the door. It's that kind of kiss you never want to remember and you never want to forget at the same time.

CHAPTER THREE

Rope Me In

Madisen

The only way I could describe it is this: it felt like adultery—the sort of thing you can't help but fumble into for this reason or that.

At a table where we eyed one another sipping drinks.

Set back amid shadows, unassuming. Her gaze catching mine. And in a voice so charming, so pleasing, she spoke—leaning tight as if I was so familiar to her. And even still, so much of that night felt unfamiliar. Inconclusive.

In the way she could unravel me. How my words kept spilling out as her gaze followed along with my every bit of nothing at all. Listening as if devouring every word. Wanting more, but in that way one would wait for that single line, that certain phrase that might tip her over the edge. How could I find that?

I wanted to. But I didn't know how.

What I know is how the night felt when it kissed my skin as we strolled through darkness led by stars so splendid and crisp you'd think they would crumble. The feel of her arm at my waist under the hazy glow of a low moon. Her scent like amber or sandalwood, reminding me of everything I couldn't have. A canopy of oaks with branches blushing in color. Bursting, really. Escorting our silence. And the sounds of our reckless steps along that pavement.

Even still, I can't help but go back to that, as irrelevant as it was. The way she tucked one heel up on the seat of her chair before slipping it off. And those creases along her forehead as she rested against a palm. Listening. The dangle of keys with her stride. And as she pulled the car door shut, reaching across my knee to the dash, then fidgeting.

Rolling that tube of ChapStick, when all I could see was a shadowed curve of her jaw.

Seeming as if she was too much yet not enough at the same time. It was all so uncertain, really. Hearing as I spoke, as I smudged a thumb across my mouth, as her gaze followed along. And the subtlety of her lips as they brushed mine right before that kiss, which threw me into a rush.

And afterward, her palm slipping up my shirt as crowds and crowds of laughter filed by.

With a gaze that never left mine as her fingers slipped into my hair, my knees pressing the gear while her palm slid tightly between them. And the taste of her breath as a chill poured in. I wanted everything about her.

Which is how it all started, at least. As we drove with a window half raised and the radio low. Her shifting to Park. Me following steps, punch-drunk as she keyed the door before gripping and tugging my fingers. As she invited me in with the taste of everything I couldn't resist.

That earthy scent of leather as her coat slipped off a shoulder and she shut the door. The sound of a lock, her shoes, mine wandering in search of a light as she wrapped her arms around me, breasts pressed to mine as my hem, my thigh, just lifted. Her breath weak, her jeans rough, rubbing, hiking my skirt, as I fell against the bed, and she weighed over me with knees fixed at my sides in a room so obscure that I scarcely noticed the slow rise of her shirt. Before I felt her skin against mine in borrowed light and she pinned me down, her strength, her mouth tracing a breeze as it trailed my skin, now damp where her lips had been. Where I needed them still. But all I could hear were my sighs in an empty room, a whimper, that ache as she slipped into me with fingers that curled into moans. Hearing the limbs of trees in the wind as an elbow braced my hips and her tongue made me wet, made me swell, insensibly lingering.

❖

"You never said," Andi says, piercing the best part of my daydream. "How was your night?" She snaps the latch of her moonroof, then opens it and proceeds to lower front, rear, passenger, and driver side windows, jerking my hair along with.

"Why can't we do air conditioning?" I say. "It's ninety degrees."

"Which is nice for a change."

"Nice for hair like yours," I say, rolling my side up.

And when I turn back—"Well?"—she says, expectant.

"It was a night," I lie and check my phone, and not for that reason.

"Did she call?"

"Of course not," I say.

"So what are you reading? Is it work?"

"It's called balance," I tell her.

"Why can't you take a day off?" she mumbles.

"As if there was anything left in that life part of my work-life *to* balance," I tell her.

"Oh, stop," she says. "She'll call."

"I'm not waiting on a call," I say, refreshing my empty voicemail. "You think you know me so well."

"Because I do," she says. "And in the interim, you have a wonderful daughter to bide the time."

"Those four days a month, I know, thanks a bunch for reminding me of that big role I play in my daughter's life. Whatever, it's for the best. *In her best interest*, right?"

"Wrong," she says. "Which means, you strategize."

Mm-hmm.

"Work on her—"

"Who, Aline? An ex is not someone you work on. It's not as if we talk—I can't. And, likewise, I'm not about to send one more paycheck to an attorney and *not* win any rights to see my own kid." *Visit*, I think. *Visitation.* Even the word devalues.

"Personally, I'd try something, I don't know, a little bit more subtle," she says. "Like maybe weaving in the subject here or there. You know, refined repetition, which you're so good at."

Refined repetition, I think. "But there's one problem with that. We don't converse."

"Well, you need to," she says.

"I know that."

"What happened to *reassess*?" Andi says.

"She'll never change the schedule. She likes it the way it is. It gives her something over me. And besides, I'm clearly not capable," I say.

"Of parenting?"

"Because when do I have time?" I say. "But sure, we can. We will. I'd love to. Reassess, that is."

"Then—"

We don't talk. "Cordially," I say. "Or at length."

"It's not hard."

"She's—"

"Jordan's mother," Andi says.

"We're not there yet," I say.

"Why not?"

"All right, I'm not," I say.

"Yet you have fifteen more years of this to go," she says. "More like a lifetime."

"How does anyone do this?" I say.

"No clue," she says. "Aline's confused."

"She's not."

"And you're enjoying that."

"I'm not. I'm just exhausted," I say.

"Exhausted—I bet you are," she tells me with this look.

"Not from that," I say.

"Lies," she says.

And maybe she does know me, given she's changed the subject to, I don't know, an ill-fitting pair of shoes, the demise of journalism. It's enough to make my mind flit off to…you know. But she couldn't possibly, and seriously, why would she call? Or maybe I'm getting ahead of myself. Maybe I am.

"Madisen," I hear. "Aren't you listening to me?"

"Of course."

"You're pining over Aline—"

"Which is the last thing on my mind," I say. "Though I'm thinking I might redecorate, remodel maybe, something. Change the place up. It feels so Aline."

"As in dark and moody?"

"As in needs more *me*. Like one of those walk-in showers, perhaps with a glass partition. I could knock a wall out—"

"Knock out a wall?" she says.

"Who needs a formal dining room? I don't do formal. I don't do banquets or entertaining or Martha Stewart or P. Allen Smith."

"Things could change," she says. "Your life could change."

"I still won't have time," I say, "or interest."

"Maybe just an aloe plant for now?" she says. "I hear they're low-maintenance. Perhaps a coat of paint."

"Paint," I echo, pondering.

"We're home," she says.

"You don't need to state the obvious," I say, grabbing my keys, phone.

When she grins. "Call this girl."

"I can't," I say.

"You know you want to."

"It was a night," I say. "A really, really incredible night. But other than that, she's…" Sigh.

"Don't be so modest," she says.

"And what if she wants to see me?" I say.

"Who wouldn't?"

My kid. "Jordan," I say, "who doesn't exactly come up in casual conversation."

Which gets a laugh out of her. "Oh, shit."

"See what I mean?"

"Did you two even talk?" she says.

"Oh my God," I say. "Of course we did."

"Of course you did," she says with that crooked smile. "Well then, tell her during one of those in-depth conversations."

"Or maybe she wants to keep it at a night," I say, "and calls for a repeat."

"And you're fine with that?"

"Most definitely."

"Well then," she says. "Tell me how that goes."

When I reach my door, as the cat stretches along the length of the living room window, there's my phone again. "Madisen"—ugh— "favor?"

Dropping my keys in the tray. "What, Aline?" I say. "Is something wrong?"

"I'm calling about Friday and this thing I've been sucked into."

"That's fine," I say. "I'll come early."

"You'll do that for me?"

"I'll do that for Jordan," I say. Which leads to some words on insurance and mail and *Have you straightened that out?* Before she pauses and, not soon enough, we're offering our hasty good-byes.

So I spend the few remaining hours of my day finishing laundry and cooking a batch of lentil soup for my rest of the week. And as much as I'd like to call Rae, text her, as much as I'm constantly thinking about her, I don't. Nor does she, evidently, not before I fall asleep or after I snooze my alarm in the morning or roll out of bed or have coffee or check Facebook and email and shower. And I get to work because, right, we had a night.

And I'd like to say it gets easier the next day, but that would be a lie as well. Because what the hell was I thinking? Doing? Sinking to Grindr levels or Tinder when I'm straight-up U-Haul material.

Focus. That's what I need to do, is focus on something other than her, like this magazine says, this piece on urbanization, on the home hub. On hearing Andi always telling me I'm overreacting because I probably am. But the truth of the matter is, she hasn't called.

So what? I still have Andi.

And how we've come up with so much to talk about every single night since—how long has it been?—is beyond me. I think it might've been that night at the pub, commiserating over her then-girlfriend who up and moved halfway across the country for some hardly worth it job—and that was that. Andi's life was officially over. And that carried back to my place, well ours then, mine and Aline's, where she crashed on our pullout sofa in the living room downstairs—because who hasn't enjoyed my bruschetta? And, besides, we made a serious night of it. That night and every other Saturday since. When pub nights became drinks and appetizers in. A routine only amplified after my divorce.

Which is how this became our thing. I call her or she calls me once I've settled in, and we talk during the time it takes for each of us to heat up and eat dinner together virtually over the phone. Or on the rare occasion, should something important in her day transpire, something *Oh my God, you've got to hear this*, our call is bumped earlier.

Like today, she's gushing over this girl she met at Jiffy Lube. Not the mechanic, who she literally goes there to see, but a customer. It was that splendid blend of camaraderie sponsored by ESPN while they were intoxicated by the seductive scent of rubber tires, or so she says.

Because they were rooting for the same team.

I don't know which team. I don't know which sport. But she got her number.

And now she's stalking her online as I select suitable work attire for tomorrow's meeting—and she's insisting I do the same, only with Rae. Stalk her, that is. But in any regard, this is how our conversation morphed from Andi's love life into mine.

As I open my closet and flip Theory, Brooks Brothers. "So navy... or gray?" I say as I switch her over to speaker where she's demoted to floorboards, freeing me to slide through all those options—charcoal, powder blue, white, pinstripe—wanting something to say *You're so worth this budget.* While at the same time downplaying my two X chromosomes.

"For the meeting," she says, "dark gray."

"Gray it is," I say. And I settle on herringbone trousers with a button-down. Afterward making my way to the kitchen.

"And how exactly did she say it?" Andi says.

"Good-bye?"

"Yes," she says, "good-bye as in *It's been nice, but—*"

"It was more like this," I say. "She didn't."

"You didn't say good-bye?"

"We didn't say good-bye or anything like that," I tell her. "She just, I don't know, kissed me."

"As in *Please don't get out of my car?*" she says.

"As in *Please don't get out of my car,*" I say.

"So you got out of her car?"

"At four in the morning," I say.

"Well, I don't know what to say."

"Is that good?"

"I don't know," she says, and I slam the microwave.

Timer-four-zero-zero-start.

"What are you cooking?"

"Soup," I say.

"I'm having steak portabella."

"From a box?" I say.

"It's not bad," she says, "seasoned."

"And that's better than dinner with me?" I say.

"As in more of your soup?" she says. "It's tempting…"

"It's lentil this time," I say. "I found this recipe online with a five star rating. I made so much."

"So make less," she says.

"How do I cook for one?"

"This is why God invented Lean Cuisine," she says.

And I grab a spoon and take a seat and prop my screen, and sure, maybe I'm loading Facebook as well because who knows…

"I found her," she says.

"Who," I say, "Jiffy Lube?" As I'm typing *R-a-e M-a-t-h-e-n-y.*

"Yes," she says and I hover over *Do you know Rae?* and *Send her a friend request,* wondering, should I? Oh God.

Wait, wait. "Shit," I blurt out.

"What?" she says.

"How do I not share something?" I say.

"What do you mean?"

"I mean, how do I hide a few pictures that are posted on Facebook," I say, "of the kid and Aline. Can I hide this?"

"Click on settings," she says. "Are you there?"

"Yes," I say.

"It's no wonder," I hear. "She works out."

"What's her name?" I say. "I'll look her up."

"She's a computer systems analyst," I hear, "from North Carolina. And she's checked in everywhere."

But Rae doesn't share much.

"What else?" I say.

"Panthers, Patriots," I hear, "and restaurants and ratings—"

"So you'll friend her?" I say.

"No."

"Why not?"

"Who wants to seem anxious?" she says.

❖

While I'm presenting the next day to a room full of people, my phone goes off and I glance down and it's Rae and my mind floats off—with five more slides and too many questions left to go. In fact, it's another twenty minutes before I can actually take my seat.

Which goes something like this:

Wednesday, 9:21 a.m.: *How are you?*

Wednesday, 9:22 a.m.: *I can't stop thinking about you*

Wednesday, 9:25 a.m.: *Call me?*

Which means, as soon as I get back to my office, I shut the door, breathe, and call and I'm just… "I hadn't expected to hear from you." Because what else do I say?

"Did you want to?" she says.

"I had."

"Good," she says. "You aren't busy, I hope?"

"It's fine," I say.

"I'm working on this thing," she says, "where I let girls wonder for days before I call."

"Is that right?"

"No, actually," she says, "what I'm trying to say is that I dropped you off, drove back, and had coffee before I got in, took a nap, made this sandwich, and couldn't find where I put your number. I searched my car, my couch, pockets, coat, jeans—and I just now, well, here it is. And would you believe I spent my entire Sunday wondering what you were up to? But maybe I shouldn't share that bit of info."

So I say, "Wakeboarding," aching now from smiling.

"Athletic," I hear.

"Not really," I say, wishing I could erase that nervous laugh of mine.

Then I hear, "Can I take you out? To a movie." And I guess I say *yes* and she's like *Friday?* and I say *sure* and she says *I'll pick you up* and I say where, and it hits, not then but later. Once I've hung up and the phone's off and docked because *shit, shit, shit,* this weekend. Didn't I just lock that date in for Jordan?

CHAPTER FOUR

Turn Left on Chestnut

Rae

When Avery gives you advice, you do the exact opposite. I know this. Which is why I'm merely half listening to her as I edge along this extraordinarily backed-up drive-through line, which is typically my moment of Zen, isn't it?

"I would call her again," I hear. "Just think up some legendary excuse."

I reach the window. "Venti macchiato with soy, please." Back to Avery, "Because—?"

"Um, she's kind of hot," I hear before that laugh.

"I'm definitely aware of that."

"This is why they always fall for you," she says. "You're so evasive. I would be freaking out, thinking you weren't interested."

Me, thinking, well, then she canceled on me. "You're wrong," I say, "and no you wouldn't."

"You've googled her?"

"Have I ever googled anyone?" I say.

"No. But I'm curious about this one," she says with that tinge of secrecy.

"You always are," I say.

"But you're not?" she says.

"Why should I be? We're just seeing a movie."

"That's so unlike you," she says. "Remind me again where she works?"

"I have no idea," I say.

"But you said she was an architect. There can't be too many architects in this town," she says. "I'll find her. Want me to?"

"Avery," I say, thinking why is it those most ill equipped to dole out advice always seem to be the ones who do, vocally at that, and so persistently? "Hold out," I add, paying for my drink then slipping it in the holder as I take off, and the wind drowns her monologue so much that I need to tweak the volume just in time to catch, "I can't."

"Can't what?" I say.

"That firefighter, I told you. She's texting."

"Now?" I say.

"Yes. It's disappointing. Look," she says, "never mind."

"Why are you so surprised?" I say, then flip the blinker, change lanes, hit the highway. "It's just that you're incompatible in that regard, right?"

"Don't act as if you wouldn't care."

"Here I thought she was over-the-top your type," I say.

"She is." *Sigh.* "Looks-wise."

"Except she's not..."

"Right," she says. And I can sense she's pretty worked up about this. "But she's not a bottom either."

"And she's not into..."

"Right," she says, pausing. "Should I even ask? I will. So let's just say this was you. What would you do?"

"Learn to top," I say. "Not that I'd need to."

"Aside from the obvious."

"Ghost her," I say.

"Aside from that."

"You asked my opinion," I say. "I'm not a bottom, dear."

"No," she says. "You just like to rouse me."

"Is that what you are, roused?"

"Call her already. I'm serious. Just say *I had the most amazing time fucking you—*"

"Because that'll impress her," I say.

"You know you did."

"I know she did," I say. And how many times have I wanted to? Try hourly. For the past two weeks. Or nearly.

"*I had the most amazing time fucking you,*" she says, thoughtful.

"Is that what you're texting your firefighter?"

"Perhaps," she says. "It's a good line."

"What a lovely way to begin a relationship," I say.

"As if you would know?" she says.

"I wouldn't want to know," I say.

"But what if," I hear, "what if this is *the one*."

"After one night," I say.

"All right, you've convinced me to call her," she says.

"I have?"

"Don't you think I've made her wait long enough?"

"And what will you say this time?"

"I'm not exactly sure. But I'll let you know mañana," she says. "And answer this time."

Which means I'm back on autopilot, crawling down this four-lane stretch of stop-and-go enjoying this Beautiful Mess playlist—on a track I'm really into, now on an emotional high or, I should say, low. Wondering why I would ever entertain advice from Avery. As I wait at the longest red in human history—tilting three vents, resetting my trip counter, flipping my visor, then checking when I'm due for the next oil change…everything I can possibly find to not text Madisen because, why? I'll see her in a few hours.

Right, so much for that. I'm sending one.

Me: *You do this thing…*

Yeah, why'd I do that? Reverting to my brief playlist as it runs its course along the next twenty or so miles of no word. I'd imagine she's in the midst of everything and I've sidetracked her, haven't I, and not in a good way.

Still two more hours pass, and nada.

Which is not an issue, since who responds in a few hours? Everyone, right? She's probably in another meeting. She has those. So again, why do I listen to Avery?

And thus continues my day until I get home and dump bags across the couch, prop feet, lift the screen on my laptop, and start googling when *near me* autofills as I type *architecture firms*, leading to such a rush because who knows. I can't do this…

M-a-d-i-s-e-n M-i-t-c-h-e-l-l

Cuffing shirtsleeves while waiting on this page to load. Then my phone goes off.

Madisen: *Go on…*

Holy shit. Now what?

Me: *You did this thing the other night.*

Madisen: *…*

Me: *You gave me this look. Maybe you don't remember. But if you do, tell me what it meant.*

Madisen: *As if you didn't know.*

Me: *I'm not sure if I do.*
Madisen: *I thought you were a rather good instructor.*
Me: *My demonstration skills?*
Madisen: *Yes.*
Me: *Is that all?*
Madisen: *Perhaps.*
Me: *Perhaps?*
Madisen: *What would you like me to say?*
Me: *That I can swing by.*
Madisen: *I'm still dressing.*
Me: *Please don't.*

I plot twelve minutes for this commute. *Turn left on Chestnut.* I make the light past Dunkin, a four-way, a field, and afterward I slow down into that perfect diagonal shade, those newly swept curbs. The woodsy scent of mesquite in the air. *What would you like me to say?*

To a neighborhood that's clearly going for some sort of Beacon Hill aesthetic with its one after another after the next lining the street— me, dodging an occasional dog, leash, dog on leash, ball, kid with ball. It's just a cool vibe, magnolia lined. Fragrant. Littered in petals this time of year.

At the second right, turn left and nerves settle in, and I'm thinking why can't everything in life have GPS? Like this, you know, just tell me what to do, where to go. Leaving in the occasional long way around and scenic drive, those messy detours rerouting you clear across town then back to the same road where you began. Back to this.

Your destination will be on your right.

Which is where I park, stalling a bit. Checking my hair, which is wrong. Then hopping the curb to a sidewalk lined in pots that are painted in every shade of white. Vanilla. Seashell. Bone. Linen. Cream. Blooms dangling. It smells of this afternoon's rain still streaming down the lips of concrete steps.

And I knock twice before gazing so far down the street thinking *Is this it?* And *chill* and *It's just a girl and a show and a couple hours.* Barely aware when the door sucks in and, with it, every ounce of my composure.

And all I can do is follow a spark of sunlight that angles its way across her lips, stepping back.

But she's pressed against me now, and I can feel her lips until I'm back on this strand of hair, looping, tucking it around, asking if she's ready.

And instead of answering, she's moved to the kind of kiss that's slipping between my knees and now hers. And I can't let her go. I can't—but I need to.

"I suppose," she says, "we should. Before I catch myself inviting you in."

"I'm not opposed to your inviting me in," I say. And we sort of stay this way, wondering, I guess. At least I am. Why I feel this way. What she's thinking. As I draw up the hem of her skirt, and she lets me. And then—

"Neighbors," she whispers. Pausing as if she has something to say, as if she's considering it. I think she should. But she turns to close the door. And with the twist of a bolt, it's painful and discouraging. As we descend the same steps and, all the while, her passing glances.

Since, leave it to me, I pushed too far.

Until somewhere between her front door and my car, she takes my hand and she laughs, hunched before sliding into my seat. Where I realize along the drive how much of this I've imagined, invented. Like how she lives. That table where she forks breakfast, drowsy while gazing out a window. I've imagined everything right down to what she eats as I filled my own cart last weekend at the grocery store.

The tuck of a towel. The scruff of hair when it's damp. The unfolding and unhanging as she slips a sleeve down, arm by arm. But here, with knees crooked, what do I really know about her?

Beyond a few stories she's shared—a few anecdotes now overlapping mine along the way.

Until we're twenty minutes in and we're sinking deep into seats, whispering, features lit by the big screen.

As she leans in, a wrist slack along our shared armrest.

"But to answer your question," she says and I peer up and there's this glow along her cheeks and that look again, unsettled, I suppose. "I can't live life only to please everyone else, not anymore."

"I never have," I say.

"Never?" she says.

"Of course not," I say.

"Do you regret that?" she says.

As I sink in my seat, sketching words along her knee before lifting my gaze. "Why do you ask?" I say.

But she glances away, resigned. "So, tell me what you do."

"What do I do?" I say. "I'm a photographer."

"How does that work?"

"I shoot magazines, catalogs, that sort."

"And do you like that?" she says.

"Sometimes," I say.

"It must take discipline," I hear before she's leaning in to me and here come those nerves again. "So tell me—what's this film?"

"What's it about?" I ask.

"Yes," she says.

"Everything," I say, "and nothing."

"And based on that poster," she says, "a drama."

But it doesn't matter what she tells me. I like listing to her talk. "Your guess is as good as mine."

"So a complicated mess of realism," she says.

"Perhaps."

"Will I cry at the end?" *Will you cry?*

"I certainly hope not," I say slipping my palm between the grip of her thighs. And maybe I'm still musing about that doorway scene—had she invited me in, how would that have gone? Flashing back to that glimpse of hair draped over the edge of my bed...

And she's smiling now. "What?" I say, dropping my gaze to her lips. But as the space around us dims, settles, her knee lifts, wedging against the pinch of an armrest. And we sink into a kiss that's hidden under a blackened theater. Until she guides my palm up the center of her thigh.

"I don't want you to stop," she says.

"I won't."

CHAPTER FIVE

Delilah

Madisen

"You sure you're all right?"

"Yes," Andi says.

So maybe I'm a little pepped up or perhaps it's just one of those days—translation: long—and now that it's over, I've caught my second wind. On the other hand, this might have everything to do with that cappuccino I was convinced into drinking at four in the afternoon under the guise of networking.

Who knows.

But in any regard, I'm picturing her slouched in one of those graphic tees dating back to God knows when, and threadbare at that. Soccer shorts. Feet propped in a new pair of crew socks. And I feel like I could talk all night.

"You're not all right," I say.

"Just work," she says, "the usual."

"You don't love your job anymore?"

"I love my people," she says, "My job, on the other hand, is maddening. Data entry. And nobody was even there today to pull me away from the screen."

"Accounts Payable…I hardly consider that data entry," I say. "And why were you alone?"

"Trust me, it is," she says. "And to answer your question, everyone's out. It's spring break. But what've I kept you from?"

"Me?" *Calling Rae.* "Just fielding emails," I say. "And I don't have a brain right now."

"I guess I'm fortunate there," she says. "I don't bring anything home."

"I don't mind it," I say. "In twenty years, though…"

"In twenty years, you'll be retired," she says.

"I'll be sixty," I say, outraged, "just barely."

"I should've gone somewhere, you know, for spring break," she says.

"Is that really your scene?" I say.

"Not exactly," she says. "But why not? I mean, what am I waiting for? A wife, a family, then what?"

"So what's going on, really?"

"Nothing," she says.

"So fullbacks, penalties, touchlines," I tell her, downright impressed with myself. "Don't I sound like I actually know what I'm talking about?"

"Of course you don't."

"I'm good at memorizing," I say, "little else."

"I beg to differ."

"So if this isn't some silly little game you lost—"

"It's Jenna," she tells me. "I just wish it wasn't so hard."

"I try not to think about it," I say. "That way, I'm not disappointed."

"But nobody gets me," she says, "instinctively."

"I thought you just met this girl."

"I'm talking hypothetically here," she says. "That's the problem—it's always hypothetical. It's not as if anyone ever hits me, like, *bam*."

"I'm sorry," I say. Because, sigh.

"Look, I know you don't get it," she says. "That's fine."

"I do, sort of."

"I need to leave. Not that I have."

"But you're thinking about it?" I say.

"Maybe," she says.

"If you're not into her—"

"Oh, I'm into her," she says.

"Well, there's no such thing as destiny," I say.

"There's someone," she says, "I'm meant to find."

"There's an infinite many you're meant to find," I say. "But I have to believe that."

"No, you don't," she says.

"I do. Because, Aline."

"She wasn't your meant-to-be. Aline was merely a stepping stone. Destiny's out there," she says. Because she likes to give me these pep talks. "She'll live to regret this." And sure, there's a part of me that wants to believe them.

"That much is seriously debatable," I say.

"And perhaps when she does, it'll be too late."

"The problem is, you romanticize love. And it's sweet and charming and so *Delilah*. But I find that rather dull."

"What is love without romanticizing?" she says.

"But where's the passion? The disagreements, the agony and arguments that always offer little reminders of all you never want to lose? Or those moments you hardly recognize who she is because she's changed so much since you met?"

"You're back on Aline," she says.

"What's that supposed to mean?"

"When it's meant to be," she says, "you can do no wrong."

"I don't agree with that. Because years later, it doesn't matter anymore. She's annoying, boring. The whole notion that anyone can find a soul mate, that someone out there knows you intuitively, instinctively. Why would I want that? It's safe, easy."

"It's not about her knowing you," she says. "Or you knowing her. It's more like that feeling you have, in that instant and forevermore."

"And what about risk?"

"Let's agree to disagree," she says.

"That glance across a room," I add, "when no words could explain that look of knowing, because she understands exactly what you're thinking. And she answers you without a sound. And afterward, you answer her in the same way. Not a spark at first sight. That sort of thing takes years and years of practice."

"Yeah," she says. "I haven't found that."

"Maybe I haven't either."

"You obviously have," she says.

"I had something," I say. "But it's not as if I knew what I had until we were years into it."

"How are we even friends?"

"You who sets the alarm for *Delilah*, the cheesiest of all radio talk shows?" I say.

"Which is not to go beyond me, you, and the wall."

"You actually called in," I say, and I can't even. "You talked to her and dedicated that song, didn't you? What was that?"

"John Mayer," she says, sounding resigned.

"That's right," I say. "'Slow Dancing in a Burning Room.'"

"Stop laughing," she says.

"Too late," I say. "I have tears."

"I'm glad you find my heartbreak amusing," she says.

"Why can't I be more like you?" I say. "I'm too busy falling for difficult women."

"One person," she says, "does not a pattern make."

"One person who somehow changed my life forever," I say.

"How do you figure?"

"Where would I even begin?"

"She deserves no credit," she says, "for your career, if that's what you're implying."

"But let's not forget Jordan," I say. "Because who wanted a family? She carried her. I just came along for the ride and a few pints of Ben and Jerry's at the crack of dawn."

"That was serendipity."

"And I wouldn't have it any other way," I say.

"Not that arguing, as you say, is emotionally stable."

"Clarification, I don't argue. I don't enjoy arguing. I'm just pointing out some of the lesser-known benefits to doing so. It's therapeutic. On occasion."

"Or maybe that was dysfunctional," she says.

"And maybe," I say, "I'm passing along my screwed-up to the next generation. Which would be why I lost the grand custody battle."

"You're not screwed up," she says.

"We all are," I say. "It's fine."

"You're just a perfectionist."

I laugh. "Unlike your ex, right?"

"You read my mind," she says.

"Let's not revisit that," I say.

"Thank you," she says. "So what's our next topic?"

"Anything. I don't know," I say, squeezing into a pillow. "Rae—?"

"And why did I know you'd say that?"

"Because I bore you," I say. "Tell me about this girl."

"There's not much more to say."

"What specifically, then, don't you like about her?"

"Specifically," she says. "Nothing. She's cute."

"Cute," I say. "Didn't you say *hot* before? You Facebook-stalked her."

"She has a good job. You know, that's important."

"It is," I say.

"And she's wicked good in the kitchen."

"Good in the kitchen?" I say.

"Yes, and not cakes or cornbread. More like fresh and vegetarian and wholesome, you know? The stuff I like."

"Wholesome?" I say.

"Would you stop?"

"Not to judge, but a decent trade and a measuring cup aren't exactly the qualities I look for in someone."

"On the downside, she's into opera."

"Okay, this is not a downside," I say.

"And her concept of romance involves Puccini with some pasta dish and maybe fruit and pastries and hundreds and hundreds of candles."

"That's sweet," I say. "It beats your monologue on the finer points of the touch pass. And Puccini is more romantic than that horrible relationship advice you hear on *Delilah*."

"It's not horrible advice," she says.

"When she insisted on the ultimatum. Really? Throw their entire friendship out the door—and why? Because the caller had a crush on her Sweet Valley High BFF? Maybe he just wanted to be friends with her."

"He obviously didn't," she says.

"According to her," I say.

"Still," Andi says, "it's best to put things out there, be upfront—like she said. Especially if he's taking off to college. It's a critical moment. That usually means it's over."

"And make life incredibly awkward from that point forward?" I say. "You're forgetting the ultimatum, all or nothing. I'm fine with saying, *Hey, do you feel the way I do?* It's quite the opposite to say *This, or else.* Imagine if that was us?"

"All right, so that went a little too far," she says.

"She always goes too far," I say. "And I only point this out because you follow her bad advice."

"But you must admit, she beats Freud."

"So now we're comparing some radio talk show host with Freud?"

"In any regard, when's our next date with the kid?"

"Wow, genius, way to change the subject," I say. "I'm already far too in debt to you."

"For what?" she says. "Pan pizza at the roller rink on you? Absolute torture."

"More like, I'm already blowing it."

"Why? Because you brushed a girl off for an entire week? Big deal," she says. "What'd you tell her anyway?"

"That I promised you pizza. That I lost a bet."

"I told you I'd sit," she says.

"Because four days a month with my kid, and I need a sitter."

"Not a sitter. I'm practically her godparent, if the two of you weren't so godless," she says. "And besides, it's the only time I get anything good out of her."

"Like what?" I say.

"There are matters a girl can't discuss with the moms. But listen, tell me more about Rae. You don't bore me. I'm just mildly defensive, that's all."

"Stop," I say.

"You do realize that a movie makes it no longer just a night?"

"It was a night," I say.

"Which is becoming something else."

"What's it becoming?" I say.

"You tell me."

"It was still a night," I say, "in disguise."

"Which means you talked?"

"We talked."

"And the movie was good?"

"The movie was very good," I say, laughing.

"Seriously, you talk about me," she says.

"She thinks I'm so perfect," I say and, God, why must I act like some dumb teenaged girl all of a sudden? "Who needs love?"

"Who doesn't?"

"I don't," I say.

"Why?" she says.

"It hurts."

"Sometimes."

"Right," I say, "sometimes. But not always."

"I want the sometimes," Andi says. "And the always."

"I do too," I say.

CHAPTER SIX

Thumb Control

Rae

I'm peering in the fridge and spot Dogfish Head when I hear, "Rae—can you get me one?" Meanwhile Elizabeth, who's normally in her gingham shirts, the corduroy coat, sits barefoot and cross-legged on her living room floor, appearing as if nobody's informed her summer has arrived—those wool shorts, otherwise known as her weekend casual, better suited for anything but, in eighty-five degree weather, I might add—improvising on an acoustic guitar strapped across her lap.

Meanwhile I'm clutching two bottles of Tropical Blonde when a flash of lightning strikes, freaking the shit out of me. Followed by her one-Mississippi, two-Mississippi, which tells us it's a good five miles out.

But back to this wardrobe thing. Avery once told me that Elizabeth spends eight hundred dollars a month on clothing alone. Not just clothing, but Daniel Wellington watches, argyle socks and leather gloves and maroon scarves, cricket sweaters, and those several-hundred-dollar wingtips and oxfords you need to actually polish. And that she does, with painstaking precision. That crumpled messenger bag, which accompanies her everywhere. She justifies the cost with, "It's an investment," a wardrobe that never goes out of style, she says. Possibly for those who attended Princeton, which she hasn't, or for those who have an equivalent bank account, which she doesn't.

The thing is, I don't know who has that kind of time but Elizabeth.

Being that if she scores one on a one-to-ten scale for casual, I'm a solid seven—maybe even eight depending on the day or weather. Give me a worn pair of jeans, loose work pants, something bendable, and

I'm golden. No ironing, no polishing, and definitely no accessories. In fact the most I've invested, or ever will, in an article of clothing would be that racing jacket, and even that's far from damaged enough for my liking.

But where we may lack cohesion in regard to style, we make up for in, well, just about everything else.

Just about.

And as I set a bottle beside the strum of her guitar, I hear, "Why is it you remember everything I'd like to forget?"

"You wouldn't shut up about her," I say, shifting my attention to a window still wide open, where it's getting dark.

"You know I wasn't into her."

"Of course you were," I say. And she glances my way.

"I thought we could be friends," she says rubbing the tip of a finger down the side of her mouth as a fan cycles by, whipping up a warm breeze that settles between us.

"No, you didn't."

And that look. "That was in my running-away phase," she tells me, "and *no*, I didn't lead anyone on."

"Phase," I say before this mild taste of sweet and cool.

"Avery rang today," she says.

"What about," I say, "her firefighter?"

"Does this one have a name?"

"Not yet. They're not sexually compatible," I say.

"Who is?" she says. "Aside from that biologist."

"She's over the biologist," I say.

"She'll never be over the biologist."

And after this comes a mini tirade about the job as I begin to daze off, picturing Elizabeth and her commuter mugs of Keurig. The doughnuts hauled in twice a week because "that's what managers do."

And she plays a little more as the wind picks up, ballooning curtains, the tick-tick, that downpour steady along steel gutters, and it grows into one of those pelting, angular storms we get all the time. The breeze so damp I can smell it.

Recognizing the scent of cedar mulch. It's the same kind they use at the café where I meet for my lunches with Madisen over cappuccinos served in those clay mugs embellished with that cursive letter *A,* short for Archipelago. If we meet before eleven, we get a patio seat in the shade. There's a breeze just like this, only drenched in sun. The heat always hitting my back.

And on any average day, we talk nonstop, unfazed even as wind lifts our napkins. Even as pigeons settle around our feet. But there are others when neither of us wants to offer a word, or perhaps we have nothing to say. I like those best. How useless it is just to be there. The way her lips pout as if she's whispering *blue* as puffs of steam tumble over the rim of her mug. Her gaze unbroken even as I bend to fix a shoelace. The way she watches me and leaves me feeling this, drowned in desperation.

"You know what really gets me," Elizabeth says. "They're buying into heteronormity. Nobody sees it as the big covert plan it is, to obliterate queer culture. Remember when we had anxiety attacks just walking in a shop with a rainbow flag since everyone knew you *were* if you went inside. Now they're everywhere—straight-owned, gay-owned. Big old rainbow flags. It's like every fucking person shouting, *We're inclusive*. Inclusive," she says with disdain. "What a privilege to be included in your straight world. I never asked to be," she says, pausing to reflect. "All of this tolerance is making everyone look and act exactly the same. Have you noticed?"

And afterward, a knock at the door that I answer, with Avery pouring in with, "I can't believe I agreed to this."

Elizabeth: "Just in time. Can I get you a drink?"

Avery: "When have I ever said no to a drink?"

Me: "Don't you look adorable in your floral rain slicker."

Avery: "You're welcome for keeping your cheese dry. I hope I didn't miss anything salacious."

Me: "Don't get her started."

Elizabeth: "We were discussing assimilation, diversity initiatives, and the demise of queer culture."

Avery: "Riveting."

Elizabeth: "Because I now have to give hour-long training sessions on diversity at work."

Me: "Because you're their token queer."

Elizabeth: "Because I'm HR and because they're coercing me into saying shit like *We're like you*. I mean, poof, evaporation of one more subculture into their nondescript norm. Fucking hetero death. My life goal is not the lesbian version of Doris Day, I'll tell you that." She directs her gaze at me. "You're so not listening to me."

Me: "I am. You're preaching to the choir."

Avery: "You are, Elizabeth."

Elizabeth: "Maybe I'm not explaining myself well."

Or maybe I'm having a harder time than usual getting into this sit on the floor as we philosophize over a couple drinks gig.

Elizabeth, trying to be cute: "Look at you." Then again, anything to hold me back from sending another text, which is what I would be doing—okay, shouldn't be doing—right now if left to my own devices. "You're smitten over this girl."

Me: "Believe me, I'm not."

Elizabeth: "It's fine if you are."

The only upside to her incessant yammering over the obvious is that I can eat and listen. And that I do, well, try to.

Elizabeth: "So this vendor shipped a box of shirts as, what, a thank-you, I guess, for spending so much. And I put the thing in the break room so everyone could take their pick on size, color, you know? Isn't that what you would do? Next thing, two whatever-you-want-to-call-them, clueless, I swear, they're outside my office rattling about some woman who took a men's because, what, she didn't want skintight? She opted for professional, if you ask me. And, yeah, they sat in on my training."

Next she scrutinizes those Warby Parkers at arm's length as if they could ever have a smudge.

Elizabeth: "I'm so tired of diversity. They take over our parades. They sponsor our rainbows. They script fake coming out speeches subsidized by McDonald's, and suddenly it's okay to buy a Big Mac? Queer is fashionable, to companies, to capitalism. And meanwhile you have these kids who are being tossed to the curb for being different…"

Me: "Not a bad thing."

Avery: "Being tossed to the curb is never a good thing."

Me: "If your parents aren't going to accept you, it most certainly is."

Avery: "You weren't twelve."

Me: "All right, point made."

Elizabeth: "Not to mention this whole marriage frenzy. And all they're hoping to accomplish with that is *Let's make history*. Fine, make it. But it's not about love anymore."

Avery: "It can be."

Avery—obviously in love again. Which is fine, since I'd rather eat and let my mind do its thing. And Elizabeth would rather go back to whatever creative process this is. She's in her listen to Bob Dylan while we contemplate politics mood. At least it's curbing my urge to text, momentarily. And while the scratch of vinyl inspires her, it only makes my mind drift to Madisen and that dull sound she makes and my heart sinks.

While Avery morphs into peacemaker: "The next time you get a batch of shirts, slip one in every mailbox or whatever you office people do. Give women men's and vice versa. Problem solved."

Elizabeth: "Right. I would be fired for sexual harassment."

I think everyone needs an Elizabeth. Without an Elizabeth, they might make the fatal mistake of feeling happy once in a while.

Avery: "So, guys, Karen Walker or Grace Adler?"

Elizabeth: "I miss *Will & Grace*."

Avery: "Are they coming back?"

Me: "You do realize, they're both straight."

Avery: "But Grace in her power suits."

Elizabeth: "Right?"

Me: "Grace has no personality. At least Karen is nonstop fun."

Elizabeth: "I'm nonstop fun."

Avery and I: "Dream on, Elizabeth."

Avery: "Erika Linder or Kristen Stewart?"

Elizabeth: "Both."

Me: "God, they're like ten years too young for me."

Avery: "Ten years is not too young."

Avery, again: "How about your best breakup?"

Elizabeth: "Isn't that an oxymoron?"

Avery: "But some breakups are beautiful."

Elizabeth: "Like the girl who gifted me one lovebird in a cage."

Avery: "That's completely psychotic."

Elizabeth: "Which is why I left. How about you, Avery?"

Avery: "Oh, so many."

Me: "Of those breakups you actually chose?"

Avery: "It's always the other way around."

Elizabeth: "I need a drink. Who else?"

Avery: "Do you have anything more upbeat, like not Dylan?"

Me: "Dylan *is* upbeat to her."

Elizabeth: "Bob Dylan is a genius."

And as disastrous as my friends might be, remarkably so after a few drinks, nothing gets my mind off Madisen except Madisen. So once I get home and take off my shoes and change clothes and get in bed, I dial her up. Okay, more like I think about dialing her up and put it off until I nearly back out. In truth, I bump her name on accident, and it starts to dial, and that hits like this rush of adrenaline. Me, hoping it's not too late. And it probably is.

Then her voice destroys me: "You sound—"

"Tired," I say. "I know."

"Not in a bad way," she says. "I waited up."

"For this?"

"I shouldn't tell you this."

Me, cradling the phone and grinning like an idiot, which I'm glad she can't see. "You must be tired."

"Not really," she says.

"Are you walking around?"

"Downstairs," she says. "For water. Tell me about your night. I hope you got there on time."

"I did," I say. "We still had takeout."

"And what'd you get? Tell me."

"Pizza," I say. "Avery bought."

"Not noodles?"

"Not noodles," I say. "They thought it might clash with our drinks."

"Which it would," she says. "How'd everything go otherwise?"

"As expected," I say. Then pause to reflect. "But how am I supposed to focus?"

"All wholesome thoughts?"

"How would you like me to answer that?"

And in her soft-spoken sort of way, "It's warmer than usual tonight, isn't it?"

"I'm not sure how I'll get to sleep in this," I say.

"Just do what I do," she says.

"And what would that be?"

"Don't wear anything to bed."

"Why do you do this to me?" I say, kicking a mound of sheet to the foot of the bed, then crossing the room, gazing out. "Now I'm picturing you," I say. And out the window, it's moonlit everything.

"Imagine that," she says. "Did you get the storm?"

"Avery drowned in it," I say.

"So did I," she says. "I left my umbrella at home. I always do."

"And where's your mind?" I say.

"I didn't check the weather," she says.

"So what about you," I say, "and your date with…"

"It wasn't a date," she says. "Andi. We went to the Cantina."

"I've never been," I say.

"It's worth a try. Margaritas, fresh—which happens to be a weakness of mine."

"I'll remember that."

"Then dinner. Came home. Closed out a few things."

"Work?" I say.

"Yes."

"And waited up," I say.

"I did," she says followed by silence. And eventually, "Why can't I be there?" Which makes my heart heavy.

"I could say the same," I say before making my way to the bed to collapse, gazing at dim ceiling tiles and wishing I could crawl through this line. "How was work?"

"I don't want to think about it," she says.

"And what would you rather think about?"

"You tell me," she says.

"Oh, I'm happy to go there," I say.

"So that's the thing," she says.

"What is?"

"I'm worried that I don't know you," she says.

"But you do," I say. Too much.

"Then tell me something."

"Tell you what?" I say.

"I don't know. Something, anything you haven't told me already."

"That my thoughts are far from wholesome right now," I say.

But the sound she makes. "Andi's been on this kick. She gets like this."

"What kind of kick?" I say.

"She's just so apathetic."

"How come?" I say.

"No sparks, apparently."

"With that girl she met?"

"Yes," she says. "Jiffy Lube."

"The dreaded friends trap."

"Not quite," she says, "just not love at first sight, which isn't realistic, I said."

I pause. "Don't you think?" But there's this emptiness on the line.

"So, love aside, you had that with me?" she says.

"Are you saying you didn't with me?"

"Oddly, well," she says, "maybe. It feels like it's going too fast. I guess that's why I'm worried."

Until silence settles between us. "Why do you say *oddly*?"

"In the past," she says, "I've really only fallen for friends. This is so different."

"I hope so," I say, trying to hide this disappointment.

"Who were you with before this?"

"Is that something we should talk about?" I say.

"I don't know enough about you."

"Well here's the thing. If I trash-talk an ex, you'll say I'm insensitive, bitter, need to get over it. If I don't," I say, "if I don't trash-talk her, you'll get suspicious and flip this around into some, I don't know, rivalry."

"No," she says. "You can absolutely trash-talk her."

"Okay. So the thing is, she was married."

"Isn't that ethical of her."

"And I hung around for nearly two years," I say. "And, yeah, I knew. I'm sure that makes me out to be some abomination, but far from it. For one, I didn't wreck a home. They're still together."

"And two?"

"There is no two," I say.

"You like telling stories with numbers, don't you? First, second, one, two."

"Do I?" I say. "I haven't noticed."

"You do," she says. "And why'd that end?"

"That's an interesting story," I say. "She wanted a ring from me—how ironic, given the state of her own marriage. I wasn't in love," I say. But I hear nothing back. "Hey…"

"Hey," she whispers.

"I was wondering."

"What about?"

"Hypothetically," I say, "if I was to ask you to come along to something, say, tomorrow, with insanely short notice like this—"

"What'd you have in mind?"

"A few friends, they're dragging me up a mountain. But I'd rather be with you."

"How could I possibly turn that down?"

"How could you?"

"Does this mean you're hanging up on me?" she says.

"Well, the hike," I say, "it's early."

"And how do I sleep?"

"I know what generally works for me," I say. "But you do whatever you want." And it pains me to end our call.

CHAPTER SEVEN

After You

Madisen

I was still on the couch with my laptop at seven this morning in what they call loungewear, otherwise known as pajamas you could potentially leave your house in should you have one of those early morning cravings for an apple fritter drizzled in icing with a barista-made latte. Which I'm not saying has ever happened.

But as opposed to basking in Friday, I spent most of my morning paying bills and wondering how Aline was able to vanish without a trace of guilt or remorse, and here I'm the one logging into my bank account transferring I won't even admit how much in support over to her.

And no mention of where it goes, either. Her girlfriend, I'd presume.

Because eight years old and, still, most of the kid's camps, her lessons in ballet, pink leotards and slippers, her violin rental—all paid by me. And it's not as if she'll outgrow her skirts or Mary Janes anytime soon like she used to. She's not two. She's not up-sizing months before they're even scuffed.

Which would be why I never saw that promotion where it counts, in Quicken.

It's also why, by the end of the day, I'm gladly ducking away from all that and my too-long day at work, plus everything else, through an unexpected downpour, lacking one extra-large umbrella I left at home, and needing a drink, as I make my way past the mural to the mariachi band and subsequently to a table lit by candles where, tucked away in a taller than average booth, I find Andi slouched, and she's making out on freshly baked tortilla chips and salsa, drink in hand, that adolescent grin. I take a seat.

"I can get you a towel," she says as the waiter steps in and we order drinks.

And afterward, I scoop a chip.

"A double?" Andi says, somewhat accusatory.

"They don't make a triple."

"They will if you ask them to."

I shake my head.

"So the latest on Rae," she's saying, lounging against the back of the booth. It's cute, the way she looks at me.

"After I promised myself I wouldn't bring her up."

"Why would you do that?"

"Because," I say, thinking I need to get a handle on this. Before bending across the table, saying, "We never seem to talk about us anymore."

"Don't we?" she says.

"And I miss that," I say. "So no Rae. And no whatever her name is."

As she looks at me, bewildered. "Then what is there to talk about?"

"Let's talk about you."

"And what would you like to know?" she says.

"Anything, really. Everything." That might distract me from the obvious. "You have a game tomorrow."

"Right," she says, shaking her head as she spins a napkin side-long. "And this new girl, she's sort of kicking my ass. And that's not okay."

"Which is to say, she's better than you?"

"I wouldn't go so far as to say she's better. Just new, and personalities, and look, I know you don't like this stuff."

"I don't understand the intricacies of soccer," I say. "But that doesn't mean I'm not interested."

"So what'll you have?" she says in hopes of changing the subject.

"No clue," I say. Then she asks about my day. "It's just busy, that's all, to the point that I have no idea where I'm going, goals, ambitions, purpose. What's next? Like in the next five, ten years. I'm starting to feel stuck."

"Who thinks that far ahead?"

"I do," I say. "As should you."

"But it all depends," she says.

"On what?" I say.

"See, that's the insecurity in single," Andi says. "You never do know."

"So you're telling me you'd up and truck your life away for some girl?"

"I could," she says. "At least, the right one."

"So your life's essentially on hold."

"I'm not sure if we should be discussing this," she says. "Isn't it borderline—"

"Yeah, you're right," I say. "So how'd we get back to that?"

"In ten years, I'll be driving a Jeep. That's all I really know."

"Which makes you well ahead of me," I say. "I need to think about that."

"When Jordan's eighteen," she says.

"My God, you're right."

"At which time, you'll be old and gray."

"Not quite," I say.

"And you'll have earned the coveted prize of primary custody."

"Ever the idealist, you."

"As if Aline could survive her teens," Andi says.

"Hey, what's a chimichanga?"

"Amazing," she says.

"So I should get one?"

"Get whatever you'd like," she says.

"Whatever I'd like...Tell me what that is," I say, "and make it something I've never had. I'm that completely burned out on making decisions."

"Yet you bring up such complicated topics over dinner," she says. "Order taquitos with me." And as I unlock my phone, the server dips in with a pair of drinks.

"Your Jeep Wrangler," I say. "But what about the sort of things money can't buy?"

"Like abs?" she says with this look. "Honestly, I'm more the type to ebb and flow. See where things go. I won't even pretend I have it together."

"I'm amazed you get anywhere," I say.

"Why, because I don't know where I'm going?"

"I would lose all shit," I say.

"But you already have it all."

"I don't actually," I say. It's crazy, though, when I think about that. How I've spent all this time planning as if life would follow this track. Then shit happens and it's all up in the air. Not that I need to think about…Look, I'm not thinking about anything. But what if? You know, one day.

"Then what's next?" Andi says.

What's next? "Maybe a larger slice of the company—twenty-five percent," I say, lifting the straw to my lips. "They make the best margaritas here."

"You could make those at home."

"I know, I know," I say, exhausted. "I could do so much more than I already do."

"I didn't mean it like that," she says. "Don't take me wrong. I'm not criticizing you. I'll make you one sometime. How about that? A triple."

"I adore you."

"And about tomorrow, the game."

Mm-hmm.

"I won't see you," she says, "will I?"

"I don't have Jordan this weekend. And you know what that means. Piles and piles of adulting."

"Right," she says, sulking. But this isn't your typical Andi upset about my not making her game. So why does it feel so heavy, like guilt?

"I hope you're not mad," I say.

"Not at all."

"What's going on?" I say.

"Just how to let this girl down without, you know, letting her down."

"So it's come to that?" I say.

"She's not what I want," Andi says, "long-term."

"Then tell her you have plans with me. Indefinitely."

"Do I?"

"It's not a lie," I say.

And that laugh. "Can I get you another drink?" she says.

"Sure," I say. "And count your blessings. It's easier to leave than the other way around."

"Right," she says. "Still discouraging as hell."

"How'd we get back on this?"

"It's who we are," she says. "Don't fight it."

"Can't we ever talk about anything else?"

"Why do you even try?"

As her gaze catches mine and we exchange this look. One that, I don't even know why, makes me weak. Not for her, just. "Andi, Andi, Andi…"

"What, what, what?"

"I'm falling so fast," I say twirling my straw. "Save me."

"She's damn lucky to have you."

She is, right? More like the other way around.

Anyway, they're words I carry into the car the next day, still on a high to the tune of NPR with its clever assortment of random bongo drums, its accidental theatrics, the switching and tapping and repetition trying to keep me focused.

All failing.

The entire drive it's failed me, but the coffee's strong. So that's beginning to fuel my personality as I slam the door shut, its *bee-beep* as I'm straightening my cap and following signs to this oddly named trail.

Where I find all three oblivious to my arrival, too engrossed in who knows, bottled water, as I near a bench now covered in backpacks—the hiker kind with too many pockets and secret zippers and ties or whatever else those are.

And let me pause right here to say that I could've spent last weekend shopping for shorts, shoes, the sturdier kind, and maybe a backpack that might've carried this lunch as opposed to brown bagging it. And had I, I would've shown up grittier, edgier, mountaineering like the others instead of, well, looking like the prima donna that I am.

Add coffee and crisp air and that fresh scent of pine. Red cedar. White oak. Bucolic. I can practically hear John Denver harmonizing as I make my way over. As I slip right in beside her at the bench, hoping to quell too many nerves. As her gaze settles studiously at my lips and she leans in for a kiss that, God, it just sort of sinks my soul.

But next I'm sidetracked through our course of introductions.

As I shake hands, pinning both in their midfifties based solely on hair, given you'd never guess from that build, those thick cycling calves and Timberlands. Their extreme low-key vibe, which is never a bad thing.

Before I'm straddling a bench in shorts observing Rae, because I can't not. Rae, who's talking but not actually considering who she's talking with or what they're saying.

But I do. I study their hands, those programmable watches, the gestures, their early start this and their turkey jerky that. True trailblazers. This is their thing.

"So which trail," says Rae, twisting a knot, "will the two of you take?" As I admire the subtle lines of her smile and that simple way she carries on, like this, only afterward shifting her attention back to me as my breath quickens.

As she snaps the lid off her ChapStick saying, something, I don't know, with such a grin.

And I guess we stay that way for a while, since they've taken off. But it's not until we reach the path and I catch my stride that I find I'm trying, struggling, to connect that girl I held on the phone with the girl I met at pool—and this one, right here. With sleeves cuffed. The cap. Extending a hand as she guides me up and along another one of those inclines.

And then she's asking, "Did you get right to sleep?"

"Wouldn't you love to know?"

"I would, actually," she says...and that look.

"I did eventually," I say, "imagining this."

Realizing this is not the coffee-toting stroll I'd expected. The conversing kind. Closer to brambles and thorns. Closer to an actual workout. "Over here," she says, pointing.

"So you *have* done this before," I say.

"Not in a while," she says. Then I catch her once-over, that crooked grin. "I see it's not your thing."

"I see it's not yours either," I say.

"I'm glad you came." But her voice is softer now.

"I'm glad you asked," I say. Then the wind picks up and I'm thinking about work again.

"Maybe you could take the lead and keep me on the straight and narrow," she says.

"Why does this concern me?"

"I don't know," she says, pausing. "Perhaps we took a wrong turn back there."

"Are you saying we might end up lost?" I say.

"Would you want that?"

"Can I just say, I didn't sleep last night."

"I didn't either," she says.

And she smiles. And, yeah. "But you do know where we're going?" I say.

"I don't," she says.

"Then why is it I'm following you?"

"Because you trust me," she says.

"I do." And that sort of hangs between us until I'm wondering why I said it. Why I feel it. Why I trust her. And maybe I don't. "So, Andi," I say, thinking something about someone else might ease this uneasiness. "Andi's at a game right now, one I should be at, but I'm not. Which is marvelous given…Jenna. Jenna Paulsen, her new fixation turned faux pas, Jiffy Lube, will come and watch, and she'll wait at the hill. And somewhere along the way, Andi's going to stroll over and take a seat…and break her heart."

And I'm learning a few things as we climb. One, that balance requires both hands, and two, that I best keep my mind on the path as opposed to following along everything so devastating about her. That firm stance as she grips my hand and lifts me up. Her fitted shirt. The way her body moves, feels when she's pressed against me. Calves that flex with each step.

"I'd love to get out of the noise more, the mess," I say. "It's a shame you need to hike so far to find this."

"Wait until you see the top."

"Will you kiss me at the summit as the sun sets?"

"I'll kiss you wherever you'd like," she says. And all I keep thinking is *get it together*. But I can't. I can't keep it together.

"But once we reach the top," I say, "it's all downhill from there."

"It doesn't need to be." And she's weaving fingers through mine.

"I know, I know. It's all about the journey, isn't it?"

"Well, that's hard to say."

It *is* hard to say. But ten, twenty, thirty seconds later and she still hasn't turned away. It's as if she's waiting for me to say something I'm not really comfortable saying.

But soon enough, we're both gazing out at this mountain's infinite, feeling ever so high as she turns to me and says, "We don't have to know where we're heading."

And we don't. That's right. This feels okay. Because I think we're heading somewhere. Yet, as I try to pull my thoughts into some sort of beautiful reply, this kiss, this wandering palm and she's whispering, "Why do I want you…like, all the time?" And my heart feels so heavy that I have to turn away.

Scuff dirt, kick this off the cliff. And she's still got her eye on me. Keeping me here, not talking, not helping matters, not carrying on. Listening. But what is there to hear?

As we manage along the path, and she hops in the lead and glances back with a curious look on her face. "Jenna Paulsen," I hear. "Does she happen to work in tech?"

"Why, do you know her?"

"I used to," she says.

CHAPTER EIGHT

The Balancing Act

Rae

Let's see. The last time I saw Jenna, she'd registered for night courses, convinced that a new degree would solve her every life's problem. And why this topic amuses me, I can't say. Given it's quite the bone of contention, making me question whether scaling up a boulder right now is the best activity for us.

What I seem to remember most about Jenna is how she would always zero in on one thing, convinced she'd arrive at some completely unrelated outcome. Case in point, cutting her hair to get me back, and why? There was no correlation between the two. Not to mention that Carnival cruise, a gift for whatever reason—Valentine's *Week*?—which only made matters worse between the two of us, as would be expected of anyone confined within such small quarters for such an unreasonably long period of time. Five days, to be exact.

Oh, and let's not forget that shelter poodle she adopted to curb her cravings for evening cocktails. Just drink, I told her. "But night walks," she said.

Good luck with that.

She was outrageously stubborn, irrationally so, with just about everything. But it's remembering her occasionally unregimented side, that's where I get into trouble. Because Jenna was my first in a string of train wrecks. Those I didn't leave for reasons I won't go into here. But it's not as if I could confess this much to Madisen.

"Surely you have a past," I say, "some of whom you're friends with—those you regret a little less than the rest?"

"I regret none of my past," she says. "So that's not it. I just don't remain friends."

"I wouldn't care if you did," I say.

"Why, though?"

"Remain friends?" I say. "There is no *why.* More like *why not?*"

"And how long does that take?" she says.

"For what?"

"You know," she says, "for the two of you to see one another as friends?"

"Do you ever?" I say joking. But maybe that came out wrong. So after reflecting on this a little longer, I clarify—or backtrack, whatever you want to call it. "That's to say, with some, you can't, sure. But most, those who were pretty much incompatible from the start, I mean, some are just wrong, don't you think? You look back and wonder *What on God's Earth was I doing?*" I stop short of blurting out *like everyone before you*—which wouldn't be wise to divulge. Instead, "I'm pretty slow when it comes to good-bye. I just don't see the need. And to answer your question earlier, nobody really left. It just dissolved," I say, "like they all do. And I think maybe a year, but not exclusive. And on the friendship front, an ex is a friend but not that kind...not like you and Andi are."

But I'm not sure how to interpret her laugh. "The line that would never be crossed," she says.

"And why's that?" I say, trying not to sound jealous. Because I'm not. Really. Curious, maybe.

"I've never really thought about it."

But if you ask me, if there's a line, it could be crossed.

And I don't know, it must be somewhere along our next quarter mile or so when I find that I'm merely half listening to her goings on about building code and long hours and a quarter past eight—half listening, that is, to those mundane ramblings, when she stops midsentence, and my mind has to wrap back to hear whatever it is she just said—or perhaps what she's saying. More like, what she's not saying.

Expecting she'll continue when I glance over. But instead she turns away.

So I ask.

"What were you about to say?"

"Never mind."

"Never mind?" I say. And she gives me that grin, you know, the overinflated *Let's change the subject* one.

"It was way off topic."

"Was it?" I say. And she jumps ahead. "In any regard," I say, "I guess I won't count on you to be there for me after our epic fallout."

"And you think we'll have one of those?" she says.

"You never know," I say, thinking *I hope not.*

"Because I couldn't imagine you…as a friend," she says.

But as we reach the summit, which is more of a flat grassy knoll, one that dives off, a bluff, if you head off too far, I find that I'm more and more intrigued, or maybe I should say concerned, about what she held back just a minute ago.

Yet here we are, remarkably the only hikers in sight, short of those two, who predictably beat us to the top, now scanning the vast valley and its treetops and rooftops and cleared rectangular farms and cloud shadows. So without a word, I unsnap and unpack as she whips open a blanket.

Madisen is on her knees right down to that inadequately buttoned tank top, hunched in that way you would to unwrap while taking your first bite. Struggling to hold that sandwich together and all the while naively sharing the edging of lace just beneath a billowing drape of hair, shadowing cleavage, making it all but unbearable to be here.

And that's when our friends catch on and decide to make their way over, eventually lazing beside. "Cheez-Its?" I say. "Vegetable Thins?"

As she slips heel-to-toe until bare ankles cross.

And lunch goes on like this, with our friends oblivious to our secret glances. As I try to hide this ridiculous grin I've had on all day.

Until a while later after we've snapped the plastic cap off another water bottle as we segue into that Tahoe story, the Airbnb, and why I despise tubing and indoor gardenias. "Imagine the six of us crammed into one hot tub with a glass of whiskey," I say, "during a blizzard, since what else was there to do?" While Vegetable Thins make their rounds and I grab a few.

Thinking it's bad enough when she leans in, sharing all that's plunging. Now I'm back on bikinis. Steamy sauna bikinis. Cold snow bikinis topped with that glass of whiskey.

And soon enough, once our partners have packed up and gone ahead, I'm lying across her lap imagining that. Air rippling. That hit-or-miss glimpse of sun through her hair.

But it's not as if I'm *not* agonizing. Especially given that far-off look, since something's going on. But I can't ask. Just let it go. And really, what would I say? And how would that sound? Ridiculous, that's how. Because it never comes out the way it should.

And it's downright gloomy by the time we do decide to head back down, overcast. Her, hoping to fold my blanket in that way you would if you were trying to save space as I collect the rest. And the wind's picking up.

But we make our way back to that lonely trail, less a bird or three, hiking along a path so thick, so layered and sheltered, it tugs us along down in its gradual descent.

"Watch your step," I say, catching her hand.

"I'm more adept at hiking than you might think."

"Were the famous last words of our slackpacker," I say.

"And we all know my reason for that," she says.

"I'm sorry," I say with a wink as a hand brushes hers in passing. "Still I'm grateful you saved me from that extreme trail."

"I thought we'd spend more time with them," she says.

"Next time," I say, "since they're in a pretty bad place if we hold them back."

"They're cute," she says.

"Marriage makes everyone cute," I say. As we fumble along, or at least I do.

"So," she says, "you shot their wedding?"

"Well, sort of."

"And when was that?"

"I was a kid," I say. "They're like moms."

"And you're the rebellious offspring," she says. "I must say, I'm honored. And surprised."

"What, that I introduced you to family?" I joke.

"That," she says, "and the fact that you'd be nervous shooting their wedding."

"Since it was their wedding," I say, "which you can't screw up."

"*You* could never screw anything up."

"Well, they clearly have no taste."

"But they clearly do," she says, meeting my gaze.

And full disclosure, I'm starting to think if we keep on, if we continue along this path, we'll be done and out by two. And do I really want that? Since we have this day, don't we?

Not to mention, this bit of rain, as I find a crook, a nook, some brush flattened down enough to tug her in. Still laughing about our rumbling storm as a gush of wind whips in and molds her shirt.

"This wasn't in the forecast," she says. "I did check." While scouting our way underneath one of those trees with roots resembling balance beams.

"They never are," I say.

And as we take a seat, she's still laughing and so am I.

Because this right here could go in so many different directions, couldn't it? If we wanted it to. As she lifts her gaze, and it's settling me. But I'm too nervous. So I take her hand, that's all.

"You know what I'm *not* worried about right now?" I say. But I'm wondering again, aren't I? "How long this storm might last." About that slip she made earlier. As she tugs the hem on her shorts. What isn't she telling me?

Since now, settled in, I'm half-tempted to ask her again. But I'm too afraid of what she might say.

Because isn't it always this way. It's what I do—skipping over it, letting it slide, hoping she means well, means something else. Not wanting to know. Then twisting this to work to my advantage. Until it doesn't anymore. Until it's too late. Until she's gone.

Those clues that never seem to matter at the time.

So for the next fifteen minutes, we talk about everything but, as in aloe plants and this paint color named Metropolitan, but it's really just another white she says. Then stand-up on Netflix and how hetero it is. And movies and television and how nothing's ever new, and how everything's remade or rehashed. And how much better we liked the originals, even if they're bad. And friendships. And why we always run through rain. And why she pulls my sheet while she sleeps. And her perfume, and how I love it, and how I'm getting rain all over me and so is she. And how we'll never get home. But how we don't even care and should we?

Then I bring up transparency, white shirts, and how she's falling out of hers. And how much better it would be if she just took it off. And how she looks at me. And how it makes me feel, like I'm someplace else. Until I'm wondering if I should care about all of those things she doesn't want to share with me.

But I do.

So I bring it up. And after that, I'm searching her eyes for a response, anything, and it's really hard to say.

And she says, "It's a long story."

And I say, "Don't we have time?"

And she's silent.

So I'm wondering, even as I slip a hand along the bend of her knee, if it's me. If it's rash. If it's futile. If I'm finding things to go wrong. If I'm running away.

And as I do, she lifts her cap in a breeze and it's spilling hair all around as she tells me, "It's complicated."

Complicated—but what does that mean?

It means I shouldn't have asked, and besides, we have this day, don't we? And she's doing this thing, leaning in until I can taste the faded gum on her tongue. Because that crazy rain is holding us back when all we had to do is walk through it, soak our clothes—I mean, we already are.

Yet we hid instead, back here where I could lift her shirt overhead without anyone ever knowing. And as opposed to going on, to asking or wishing, assuming, I'm pinching that hook at the center of her back. Then straps slip down along her elbows, stopping at the crook. And she falls right out.

With this spray drenching her skin all the way down the front, and between her thighs. Until she draws me up and we're standing and hair clings all along her face half drenched. Rain coursing down my hand to the flesh between her legs. It's weighing at my clothes.

Knowing in my heart that had we gone in that other direction, she wouldn't be here, resigned, her slipping out of this, her breasts heavy, her fingers gripping me, unsteady. She wouldn't have guided my hand here. To unfasten, unzip. To slip inside her. To hear her breathless. Or to taste her. To breathe her in.

The next day, we meet for brunch and she strides into view in that casual way to the crosswalk, watching cautiously as she waits at the curb for brake lights to flash, that hand shading a brow with fingers casting shadows along the bridge of her nose.

It's our standard seat at Archipelago. Somewhere beneath the canopy, I always say. And this is your typical weekday with a pinch of damp in the air during that stretch sandwiched too tightly between a.m. and p.m., offering no shadows or reprieve unless you're tucked beneath a broad-spread canvas, which I am, separated from pedestrians by a draped chain suspended on knee-high posts.

And I'm listening to that musician play James Taylor. Meanwhile, engines roar along a scarcely populated stretch that goes only in one direction—its line of traffic hush as legs like hers hop the curb to cross its white painted lines. And as soon as she comes into sight, that plunge at the pit of my stomach.

Catching a draft that's carrying that scent of everything grilled from indoors. Sweetened with magnolia that blooms right above. As I take a drink of water, then set it down.

Following meter after meter as she passes—chin tucked, focused more on squares passing underfoot.

Her stride that shouts, *Don't bother.*

At least until she nears, until she's making her way around, tucking knees under the table, pulling hair into that mess before she lets it fall over her shoulders, and it's framing her face, her gaze now resting on the heels of two palms. While our stout waiter tucks in. And she's ordering her espresso.

Me, bending across the table to take her hand.

"So, how are you?" she says.

"They like your skirt," I say.

"I didn't wear it for them, you know?"

And I smile, leaning back. Then cross a leg. As a car pulls up to the curb and some guy gets in and they take off. "I love summer," I say.

"Why," she says. "For skirts?"

"For that, yes," I say, leaning in only to realize I'm mirroring her cheesy grin. "And this."

"Lunch by sunlight," she says. But my heart won't slow.

"With the occasional storm to cut the heat," I say, and her ankle brushes mine beneath the table. "Or something like that." But I can sense my voice waver as I take this in. "It's just bad for the drive."

"I know," she says, reflecting. Then her phone goes off again. But she ignores it. "And where has the day gone? It makes me wonder why I did this…chose this career. Until I remember, right, I didn't. It's good to step back."

"When you can," I say.

"If you can," she says.

"It's never fun when you're paid for it."

"It's *only* fun when you're paid," she says.

"No, I mean, the minute you do it for a living, it loses the thrill," I say. "But what'd you mean, choosing?"

"It was never my decision, just expected," she says. "And I don't mean to complain. It's food, this, a roof over my head. So let's change the subject."

"A roof that I've never actually seen."

"And why is that?" she says.

"I don't know," I say. "You tell me."

"Because I always stay at your place," she says.

"Invite me over," I say.

"To help me repaint?"

"I can paint," I say.

"That's what I'm afraid of," she says.

"Don't be afraid."

"It's just easier to stay with you," she says.

But her phone breaks in again and she excuses herself, stepping away, covering an ear. And just beyond that, *Don't Walk* blinks to the negligence of a woman texting up the curb past a guy who just stepped out of the Apple Store, now drawing up a cigarette, then dropping a match, smothering it.

And by the time she gets back, I'm still working over what I want to say. Or where to even go with this. So I ask without asking...

"Mother," she says in this matter-of-fact way before hiding her phone. "I'm sorry. I knew I shouldn't have called her in the first place."

Me, squeezing palms: "Sounds important."

"If driving to hang out in my old room is what you'd call important," she tells me.

"I can't imagine that would be a good time," I say.

"Just tell me you agree," she says.

"And what am I agreeing to?"

"That sometimes you ask for advice without actually needing it. Just hoping to have a polite enough conversation, to find some common ground—to flatter, maybe. As opposed to needing this lecture. As opposed to hearing that you're inept at all that you do. But yeah, if I don't get down there soon, she'll likely find me."

"And you don't want that?"

"Would you?" she says. "I'm sorry. I've tried—I have. It's just that, it's hard to explain. She's critical. I am her competition, or that's how she sees me. She really always has. So the only way to win with her, I know, is to fail...and I can't do that," she says as lunch arrives. Then silence again.

"I'm heading out in a few," I say if only to cut this tension. "Boston, I'm told. We'll see. But this wouldn't be until next week if it even happens," I say, and she gives me such a look. "I'll miss this."

"Is this work?" she says.

"Yes."

"So will I," she says, "miss this."

And I'm not sure why this feels so heavy. Why she feels heavy. She always does. And by heavy I mean, what is this? And why can't I figure it out? But instead I shake salt, watching her, wondering when have I ever anguished over having to leave...over this, work.

"What'd you tell them," she says, "you know, about me?"

"I said you don't hike. That's all."

"So the obvious?"

"And that you love white chocolate, the worst kind."

She laughs.

"And that we do this," I say, "but other than that, you're just a grand mystery."

"Why is that?" she says.

"I'm not really sure."

"Because I've never had you over," she says.

"Because you've never had me over," I say.

"And because I take it too slow," she says half mocking herself. And even she can't stifle a grin.

"Slow," I say. "Right." And this look she's giving me.

As she takes a drink. And so do I.

"What else did you say?"

"Nothing," I say.

"And why do I worry about what others think of me?"

"Why do you?" I say. And she smiles and so do I. "Because they loved you. They think you're gorgeous."

"Gorgeous," she says, scoffing, taking a bite, peering up.

"Gorgeous," I say.

And again there's her ankle brushing mine as a flurry of petals breeze down from that messy magnolia. Still wondering, as they settle, how an ankle, how a look so simple, can feel this euphoric.

CHAPTER NINE

Campbell's Soup

Madisen

Where should I be right now? Likely idling near the water cooler waiting for my Lean Cuisine to *bing* while humoring our CAD guy as he deludes himself into believing he's the only one with enough machismo to flip a five-gallon water jug. Or assuring my colleague, albeit unenthusiastically, that *it* only happens once as she carries on about her nuptials and a gown she says won't fit after too many rum balls she's quote-unquote *taste-testing* for their red barn reception.

All varieties of which I won't be sampling. Instead I'll be slipping back into work after the longer than usual lunch I'm about to have with Rae.

Since when do I, ever? And because, after their five o'clock commutes, after they've prepped real meals and shared anecdotes around familiar kitchen tables, I'll still be at the office plugging away.

Which leads me here to our table on the patio at Archipelago tucked beneath a tree that provides more privacy than it does shade as she brushes petals off the edge and asks about Andi, who's currently home sick with the flu.

"She was hoping to land something stronger than the bottle of Robitussin I dropped off this morning," I say. "My care package of Campbell's soup, two packs of Kleenex, Lysol, Zyrtec—since I told her it was just allergies, and those mmm-flavored cherry lozenges. Her voice, though, you know what I mean? I think I'm in love. I said so, and she laughed into a cough."

"Allergies?" Rae says. "I'm glad to never get those."

"They're really bad this year," I say, "with the rain and all."

And where am I going with this?

As she's bending across the table, taking my hand. And these nerves, God. "And so we meet again," she says. It's all she has to say to set them off.

And I'm back in a whirl. "And so we do," I say.

"How long do I have you?" she says.

"However long you want."

If only that was true. In reality, work has piled so high thanks to my being unusually unproductive all morning, as I run over this in my mind, what I'll say and how, convincing myself it's time, that I should, that I'm going to bring up Jordan.

To the point that I don't even realize this whole dialogue I'm having with myself.

But apparently, she has. "What could you possibly be thinking?" she says.

"That it's hard to break away," I say.

And that knot of tension builds as they argue at the next table over some op-ed published in *The New York Times*. And I'm listening in.

Asking her, "Have you read it?"

But what I wish I could say is *Would it matter?* Because it doesn't even feel as if she knows me right now.

Then I say, "You seem...I don't know."

"Overwhelmed," she says, kicking back.

"Definitely not that," I say.

"Nervous."

"As if you're ever nervous," I say.

"I'm always nervous around you," she says, and my heart skips a beat.

So before I'm able to regret it, I blurt out, "There's something I've been meaning to say."

"I can tell," she says.

As I stumble. "It's just that..."

"It's just that what?" she says.

"It's just that we met in a weird sort of way," I say.

"What way would that be?" she says, but she's slipping a hand up my thigh, which does things.

"You're sidetracking me," I say.

"Am I?"

"I don't even know where this is going," I say.

"Neither do I," she says.

"And it doesn't need to, I mean, go anywhere."

"I like where we are," she says.

"Well I'm concerned you might feel obligated," I say before I realize what she just said, that she likes where we are. So I say, "What's that supposed to mean?"

"Just that the more you stall," she says—and that look in her eye. That wonderfully agonizing look when I'm hoping to play serious here. Thinking, why does this have to be such a hard thing? Any of it. All of it. Because she wants me to be this: a girl who cappuccinos. The girl who lunches. Not charades, not Kidz Bop, not TeenNick.

So now what, I'm backing down?

"Let's see," she says. "I'll take a wild guess. You're either going to say we've gone too fast or there's someone else."

"Someone else?" I say. "That's not what you think."

"I'm not sure what to think," she says.

"Well there was somebody else," I say in this flippant sort of way. "But there's not."

"There was?"

"We're divorced."

"You were married?"

"I was. But it's over. It has been." As one confession spirals into the next until it dawns on me that I've said way too much. But not nearly enough. Not the right stuff. Not the planned stuff. But why does it matter? Since I'm waffling again, doubting, second-guessing, wondering if there might be a less apocalyptic time to finish this out.

And as I do, she's off on another topic.

"Will I see you tonight?" she says.

And with that, it just seems as if my moment is gone. "Would you like to?" I say.

"You should stop by," she says.

But it's close to nine when I do, and we're beat and she's cooked this meal and starts telling me about her day—in an unusually long and arduous way. And though I do flip back a couple of times, I never quite know what to say. Or how. And she doesn't bring it up, either.

But it's not as if that ends my preoccupation.

Which builds well into the morning when she slips out of bed and brews coffee as I wrap myself up in her robe. As we caffeinate half dressed. As the day sprawls out.

As my calendar fills in. And as my week flies by. Before it all wraps up.

And the subject is so far buried under good-byes by the time she heads out of town.

So by Friday, I'm sharing my version of our confessions over cappuccinos en route to Aline's with Andi before our night of Chianti meets charades.

"And that's it—that's your big reveal?" Andi says, sucking so hard on that bottle of water that the side sinks in. "A little anticlimactic, don't you think?"

"So it didn't go according to plan," I say.

"And therein lies your problem," she says. "You don't need a plan. You just slip it in, you know, like casual conversation."

"And how would you suggest I do that?"

"*My kid's totally into that,*" she says. "*My kid asks for that all the time.*"

"Why are you so much better than me, at parenting, at everything. And how do you come up with this stuff off the top of your head? And why didn't I think of that?" I say. "After I've agonized and planned. Still it comes right down to timing, which I never get right."

"Much like me with breakups," she says.

"There's never a good time for a breakup," I say.

"But for ten dragging minutes at least, she sat there sulking. Or watching the game. I guess it depends on how you look at it."

"What do you mean?"

"I mean, I had a game. I couldn't hang out and explain why our two-week relationship wouldn't go where she wanted it to go. And she wouldn't leave."

"Well I, for one, am grateful it didn't work out," I say. "Since I can't have you hooking up with someone my girlfriend used to date."

"Eons ago," she says.

"It doesn't matter," I say, dumbfounded that I just referred to Rae as my girlfriend.

"Anyway," she adds, "we have plans to see a show."

"But I thought you just ended it," I say.

"I did."

"Then why are you seeing a show?" I say.

"Why?" she says. "Because she invited me, that's why."

"Shouldn't you draw a line?"

"I did," she says. "It's over. I just wish it wasn't so hard. God, it's no wonder half the nation does this by text."

"You're giving me ideas," I joke.

"And yeah," she says, "don't."

"You know I'm not serious," I say.

"But you are. And you would. And it's wrong," she says. But I didn't mean a *text* text. I thought more along the lines of an email. An email wouldn't feel so utterly terrifying.

Still, why does it matter? She'll leave regardless, the minute she finds out. I'm like the worst ball and chain ever. At least it feels that way. But why should I apologize? I won't.

"That's fine, Andi, but this is not easy. So don't expect me to pull out violins for you if you can't for me," I say. "You're acting as if this girl was any different than any other. You do this all the time."

"No, I don't."

"Yes, you do," I say. "I mean, really, what are you even looking for? And how is this any different than all the rest? And why are you still hanging out with her?"

"It doesn't matter," she says.

"It does matter. You who always tells me to move on, get over it," I say. "You weren't in love with her."

"Like I said, it doesn't matter."

"It was two weeks!" I say.

And, again, this is not your typical Andi who honestly couldn't care less about what I thought, especially when it comes to this—to moving on, to getting over it. "Look, maybe I just wish I could find someone I click with," she says, "half as well as I click with you." And here, it all shifts. It changes, her posture, mine. "God, how do you get me to say this stuff?" But what is she saying? And what's changing? I'm not sure. All I know is that it feels somehow…wonderful. If anything could feel wonderful and tragic at the same time. "Look, can we not get into this?"

"What are you saying?"

"I'm saying that, look, timing is an artificial concept. It's right up there with closure, that stuff that never happens. Besides, the girl's totally into you. How could you not see that? And how could that possibly change because of this, because of Jordan?"

As we pull up to Aline's, which is the answer in and of itself. Proof positive that I could do or say the wrong thing and turn her off. And as much as I'd like to continue this conversation, we're here, and I'm not exactly sure if she really meant it that way. And besides, she's in this mood.

Aline's landed one of those downtown Victorians they've split into condos. With that sunny-side addition, scarcely in line with its whole multicolored Easter egg aesthetic, its asymmetry. And here I am, realizing that my wishing Aline had good taste and wishing she hadn't come upon it can be felt simultaneously.

It's usually back there behind that glass where Jordan waits, where she bolts out from to see me only to trip us up as soon as we near the front door.

And that's exactly what we get.

The kid dragging Andi inside. As I stay out here, understandably so, basking in a glint of sun after an awfully long week of fluorescent. Tense but trying not to be. Her peonies and poppies, her stone retainer wall. That thick-painted porch with its glossed-up ceiling, reflective even now.

As I catch, out of the corner of my eye, Aline, those leather flip-flops settled on high-cut grass.

But how long has she been there?

And why is she coming over?

Then with a voice so soft, so capable of stirring up a whole mess of possible replies, none of which I actually intend to use, she says, "You look nice."

Simple.

But not.

Wishing I could feel angry, not taken by her. Not flattered. But I am. Where is my *Fuck you* when I actually need it? When she's right here in front of me, spilling up nerves, while I wait for our usual, I don't know, *See you Sunday* or *Plans this weekend?* When I'm waiting to hear her say anything but *that.*

"You're welcome to come inside," she says.

"And why would you say that?"

"Because your daughter's in there," she says.

"Not that."

"Are compliments now out of bounds?" she says.

As I take a step back. "How is she?"

"She's great," I hear. "And you?"

But I am, I'm hoping she'll say it again, aren't I? "I'm fine."

"And I never did thank you for covering," she says.

A remark I'm quick to brush off with, "Sure."

"And have you been to the lake?"

"What are you doing?"

"What am I doing?"

"Yes, Aline, what are you doing?"

"Maybe I thought we could have a conversation, that's all."

"I see. Converse away."

"Please," she says.

"Converse, Aline."

"Why do you have to make this into a scene?" she says. "Consider Jordan."

"Who's nowhere in sight," I say.

And her ease, this way she settles on me as if I was hers.

But I'm always forgetting. I'm always flowering her up, holding her in my pocket no matter how inconsolably I lost her.

"I don't hate you," she says.

"Keep reminding me."

"And I'm not angry."

"I'm not either," I say.

Wishing I could find the agony and panic and rage she left me with. When it seems nowhere to be found.

As the kid comes dashing out and startles me.

With Andi seconds behind, and she's giving me that *What the hell are you doing?* glare.

"So. I'll see you Sunday," I say.

Wondering, as I do, if I'm always going to feel this.

Sometimes I do. Usually I don't.

Wondering, too, if there's any truth to that story I made up in my mind—the one that began soon after our real story came to an end.

And the look she gives as I turn away, it's hard to say.

CHAPTER TEN

Chopin

Rae

I'm working on my umpteenth bottle of VitaminWater Zero while flipping through this complimentary copy of *USA Today* that I found in my hotel room when I see Madisen's name flash across my screen. I pick up. "I forgot my umbrella," she says with this beautiful sort of sadness to her voice.

"At my place?" I say.

"That would be where I left it. With this eighty percent chance of rain today," she says. "How very *me* of me."

"Want me to head back and get it?"

"Would you?" she says.

"I would love to," I say, feeling this ridiculous grin come on. "I just got back to my room. And you would not believe the gym at this hotel. It's like Times Square—those LED video walls they have?—meets the Death Star. Spotlights. Disco balls. The only downside being this grandiose hotel room. Why do five-star hotels still look, I don't know, like the worst possible polyester print bedding they could find leftover from the seventies?"

"Because you happen to have exquisite taste," she says.

"As I dine at this mod, faux-wood desk between a Keurig machine and an ice bucket," I say.

"And why is it hotels leave ice buckets in every room?" Madisen says. "Do you think there's really a strong demand for ice? I mean, how many people tote champagne in their suitcase to celebrate tomorrow's sales meeting? TSA would never let me board a plane with liquids."

"You ponder such inane things," I say.

"Well, you figure companies cost-cut just about everywhere these days. Why not consider the most obvious source of waste—the unused ice bucket?"

"I think it's a rather nice touch, nostalgic," I say, reflecting on my outdated surroundings, this dry tuna sandwich.

"It's true," she says. "I suppose this latest influx of miserly clients has broken me down, wanting to trim this or cut that. It's been the theme of the year, exhausting, with no real thought to practicality, safety, compliance. Let's just make it pretty. Who cares if it works? Imagine how much more we might accomplish over the long haul with a bit more efficiency in x, y, z?" As my air kicks in and deep voices travel along the carpeted hallway just outside my door. But it's cold in here already. The place feels still, unsociable, settled, aside from her voice on the line, breathy. "I'm sorry," I hear. "I didn't mean to go on."

"I appreciate when you do," I say, realizing I've sunk into a whisper.

"So what are you having? Room service, I hope."

"Try a tuna sandwich, you know the prepackaged kind they sell in plastic at the convenience store? With too much celery. And never enough mayonnaise."

"Isn't room service," she says, "one of the only perks to staying at a polyester hotel?"

"There really are no perks to staying at a polyester hotel," I say, "unless you're in my bed, which you're not."

"Polyester hotel," she tells me, "or this conference room."

"Such a toss-up," I say as I finish my last bite, then bunch the wrapper.

"I'm picturing your room, though."

"You mean that chic headboard bolted to the wall?" I say. "Flowers in the bathroom—a nice enough touch. My laptop, charging. There must be fifty Wi-Fi networks all vying for my attention with names like *Get Off My WiFi* and *The Password is LOVE*. And a chair near the sitting table over by the door where they left today's paper. One hundred eighty cable channels I have no desire to watch. The most delicious smelling soap you could imagine. My hair's still wet. Room 514."

"The fifth floor?" she says. "I bet you have an amazing view."

"I do. It's a shame you're not here to enjoy it," I say. "But you'll never guess what I'm doing."

"Let's see. You must be sipping champagne they left chilled in that little ice bucket."

"Had they left me a bottle of champagne, it would be gone by now. I assure you. More like trying to clear off an old memory card. I'm uploading those shots I took of you on our hike."

"Of what," she says, "my promenade along a steep mountainside, Starbucks in hand?"

"Not quite," I say.

"What, then?"

"You don't exactly have a shirt on," I say. "Fully, that is. Not fully."

And as soon as that sinks in, she says, "You didn't—"

"You didn't honestly believe I was out scouting a path like some well-behaved Girl Scout, did you?" More like eighty-seven pictures, all at 3.5 megs. Not that I share that part of the story. "And let's just say for the sake of argument that if you were to, I don't know, stop by unannounced and surprise me, you think you might wear this again?"

"What is it you're trying to say?"

"That I kind of like this ensemble," I say.

"Maybe we could continue this conversation once I get home from work?" she says.

"I wouldn't mind having this conversation right there at your office."

"Yeah, and like I said, I'll call you just as soon as I get home."

And that she does.

Me: "I thought you'd never call."

Madisen: "I'm sorry…I was stuck in traffic. How was your shower?"

Me: "And why is that?"

Madisen: "Why was I stuck in traffic? They've set up road construction everywhere."

Me: "I was imagining, hoping, you might be on your way…to bring me room service."

Madisen: "I could pull off room service."

Me: "But you would've caught me in the shower."

Madisen: "We have universal room keys, you know. Hotels always do."

Me: "Would you wait for me to get out…to get your tip? Or would you join me?"

Madisen: "I like that those are my only two options."

Me: "I would want you to join me."

Madisen: "Still, I think I might rather be management."

Me: "You'd rather be management…why?"

Madisen: "Because they wear suits, and that's what I happen to be wearing."

Me: "Management you are."

Madisen: "And it was brought to my attention that you weren't particularly pleased."

Me: "Not with my order, no."

Madisen: "How can we make that up to you?"

Me: "What are my options?"

Madisen: "I see you brought Taittinger for your stay."

Me: "I'm making use of your rather nice ice bucket."

Madisen: "We do aim to please."

Me: "Then maybe you could rectify this situation."

Madisen: "Tell me what you're wearing right now."

Me: "Who, me?"

Madisen: "Why are you so cute?"

Me: "Can I just say I'm wearing Diesels? I'm not, more like pajamas, but…"

Madisen: "You're really good at this."

Me: "You know, I'm not."

Madisen: "You are. And I love your Diesels."

Me: "Do you?"

Madisen: "I'm taking my shoes off. I'm at the edge of my bed."

Me: "And you're still in your suit?"

Madisen: "Or something like that, trousers, white button-up…I'm picturing your room."

Me: "You're picturing a gigantic polyester bed. I'd rather imagine yours."

Madisen: "You don't even know what my room looks like, do you? So, I have this high headboard and tall ceiling, plaster coving."

Me: "I don't know what that is. But say I walk in…"

Madisen: "Say you walk in. If you look to your right, you'll see an antique card catalog about waist high. I had it restored. And if you look to your left, you'll see my bureau, my closet. And beside that, a leather beanbag, which is tan and sort of distressed. I pile clothes on it, like now. But say you're looking straight ahead…that's where you'll find my bed. And I have two lamps, one on either side. My window's open. It's not dark. So there's tons and tons of birds outside, and my neighbor's playing the piano. And I'm rather hoping that you might take those off."

Me: "Take what off?"

Madisen: "Your jeans."

Me: "Oh."

Madisen: "I seem to recall you starting this."

Me: "I did, didn't I?"

Madisen: "So what are you thinking about now?"

Me: "You wearing that suit."

Madisen: "I'm out of that."

Me: "Seriously? So what're you in?"

Madisen: "I guess you would have to describe this as…"

Me: "As what?"

Madisen: "As my hiking attire."

Me: "God, how you do this to me."

Madisen: "I think you started it."

Me: "So you're basically in, *ahem*, that. On your bed…right now?"

Madisen: "Well, yes, and this stack of pillows, too many."

Me: "And that's what I see…as I'm leaning against your door…"

Madisen: "But eventually you do come closer, I hope…"

Me: "And I just sort of take you in…"

Madisen: "So I'll need to pull you down and just sort of straddle you."

Me: "Wait, wait. You're falling out of this. And your hair's all over my face…"

Madisen: "There, I'll flip it to the side…"

Me: "What'll you do next?"

The sad part being, some meeting she has, early, she says. So I end up falling asleep, more like not sleeping, more like racking up mental notes all night and day on what I should—and shouldn't—say. So much that this gone-for-a-week is beginning to feel like a string of sad events I'll need to endure so I can get back to my room.

And call.

Like tonight again, because—yeah, I know. I shouldn't.

As I collapse across my bed—and by that, I mean flat on my back on this enormous king-sized mattress made for plenty more than one.

And we begin again as if there were no in-betweens. No days. No nights. No life outside of this right here. "I did," Madisen says, "before Andi sent me four emails in a row, and anyway, she's coming by."

"Which means her voice came back?"

"It did…just in time for Chianti," she says followed by a long battery-draining pause. "Chianti and charades," she finally says. "This weekend." And then again, radio silence. Which just sort of freaks me out, and I'm not sure why. But, whatever, it's late and she's exhausted and so am I.

"So, is everything all right?"

I hear her sigh. "I'm sorry," she says, "just reading her millionth email."

"And it wasn't laryngitis?"

"Allergies," she says. "It's like that perfect storm right now of single meets suddenly sick, or recovering. So days of Delsym, documentaries. Right now, she's trying to convince me to go vegan."

"Don't go vegan," I say. "They can't eat cheese."

"I love cheese," she says. "I think she might also be having some sort of meltdown or midlife crisis."

"I still remember my first."

"Your first midlife crisis?"

"Yes," I say. "I think I was twenty-six. I lost my job."

"I was fired one time for sending an email to the wrong distribution list. I was a temp. I can't even remember what they did anymore. But that went out and calls started coming in from their Northwest customers asking about this Greek potluck and why were they invited."

"Epic."

"It was great PR," she says. "Why were you?"

"Insubordination."

"That's a thing?"

"Subordination, apparently, is a condition of employment."

"You don't subordinate well?" she says.

"I wouldn't say so, no."

"Andi found gray hair. One strand. But not just that. She's all about endocrine disruptors and hormones and UV. And she's giving me all sorts of advice."

"About tofu and quinoa?"

"About sunscreen. And bad choices. She's sort of on my case," Madisen says. "But we won't talk about that. I was thinking today again about how you've never actually been to my place."

"Forget I said that."

"Why…don't you want to?" she says.

"You're inviting me?"

"I might be," she says.

"So why is this girl on your case?"

"I can't really say. It'll ruin your night."

As if that wasn't the case already, being miles away. "Then ruin my night," I say.

"You tell me that now."

But I'm still thinking about her offer. "Write something down for me."

"What?" she says.

"Beer to Drink Music to '17 Tropical Blonde."

"And what's this?" she says.

"It's my drink request for the night I swing by," I say. "Don't take her advice."

"Why not?"

"Because."

"You don't even know what she said."

"It doesn't matter. Just be you."

And I'm fixing my hair in this mirror when I hear all of that. An uproar and commotion and, "Traffic," she shouts. "I'm heading out. It's pouring—oh my God!—and you have my umbrella," and then, "Shit," before a whoop and the car slams shut, and then it's calm again. "I'm. So. Drenched," she says—and I hear it like that, in staccato. So now I'm just laughing. "I could seriously wring this shirt out."

Which is what I'm thinking about as she makes her way home, and I shower, change. And afterward she calls, and I'm hoping to explain something technical while she loads dishes. Utensils. Rips an envelope. Then more thuds and she's bringing up work again. So during the time it takes for her to undress and get dressed, I offer up my generic advice. Until she slips into bed. Until I'm falling asleep feeling *if only* she was here beside me. And feeling as if everything was possible. It's just the most powerful thing.

So I call the next day.

"Cameron," I say.

"Cameron?" Madisen says.

"She's the one who got me arrested last year in DC thanks to her protest on climate change. I haven't seen her since...I don't know. We met for sushi, tempura, but she kept on about old times. About some trip she took to Stockholm, someone she knew online. And it beat my end of the day, as ten of my opinionated clients tried to head up one simple decision, but they can't." Then it turns into this thing. I don't know. Her MacBook powering down. And a key and a lock and heels echoing along some hallway.

"Do you find it easier," she's saying, "when you're having those conversations in person, like that?"

"Instead of what?"

"Instead of this, like on the phone or email," she says.

"I don't care either way," I say drawing drapes—layer after hotel layer, thinking this is the best part of my trip, and she's not even here. As I'm watching that transitional sky as it sets, not dark but not daylight either. When streetlights flick. That pulse of neon.

"And lunch, sushi, your Friday thing."

"She's starting a new job," I say, "on Monday, and she talked about that incessantly," omitting the fact that I talked about Madisen incessantly. Pretty much. And we commiserate some more. "I won't really see her after this." And as soon as I finish one thought, she's on to the next. Until two hours pass just like that, and I say, "Whenever you get quiet like that, it's like you're hanging up."

"I'm not," she says in that lying in bed voice. "I was just thinking."

"About what?" I say.

"How once you go down a certain path," she says, "you can never come back."

"What path would that be?"

"This one."

And the thing is, she doesn't call on Friday. I don't, either. Reason being, she's now committed her weekend to the BFF. And I've committed mine to dinner with Cameron.

And the gym, and laps, the pool, and *Why not?* I figure as I order a plate of room service to accompany my in-room on-demand double feature.

The following Monday, I'm texting *good night* before squeezing one last time into hotel-tight sheets. And on Tuesday I'm lugging bags down the hall to the elevator downstairs where they're serving blueberry scones and bourbon caramel glazed upside-down cake, which is even better than it sounds, plus way strong coffee and that *USA Today* I've tucked under an arm, only to segue into hours of highway hypnosis hosted by Simon & Schuster audio.

And somewhere in the hundred and twenty-five miles or so between Boston and back home, I give her a ring. "I'm still on the road," I say, "running late."

Hearing the only thing I didn't want to hear when I got back, which is, "Me too." And not just today. But day after day after day.

Until Friday, when the last thing I care to deal with as I make my way over to her place is this call from Elizabeth. "Has Avery rung you?" she says.

"Not recently," I say. Can't this wait? Especially given the fact that I've agonized through the most convoluted traffic detour anyone could ever imagine, and here I'm minutes away. "I'm meeting Madisen."

"I heard," she tells me.

"You heard what?"

"About your ooh la la with your new girl."

"Then why'd you call?" I say.

"I wouldn't have," she says, "except they're on their way."

"On their way?" I say.

"To Paris," she says.

"Who's *they*?"

"Avery and some girl she just hooked up with. For something, I don't know, spontaneous, romantic. I call it insanity, and really, you need to talk with her. She listens only to you."

"Avery never listens to me," I say.

"She only listens to you," she says.

"Is this her firefighter?"

"It is," she says. "And guess who's moved in?"

Wondering, as I dial Avery, why the crisis of the year needs to hit today.

"Avery," I say.

"And where've you been? You've talked to Elizabeth."

"Yes—I mean *no*. I mean, I only have a few. So I wanted to play catch-me-up CliffsNotes style before unplugging for the rest of the weekend. And please tell me you didn't move in."

"She makes me breakfast, Rae, and let's just say there are so many ways you can dine in bed."

"You can spare me the details."

"I'm thinking she'll propose," she says.

"And what would you say?"

"When I get back, we'll have drinks. I'll buy. And I'll show you my ring."

Thinking Elizabeth is going to kill me, but do I care? "Do that," I say.

Because my lungs are filling with the scent of TGIF as I dive across the seat to grab my bag, then hop the curb, hoping to quell this influx of nerves. Yet failing. Catching that echo of an old piano until her door sucks in, and I'm accosted with way more skin than a girl could possibly handle with any sort of composure.

And let's just say that I don't.

Or, I should say, I didn't, during the next however many hours during which I could scarcely muster up enough eloquence to break that awkward silence, let alone hope to impress. And after…how long had it been? But all I could think to say was, "Hi."

And she said the same.

And I said, "How've you been?"

"Good."

"Good," I said. Half confident, half trembling.

But she kissed me, and well, that was it. It's when I backed her up inside. When I reached behind to kick shut the door. Then pressed her up against it, feeling my way down. It's when the best part of our evening began just as easily as my bag slipping to the floor.

Because I was thinking about her call or something like that when she led me along this hall with tall walls in bare feet just past this and over there, where I kept glancing. I kept peeking. Into the next room with every turn—everywhere I'd never been. As if I might find something that would tell me a little more about her. Even though I never did.

Until she was at the fridge, peering in, bent, glancing back, grinning in that way, in that narrow galley of a kitchen. Until she was leaning beside me, hair loose, tousled, and I caught that scent. Her rosemary mint, it tickled my lip as twilight streamed intermittently through the swell of another curtain.

And wearing that, when something more conventional, more conservative would've sufficed, something buttoned or zipped. Or jeans like me, loose. There were so many other options. But instead she chose that skirt, which I could easily hike if I wanted to—even as she stood beside that counter popping tops off bottles, then handing me one.

Before I felt that taste lingering on her tongue.

"You must do this often," I said, but my heart was racing.

"What's that?" And she kept on.

"Invite girls over to your digs…then seduce them."

Because where had my mind gone? I was talking then about neighbors instead, that somber tune they played, their drowning us out. Even as that chair went crashing against the floor, as I backed her up, as we pressed against the table, as she fingered along its edge, and my heart rushed. As I lifted her. As she climbed up. Watching her flush-faced as she drew me higher, that wrist slack over its lip as I found my way down. Raising hips to the sound of her sigh, her trembling, her knees lifting. Then bracing her down with my arm when she wouldn't stop shifting.

CHAPTER ELEVEN

101 Conversation Starters

Madisen

Were this any other weekend, I would be spreading butter along with wild blueberry jam on my sourdough toast, then making my way out, where I could sit in the still breeze, a glint of sun peering through those leaves, planning out my day. Anything but this. Because Saturdays are my errand days, my get it done before noon days, shopping before cleaning, then everything else.

But I'll accomplish none of this.

Instead I'm entertained by a brisk beam of sun now shifting its way across her lips as we figure out just how highly irresponsible two adults can be when wrapped in little more than our own exhausted euphoria.

"So how well do you know your neighbors?" she says.

My neighbors are far from neighborly. There are fences framing courtyards that are hardscaped and adorned in potted plants. And in the span of three or maybe four steps out, we latch car doors and tune radios without a single *How's it going?* or even a *Good morning*.

"Why do you ask?" I say.

"Because we left that window open," she says.

All night? And, sure, I'm mortified, I mean, how loud did I get last night? Though I do manage to crawl across and snap the latch, as if that would do me any good. "I love how you laugh about this," I say as I slip back into bed.

"So you had a good time," she's saying. Then she tugs me down. "No harm in that." And I'm really getting into her consoling, like almost to the point that it's working, when I hear that noise—thinking *What is that?* And she's grabbing her phone from the table and shutting it down. "Nobody heard a thing," she says, "I promise," as her palm slow dives under a pillow.

And who knows how long we stay this way?

Or what time it is when we make our way downstairs. I only know it's cool once the air settles into that heavy kind of dense you wish would just pour.

"I wouldn't call it that," she's saying. "More like insurance. But what about you?"

"So when you think someone's ready to leave, you just—"

"Secure the next," she says.

"Sometimes?" I say.

"*That* time," Rae says, laughing in this way, and I'm suddenly furious or jealous or—who knows?—slightly devastated. "Which isn't what you think."

"And that's how you justify it," I say, "overlapping?"

"She was polyamorous," Rae says.

"So you're seeing this girl who was polyamorous," I say. "Which means you could see other people. And how does that qualify as overlapping?"

"She wanted to be more involved in the other people part."

"And were you ever," I say, "involved?"

"You should see the look on your face," she says.

"It would matter," I say, recoiling.

"Would it? Listen, it was her way of saying *We're through*. Or maybe I'm not the wait-around type," she says. "Either that or, look, I didn't even know she was. So tell me about yours."

"My ménage à trois?" I laugh.

"Was there?"

"No!" I say.

"Deal breakers," she says. "I mean deal breakers." Which might be something we should, I don't know, go into more at some point, or not. Since I've never really thought about my own—just worry about hers. "Because isn't this situational?" she says.

"Situational?" I say.

"Overlapping, I mean, it's not black-and-white."

"But it's not right," I say.

"It can be," she says.

"Why is this so disconcerting?"

"The only thing I'm saying is, look, there are times when it does make sense," she says, adding this rather intense gaze. And if I didn't know any better, I'd think she might be questioning me as opposed to the other way around. "I'm referring to situations where you dive in too quick, not knowing what you might've gotten into—that's all." Which might be why that knot in my stomach churns. "When you get too serious too soon before ever really knowing who they are. Or when they change that drastically midway."

And who would not read into this?

Because next I'm hearing Andi, and I'm thinking *Slip it in*. Like, now.

I mean, talk about timing. So once she finishes up, I say, "What would you like to know about me?"

"Just the important stuff," Rae says.

"But what's important to you? I've been curious about that."

"Have you ever," she says, "overlapped?"

"No, the absolute worst you could do," I say, "is betray someone's trust."

"Well, how long have we known each other?" she says. "Not long."

"In lesbian terms, we should be celebrating some sort of anniversary today."

"Would that be paper," she says, "or cotton?"

"I think it's our trip to the dog shelter anniversary," I say, "where we adopt a stray."

"Well, I don't do lesbian terms," she says. "Nor do I expect to know all there is to know about you right away. So I really don't mind if you're holding something back. Aside from, well—"

"Aside from what?"

"What would you like for lunch?"

"You're asking me about lunch?" I say, wondering how I've gotten so sidetracked. "I'm open to whatever you are."

"Then how about grilled and smothered in cheese…not vegan? Where could we go? Say, pub cuisine. Then after, we could hit that market on Burnside on our way home." Home, I think. Why does that sound, I don't know, so perfectly wonderful? It all sounds so perfectly wonderful coming from her.

We don't broach any of those weighty topics along the drive. But it's not superficial, either. And after the heat of our day, as we step inside this air-conditioned pub, as I catch my reflection in a mirror, after realizing how I look, as if surfacing from some sort of night and, well…

To think we left that window up.

As our host walks us back to the table along this winding path until we're hidden against this endless stretch of brick, which divorces us from the main dining area. As Rae comes up from behind and grips around my waist, and we're walking that way. And she's pulling my chair. Where it's quiet, aside from that music, which is low and slow and unrecognizable.

As I'm trying to recognize that unrecognizable and she opens her menu with, "Social justice advertising."

"Where do you come up with these topics?"

"Elizabeth," she says, "who's having it out on Facebook. She despises companies that hijack a cause."

"You mean like Nike and Gillette?" I say.

"I mean like Nike and Gillette and McDonald's, with their gay coming out commercial."

"Advertising is the new religion," I say as I scan four pages of menu clipped to a board.

"Advertising is the new activist," she says. "And corporations are people with thoughts and beliefs and views...and where do you draw the line? Do we start shaving our legs with Gillette to support the cause?"

"Aren't they still gendered, pink and blue?" I say, glancing just in time to catch her gaze from above the menu. "Have I said something wrong?"

"You say nothing wrong," she says.

"I say everything wrong."

"I just don't usually meet people who think the way I do," she says before silence. Then we're both back to our menu. "But remember those milk ads and that mustache?"

"I thought I could look like Lara Croft," I say, "or Kate Moss."

"As if Kate Moss drinks milk," Rae says. "Mac versus PC. Iconic."

"No, Calvin Klein."

"Again, Kate Moss," she says.

"I love Kate Moss," I say.

"She's a hot mess."

"She's a hot mess who sold every perfume he ever made."

And we share something again, this look which feels, I don't know, settling? "I think it cheapens a cause," Rae says, "when they tout morality through a product brand—for monetary gain, to up their stock."

"But they always have," I say. "Corporations always have. Think

Coca-Cola. As if hippies were all about peace, love, and high fructose corn syrup."

"You're so right," she says. "Caveat emptor."

"Caveat emptor," I say. "It's not worth the fight."

But back to lunch options, which sound too amazing right now. That and…déjà vu. Glancing up only when she sets her menu aside with, "Such the look you're giving me."

"I'm sorry," I say. "You reminded me of someone."

As she bends across the table. "And that's a good thing, right?"

"Absolutely," I say. Grateful when the waiter breaks in with our water. So I thank him. Then order a mimosa, as does Rae. And when he leaves, she prompts me for more.

"It's nothing," I say because we can't go there.

"Who'd I remind you of?" she says.

"Long story," I say.

"But we have all weekend," she says. And why does she always do this?

"It was just someone I spent a lot of time with," I say, "for a while, which wasn't technically necessary. More like a client. And she just so happened to say the same thing you did. *I don't think I've ever met anyone who thinks the way I do*, or something along those lines. That's all."

"You're not as harmless as people may think."

"Don't read between the lines," I say.

"Am I?"

"I'm talking about a long, long time ago when I was so wrapped up in myself. You wouldn't have recognized me," I say. "You could say I wanted her business, and I got it."

"That's what I thought," she says.

"But not in the way you think."

"No?" she says as our drinks arrive.

"What time is it?" I say.

"Two thirty," she says. "So tell me."

"Ask me something else," I say.

"You would, though," Rae says, "wouldn't you?"

"Have you?"

"Possibly."

"You've slept with someone to land a job?" I say.

"So you did," she says. "Don't you think that's unethical?"

"We were just two people."

"So to answer your question," she says, "I haven't slept with anyone to land a job. I'd be more afraid to lose that job over it."

"I'm sure you could," I say, "and I'd never do it again. But she was oddly interesting. And had it not been a client, who knows? I would've enjoyed knowing her. It sort of broke my heart. And as you might imagine, I don't feel comfortable talking about it—for obvious reasons. So why don't we change the subject?"

"To what?" she says.

"If she was straight," I say, "would that stop you?"

"If it was you," she says, "no."

"And if she lived miles and miles away?" I say. "Would you wait?"

"That all depends."

"Would you wait for me?" I say.

"Yes," she says.

"How about…"

"What?" she says.

"Would you date someone with a child?" I say, taking a deep breath.

"All right, not expecting that one," she says. "Have you?"

"I haven't."

"Well, neither have I," she says.

Later we swing by the market, where Etta James is having "A Sunday Kind of Love." I pick up what I need for the week, adding a bottle of prosecco (make that two) along with Florida orange juice sans pulp. And by the end of the day, we're stepping onto the terrace, barefoot on tiles, accompanied by my perfect attempt at mixing up a few more drinks at home for the two of us.

Thinking it's not the first night I've been out here entertained by more than just muffled jets overhead, those dark notes drifting from their piano, with the sky and its glow, turquoise, clear, that unsettled haze. Yet this feels like a first.

With that scent of moisture in the air, but cooler now, relaxed, as she gazes in that scholarly way, fingers woven between knees, making her seem so held together. Even now, with that touch of apprehension about her.

So I ask, "Is everything all right?"

And she says, "Yeah. Why do you ask?"

"And so what were you thinking just now?"

Then she says, "Who's to say?" And while she doesn't exactly go on, it's enough to hold me entranced by the sound of her voice. "It's not always a bad thing," she says, leaning in. And still I can't turn away.

As she peers into the night, into her glass, into that window on the second floor—then down to a potted plant. Until she's back to me again. But how long have I been watching her like this as I ponder last night with my skirt hiked up at the table? Those slow lips against mine. Her breath as it touched my skin and parted my legs.

It's that same sound, just still. Just silent and loud like that, since I'm drowning in thoughts. As her knee keeps nudging against mine.

As she devastates me. Because what would she like me to say? That I want to stay right here wrapped up in this every single day? With my heart racing—from what? From a knee that can turn my every last nerve upside down. That I'm terrified. That I haven't stopped thinking about her. That life, that work—that everything on every day has become such a huge sort of intrusion anymore.

As the cooling hum of twilight settles in and I hear, "Tell me about family, then. Kids," casually like that, as she's edging off the chair. As she sets her glass down. And it makes that sound. "Have you ever thought about that?"

And I guess you never really think about those things you do when you feel cornered, uncomfortable. But they all seem magnified now. My face as it warms, my arms as they slip into one another. Our distance.

They're shutting the window now, turning on air. It's loud. And all I can hear is the hum of a motor. My heart racing. Or maybe it's the clicks of cicadas, as she waits for my response.

"Are you always like this?" I say.

"What's that?"

"Proposing barefoot over mimosas?"

But that laugh is far from shy. "Is that what I'm doing?"

"Why not tell me about yours?" I say.

"What, family?" she says. But does she even need to? She didn't even need to do *that* to let me know I've gone too far.

"I've said too much," I say.

"You never do," she says.

"I always do," I say.

"No, you don't."

"But you never bring it up," I say.

"Since there's nothing *to* bring up," she says.

"Because we're not there yet?"

"Because of a lot," Rae says.

"Because you'd rather I not know," I say.

"Because they don't want me," she says. "They don't want me. Which means I've thoroughly impressed you."

"You've thoroughly impressed me," I say.

"I don't think I have."

"You really have." But there's so much more I could say.

"Then when will you make the time," she says, "to meet Avery, Elizabeth? That's family." And she's back on that again. But I'll have Jordan.

"We'll see," I say.

"And what does that mean?"

"It means that we'll see. How you feel. After this." And I bottom my drink.

As I set it down. As she sinks in her seat. As I bend over mine.

Glancing to the side, where I find her shadow of a kiss at my lips, its citrus and prosecco. Her voice tickling my ear, or maybe it's a breeze, weak, when I hear, "I'm so in love with you."

CHAPTER TWELVE

My Worst Possible Timing

Rae

You know that hidden stretch of road out where nobody goes, and that feeling as some old song comes on and you sing along or just go there again, wishing you could dance or cry alone out in the middle of it all with those windows rolled down until the odometer slides into view and you're, like, *oh shit*. But it's not as if you can pull back or slow down or anything like that. I mean, it feels too good to just go there and stop watching your speed for once.

It's where Elizabeth would tell me to chill. And when that didn't work, *What the hell, Rae?*

So what if I did the whole *I love you* thing first? Haven't we shared everything right down to my vast collection of rare seventies DVDs? Even those awkward shots of me in that jester suit they convinced me into wearing Halloweens ago.

Because were it not for that song ending last night, me having to get up and go inside and start it up again, then her coming in to pour another glass, it shifted the mood. And if it wasn't for the storm passing through, that downpour soaking my shirt as I ran back outside to grab my glass, we might've sat out there gazing at the haze of a moon all night, and maybe then she would've said it right back.

At least that's what I'm trying to convince myself as I kick it, weekend style, on her couch while she comes in carrying two mugs of coffee, hands me one, and takes a seat. Then she does that thing where you rest your chin on the heels of your hand before glancing up, as if I've caught her in some sort of lie. It's a look too easily camouflaged behind that wide-rimmed mug.

Still, haven't I walked out with less of an incentive than this, too ready to wrap things up at that first hint of hesitation? When it starts to feel unpredictable, uncertain, like now.

Because maybe this is it for her. Maybe I blew it, jumping the gun, and there she is over there thinking up ways to cut this long story short. What if we're at that point of the show where it ends and we're faced with empty seats after curtains fall, when we all file out, house-lights blind, and you look around to find that it was all just an illusion. Some kind of cruel masquerade. Theatrics. They're not who you thought they were.

Really. Maybe she isn't. Maybe none of this is. Maybe I'm fooling myself.

Still, why does it feel as if I'm riding a crescendo, deep and dull and reverberating? As I shift my gaze out the window.

"Tell me what an awful host I am," Madisen's saying. But she's indulging in this, reveling in it all. In my worst possible timing because, let's face it, there are things you just don't reveal this soon.

"Please don't host me," I say, feeling as I speak that I should run, leave, something. But I can't.

"I'm sorry—I've just never been good at entertaining," I hear as her posture softens, unlike mine.

"Well, that's fine," I say, "because I'm not your guest."

Next she's propping feet up on the couch, then nudging me. And every once in a while, she'll raise a knee to run her palm up the length of her shin, that same way she fingers her lips when she uses that balm from a tin, the kind that tastes like watermelon and honeysuckle and rainbows full of infinite promises. Sweet and succulent and new. And she's gazing at me over a lifted knee.

While I drape an arm along the back of the couch, which she doesn't catch, but the cat does, nudging my knuckle with her nose, then off behind the curtain to the window she goes.

"I've been thinking," she says, "about what you said last night."

"I said a lot," I say, admittedly sulking.

"I meant that part about family," she says. "Because I've never really understood why their stamp of approval means so much. They're all just flawed and damaged like the rest of us. Yet when they criticize, our world closes in. I wish I didn't care so much."

"Then don't," I say.

"I do," she says. "But maybe I'm reevaluating, I guess."

"Look, you can spend your whole life waiting for someone to love and accept you," I say. "Or you can live it instead."

But it's as if being here seems endless and longer and extra everything. At the same time, it's just a lot of nothing, like this. There are no someplaces to be, no anythings to do. We just laze around and talk about nothing at all until we run out of that and begin again. It's that sense you get when you're off on holiday, strolling through everything new. And even as they're hurrying around and running about, serving, hosting, waiting on you, it doesn't click, that everything goes on with or without you. Because life has paused for one brief, perfectly idyllic moment. Right here in this.

"Then tell me why it's so hard for me to reconcile?" she says.

"I don't know," I say. "Why is it?"

"To me, it feels so polarizing. How could someone give up on their own child?"

"That's because it is," I say.

"Well, I'm trying to put myself in their shoes," Madisen says.

"You can't," I say. "They live in an echo chamber. You don't."

Next she's giving me that look again. It's the same look she gave me last night in that shared mirror in the bathroom, which feels unnerving, so much that my heart's now pounding uncontrollably. Because I don't know what she wants from me.

Remembering the way she said: "You just act that way, as if nothing ever bothers you."

"Maybe I just wanted to get you home."

"You'll say anything," she said, towel-drying her hair. "You're doing it to me now."

"What am I doing?"

"Saying everything I want to hear," she said, "just to draw me in."

"Have I drawn you in?"

"Of course you have."

Me: "But you don't think I'm sincere?"

Madisen: "I didn't say that."

Me: "Then what are you saying?"

Madisen: "Just that you don't know me."

Me: "Don't I?"

Madisen: "Not completely."

Me: "You're not at all what I expected."

Madisen: "What'd you expect?"

Me: "Things."

Madisen: "When we met?"

Me: "I thought you were hot. Still do."

Madisen: "And what else?"

Me: "Either straight or taken. You came with somebody, and I don't know…"

Madisen: "If I had been taken, would that have stopped you?"

Me: "Obviously it didn't."

Madisen: "You were interesting."

Me: "That's it? You found me interesting? I find you extremely hard to read."

Madisen: "And that goes both ways. Now I'm worried."

Me: "About?"

Madisen: "I don't know. That I could lose this. I could say the wrong thing, and that's that. So I'm trying to be rational."

Me: "Which is why you're agonizing."

Madisen: "The good kind of agony?"

Me: "The only kind."

Madisen: "So what if this ends? Like, say there's something about me that changes it all."

Me: "Nothing could."

Madisen: "Yes, it could."

Me: "And do you think it would be a pretty end? Where we traipse off into the sunset, remaining friends forevermore as all lesbians do?"

Madisen: "It won't be pretty."

Me: "And why is that?"

Madisen: "I think you know."

Me: "And I think you're madly in love with me."

But that glimpse beneath her shirt was so distracting that I didn't care what she said back. Much like now, with that sheen settling along the groove just above her lip as she tries to cool off, reclining against the couch, her skin so radiant and honeyed at ten a.m., haze shifting along her jaw, down her neck.

Until I'm back to the curtain ballooning in the breeze, offering a peek of life outside before the screen sucks it flat again. As that roar of diesel pauses at the curb and I glance out and see UPS, and that uniform shifts me back into everything ordinary. To packages being tracked. To morning radio, to DJs, to banter. To news reports and social media. To road rage. And all the while, we're here, partaking in none of that.

"I've never in my life done that," she says. "I don't meet up with girls at bars and go back to their place."

"So how does it work?" I say.

"They start as friends."

"Or clients," I say.

"As if I've had so many," Madisen says. "I was married."

"Yeah," I say. "Don't remind me."

"Everything about you is so wonderful. But that's so overwhelming, like I can't get out. Like I can't stop. Like I can't slow down enough to think, and it's not as if you know me. And you should before—"

"Before what?"

"Before…you know," she says.

"Is this about last night?"

"You don't know enough about me yet," she says. "So how could you love me?"

"So that's what this is about."

"No," she says.

"It's about you and your slumber-party sweethearts braiding hair, waiting however long before ever actually doing it, and that's *knowing*? How charming. It's not about knowing, trivia, Twenty Questions. Who even cares about knowing? It's how I feel. And I think you do, too."

"How would you know what I feel?"

"Because you just told me," I say.

"Told you what?"

"You told me everything I need to know," I say.

"But I'm just some girl you met by chance at the bar," she says.

"You're not some girl," I say. "Well, *were*—perhaps were. But had I thought that, I wouldn't be here. I wouldn't call. I wouldn't want you to call. And really, how do you think this is for me? You were married, you said, for how many years? Because when have I ever had anything real like that?" And shit, maybe I'm just done. Not with her but with me. "Listen."

"What?" she says.

"This is going nowhere," I say. "Plus I have messages, and everyone's in a crisis right now, and I've just deserted them."

Which leads me to the second floor and down a hall to her room where everything seems more amusing, more inviting for some reason, now that I'm alone. This leather tray and a stack of coins. Wrapped candy. Some random key. This tube of hand cream crimped at the end. And another tube of lipstick, which I snap, then reseal, feeling more than slightly voyeuristic after I do. And there's that balm in a tin that she carries around.

But what am I trying to find? Some random simple object in her room that'll answer every question I have?

She has no television. No photographs. Nothing on top of her bureau. Just a half-melted scented candle under an open window, where you can see right down into the neighbor's yard. They're fueling up the grill now, their cloud of smoke, mesquite, deep voices, indiscernible from this height. It's more like mumbling. A woman's laughter. As I try to imagine our pianist among the crowd.

Then I notice a baseball cap on a hook on her door and I try it on.

And my phone rings. It's buried under yesterday's jeans. But I don't pick it up.

Instead I head down the hall to the bathroom at the end where, on a shelf near her sink, there are bottles and bottles of Aveda. More of this and that. As I twist a faucet to wash my hands and reach for the towel and find a hook, empty, until I'm walking along the hall past doors that are shut, and I'm opening one, then the next.

Eventually reaching this closet with linens and a couple bars of soap, hand cut. And I dry my face, then hang the towel on that hook.

Before bouncing down and spinning around the banister to the hall. My chin rests against her shoulder, and I glance at her screen.

"All caught up?" I say.

And she is. So I pull a chair as she twists waves of hair above her head. That scent of hickory breezing in, heavier now. As she hides her laugh behind a mug the color of this teapot, olive, like something you'd find in an import catalog.

"What?" I say.

"You're wearing my hat."

"And your neighbors are having a party," I say because, yeah, I forgot to take it off. "We should grill. Can I make you lunch?"

"You don't have to cook for me," she says.

"Of course I don't have to," I say, then follow along the ledge of her counter. "And by the way, how about that room you have up there?" As she closes the window to dull the noise. "You must have a niece?"

But what'd I do?

Because she's leaving the room, and all I can see is that hand trailing down the back of her neck. Before she turns and settles on me, grave and, dare I say, apologetic? At least it seems so.

"That room," she begins to say, "is for my daughter."

CHAPTER THIRTEEN

Cursed

Madisen

How there are two remaining doughnuts left on the counter from this morning's meeting is beyond me. What's more, I'm half tempted to grab one for dinner. Make that I *do* grab one for dinner. And as I do, as I crumble a piece over the sink, I wonder why it's always the plain-Jane glazed they leave for last, when I happen to think they're the be-all.

Either that or apple fritter. Okay, chocolate glazed. Seriously, though, a good doughnut is just about as mind-altering as sex when you haven't had one in a while.

Or maybe I should start making something better tasting than lentil soup and crackers if I'm going to start comparing this plain-Jane doughnut to sex. And when I think about it, I might need to find something more satisfying than chocolate protein bars in the morning, add those Stouffer's pizzas I've nuked for lunch every day this week.

Still, as I finish the last of the glazed, I'm reading this note taped to the fridge in here warning of consequences should food not be cleared out by the end of day today.

And I can see why, as I fish deep into tubs of plain and light cream cheese, coffee creamer, two liters of Diet Coke, one sad looking bottle of soy sauce, not to mention a few SlimFast shakes before finally uncovering my lunch bag, which is empty, less the few table grapes still on their vine, something I could've eaten instead of that doughnut.

"Packing up?"

"I didn't realize you were still here," I say, catching Kristen, our account manager, at the sink. And when have I ever blocked that out, her keyboard, the tapping, the smooth glide of that drawer on her desk.

The file cabinet. Her occasional nonsmoker's cough. And did she hear my call?

As she washes another mug with those cared-for hands. And even her hair bounces fresh as if it was eight a.m. I'm not, more like strung together like taffy and lacking sleep, lacking everything aside from the strongest grind of coffee set to fine. Still she glances at me in that unsure, because this is my boss sort of way, then opens the cupboard to line the last few mugs mismatched on the bottom shelf.

It's late. And I want to say *Go home already* for another home-cooked meal—what I wouldn't give. But the honest to God truth is I'm really glad she's here—to the tune of her goings-on about her orbiting ex, and that cabin, and its plumbing, and had she mentioned all of that work she's put into it? Every weekend, she tells me, amid occasional jokes and remarks. Amid questions.

Questions I don't even know how to answer. As if weekends always consisted of car trips, of lake dips, of ordinary, when mine was anything but. After which you wander around in a fog not knowing, not rational.

So I fall back on my generic response. "I decided to take the weekend off."

And she laughs before cleaning up, before setting the place up for tomorrow. The coffee filter. Twelve cups of water.

But here's the thing—I'm at work. Which means I talk about work. I only talk about work because nobody wants to hear about life, and besides, as much as they say they get the whole gay thing, they never really will. Which is why I steer this whole conversation back to where it belongs and say, "There's something I've been meaning to bring up." Amid the lingering scent of lemon verbena counter spray. "Though," I say, "it's not the time or place."

"You need that budget."

"I do need that budget," I say. "But I wanted to talk to you about marketing…that we've contracted that out to an agency. But really, I've been thinking about this, and we might be better off bringing that whole function back in-house, given the expansion, and maybe we could shift some of those responsibilities, all actually, to someone who knows our business." Then I dry my hands. "Like you. Since you do have a marketing degree, and I don't think it's really being utilized. And, well, if we were to do that, it would mean a larger role…if that's even something you'd be interested in?"

"Interested," she says.

"Is that to say you are?" And her gaze, once blank, now softens. "Then let me see what I can do."

And it's on that note that we leave, me ill-prepared for the wall of heat that greets me just outside the double doors as I rearrange keys on my ring, making my way down our sidewalk, which is lined on either side with beach-sized houses that show all of the elaborate trappings and features of being large. The kind with window fans facing inward— their stone walls, their cracked drives. Adding to that, the aroma of evening cuisine.

As I round the corner just past the jeweler, the chocolatier, the shop that sells lighting decked with its sparkling display of fixtures and chandeliers.

And here's the darkened pub, where I step in, gazing across shoulders to find Nelson before he's shaking my hand—squeezing it, actually. And I'm noticing their drinks, low, as I join in on their conversation about staffing and morale and network security before they're sinking into a blur of NBA, which is when I tend to drift off, imagining Rae in that thin shirt with the insignia on the back, and I can't help but grin. So by the time my drink arrives, I'm turning in my seat to check voicemail.

*Stanley Porter…Madisen, it's Stan…*which I save for later because *Madisen, Juan Alvarado…I need to get your decision on that by next Monday, no later…Katrina Strojko…Ms. Mitchell. Wednesday morning is perfect. I have to thank you for being so flexible.* And afterward *Rachel Matheny…*and my stomach tanks. *Hey, it's Rae. But you knew that, right? So I'm stuck here in rush hour traffic thinking about you, and well, you have the sexiest voice on that message. Have I ever mentioned that? Anyhoo, don't call me back. I'm heading home. But, yeah. I miss you. Bye.*

Which makes the next hour of modular this and poché that seem that much more bearable, in a way, at least. I add a glass of wine. And the next time I catch our waiter, I ask for a spread of hors d'oeuvre.

Until a few hours in, it's Taylor who mentions it first. That she needs to head out. So I do as well.

Attentive now, somehow even though I'm exhausted and anxious to get home thinking, how is it I've never really noticed the enchantment of this shop—as night sets, illuminating Taylor's cheeks as we pass, as we laugh. As we go our separate ways into a lot where I've parked and where, once inside my car, I play that message over and over again as I'm gazing at the glow of my screen because, yeah.

Because I should be doing something more productive, like driving or, at the very least, calling Andi.

Which is what I eventually will myself to do. Call Andi, that is.

"The pub," I say, "we just had a couple drinks."

"Drinks and things?"

"Drinks and hiring and moving and a bigger, brighter place—I told you that. I'm meeting with a Realtor tomorrow."

"You already ate?"

"Yes, mom, doughnuts," I say, "and drinks."

"Please don't be serious."

"It was just one drink. Plus a few mozzarella sticks."

"You'll never guess what arrived today on my doorstep. Or better yet, don't guess…I'll tell you. Mail-order food. It's apparently a thing, a care package from the 'rents since, you know, the flu equates death in their mind. So why'd I even mention it?"

"What, that you were sick?" I say. "It was allergies. And I'd love to get that."

"Have you tried fried rice on dry ice?" she says. "Because you can. I'm on this weekly plan for who even knows how long. They didn't say. And have I mentioned Styrofoam coolers, if you're ever in need."

"Weren't those outlawed?" I say.

"Apparently not," she says. "And for the record, you were right."

"Of course I was."

"She read so far into it."

"Your friendly dinner date?" I say.

"My dinner date, yes. So why'd she even go?" she says.

"Because," I say, "subtext."

"What do you mean?"

"I mean it's an evening and dinner with an ex. There's subtext to that. Read between the lines."

"I guess I'm more literal," she says.

"When you dish more subtext than anyone I've ever met," I say.

"What are you trying to say?"

"I'm saying, don't act as if you've never done it. It doesn't soften the blow. It just prolongs the agony. Don't do that to yourself. Don't do it to her."

"I wish you would've warned me," she says. "It was that awful."

"I did warn you. There are platonic and nonplatonic venues you could've taken her to."

"And platonic would've been…?" she says.

"Wakeboarding. Shopping," I say. "Okay, nix wakeboarding, given the lack of clothing involved. But afternoon or lunch…not dinner, not some darkened booth with an ex who has sordid expectations."

"Whatever," she says. "You and I have dinner all the time."

"And we've never been more than friends."

"Unfortunately," she says, and I just roll my eyes like I always do. "Jordan called."

"Did she ask for me?"

"Not this time," I say. "She was crying. Me, thinking it was Aline when my phone rang so I almost let it go. And can I just say one thing? If you ever tire of adulting, two words: third grade. Those girls put a curse on my kid."

"A what?" she says, cracking up.

"It doesn't really matter, does it? Some mean girls, with nothing better to do than burn sage and curse my kid, who was petrified. She thought she was dying because of some spell kit they bought online. I calmed her down. We don't believe in that, I said. And given *Mom said the same thing*, that was that."

"Kids today," she says. "The most we had was, what?"

"We had a lot," I say. "You're forgetting third grade."

"All right, I'll give you that," she says, "but it's worse now."

"I've already banned social media," I say.

"Oh, not to change the subject," she says, "but why were you freaking out?"

"Oh my God, I was *not* freaking out," I say. "Where do you get freaking out? I was cautious, that's all. Then it started to pour and we went inside."

"*I'm not exactly sure how to take it* were your exact words." Okay, so I was freaking out, but not in *that* way. And Andi wouldn't get it, and besides, she doesn't need to know every little thing.

"Yeah," I say, "before our talk."

"Your talk?"

"We had a talk," I say, "about Jordan."

"So alas, you told her. You were so freaking out," she says.

"You're reading way too far into this," I say. "It's just going fast."

"I'm empathizing," she says.

"You're not empathizing," I say.

"So you told her about Jordan, and she's in love with you," she says, clearly bitter. "I was honestly waiting for you to tell me you'd eloped."

"How does one go from freaking out to eloping?" I say. "And besides, it was the other way around. I hadn't told her about Jordan yet."

"You freaking out always means something good."

"But here's the thing, though...Why? How, when she doesn't really know me? Not in the way you do. After a few weeks. After some happenstance encounter at a bar and now this. So what, am I to throw caution to the wind, like one more thing I'll live to regret—or what I really mean to say is, one more thing she'll live to regret? I'm not sixteen. I'm responsible."

"You could never be irresponsible."

"But she'll break my heart."

"More like, you'll break hers."

"But I have a kid," I say.

"I cannot stand fried rice on dry ice."

"Why are you changing the subject?"

"Because," she says.

"I brought up the marketing thing," I say.

"At work?" she says.

"She's interested," I say. "Now it's up to me to convince the others."

"You're pretty convincing," she says.

CHAPTER FOURTEEN

Checkmate

Rae

I'm at my stove reading a packet of authentic Cuban black beans and rice that I picked up because it seemed healthy enough, which is what I'm going for, prepping broccoli to steam, tipping a glass into the dishwasher, when I get this call from Rebecca telling me, "My only friends are Sangiovese and *Jazz à la Mode*."

Because whereas Elizabeth is the epitome of chill and Avery my glowing breath of sunshine, Rebecca lands somewhere in between.

"And this would mean your adoring wife is where?"

"Where else?" she says. "Come commiserate."

"I may take you up on that offer," I say. "I just learned that Madisen has a kid."

And what her silence really means is that right now she's picturing the mom bun. Madisen slogging over sandboxes in fleece, flipping bubblegum novels, and tugging apart a bag of Lay's potato chips at the kitchen counter—screaming at someone.

As opposed to houndstooth, pinstripes, dry-clean only. And have I mentioned hot?

Because what kind of response do I get? "Interesting." Mind you, Rebecca's the type who could say *fuck* and make it sound cultured and sophisticated—of course with that undercurrent of something, I don't know, conniving perhaps. More like judgmental.

Which is fine. It's not as if I'm the archetype of family, settled down, two-car garage stuffed with dirty lawnmowers and coiled up hoses. Recycle bins. My loft has no yard. I sleep on a platform bed made of leather with a kick-ass Alex Kanevsky oil on wood hanging just above. And I dine on my couch most of the time.

"Big glaring U-turn, right?" I say.

"It's her kid, not yours," I hear. "But how old a child are we talking?"

"She has an eight-year-old," I say, catching that voice in the background, so I ask.

"It's just Elizabeth," she tells me, "with a mix of Bob Dylan to cheer me up. Did you tell her?"

"What?" I say. "You mean about Madisen? Are you kidding me? No. And hey, I'm sorry about Dylan. I'll be right over. Just give me forty-five, give or take."

Which means I'm back to spooning broccoli and grains, taking an off-the-edge seat on my couch to ring back Avery, and this doesn't taste half bad.

"You're never going to believe it," Avery says.

As I stir my bowl. "Try me," I say.

"Why do they always come back asking to be friends months later? But you know what?"

"What?" I say.

"I'd rather not hear about their matching tattoos."

"I'm sorry."

Avery, who has this way of never getting over anyone, even if she's the one to leave, which is more guilt than anything else. "Never mind. I'm over her," she says, clearly aggravated.

"Why'd she call? I mean, this time? What was her excuse?"

"She seriously thought we could be friends. Friends, like I'm over her. Like I'll ever be over her. The only good thing she gave me was that aching breakup scene at the front door. God, that really was the most beautiful breakup of my life," she says with a sigh. "She dropped to her knees sobbing—" And, "I can't go there again. I want your news. Why'd you need to talk?"

"She has a kid with this woman," I say.

"Who has a kid? Madisen?"

"Yes," I say.

"Sorry, love."

"And—?"

"And, you know what they say. If it sounds too good to be true, there's always a deal breaker."

"So you think this is a deal breaker?" I say.

"Don't you?"

"Well," I say, "would it be for you?"

"It might," she says. "That all depends."

"So even if..."

"Even if what?" she says.

"Nothing."

"No, really," she says. "What's going on? You're acting strange."

"Nothing," I say, resigned.

"You give me so little credit sometimes."

"It's just that, coming from you—you're usually so off the cliff in love with a girl," I say. "I can't see this being a deal breaker."

"In love," she says. "Have you fallen in love with this girl? Holy shit."

"I didn't say that. Look. I don't know."

"In that case, okay, we need to go all out," she says, followed by, "get this kid loaded on chocolate, and not the hollow kind. Hollow chocolate says...you know. Chocolate is highly symbolic. So truffles maybe, but this needs to be exquisite." *Symbolic*, I think. "Let's hook up. I know this place where they sell everything decadent."

"So you're not just saying that?"

"It's a child," she says. "Not a big deal."

"So you would do this?"

"I wouldn't hook up with a mom, no."

As I fork broccoli.

"Thanks," I say. Then I start sharing more than I should. And, in turn, hearing more than I want to. Correction, wondering if she could possibly get to the point. But instead she gets way long-winded about domesticity and that dreamy-eyed firefighter of hers.

But in any regard, after dinner, I head off to Rebecca's, thinking a drink will do me good. In fact, I'm feeling pretty grounded like *Sure I can do this*. As I belt out this tune en route, lowering the window to a hot breeze, remembering what's-her-name who loved Portishead, God! And that would be why we split. I split. I can't stand Portishead. She played it all the fucking time, like incessant, and I do firmly believe in music compatibility. But why she comes to mind, not a clue. That must've been, what, a good decade ago? Come to think of it, that would be around the same time Madisen would've been walking down the aisle starting that cute little textbook family of hers. Not that I care.

So how does one even begin to converse with a child?

At the age of eight, I'm pretty sure my biggest complaint was being an only child. What I would've given for a sibling or three, those unforced conversations. That meant everything. Family, a big one, life overflowing with sarcasm. And a sister I could toss off the top bunk.

Now, though, the very thought of passing my anything off to a pint-sized human being, the fact that I can't even focus on a single thought for more than two seconds, like right now…

I cut the engine, still trying to figure out whether I'm floating on air over this girl or closer to calmly unhinged. So I make my way to the door, where Rebecca greets me with this paltry excuse of a hug, one I'm not okay with, and next thing, Elizabeth is rounding the corner gushing. "What the hell, Rae?" As I slip right past and into the kitchen.

"I can't believe you brought Dylan to her pity party," I shout over those incessant rhymes. "Way to cheer a girl up." But she follows hand to mouth.

"Look at you," she says. "You're all *Leave It to Beaver* lesbian style."

"Nice jacket," I say, deflecting.

"You like? Light enough for rain…It's called a sailing jacket."

"Very nautical of you," I say. "But you don't sail."

"I'd like to look as if I do," she adds to my blank stare.

"A latte deckhand," I say, redirecting my gaze from Elizabeth's bullshit to Rebecca as she pours—rather diplomatically, I might add. Meanwhile I'm busy switching "Like a Rolling Stone" to EDM, effectively transforming the kitchen into an old-school gay bar.

Still sensing that weight of scrutiny as I redirect my attention to our sailor. "Are you not having a drink with us?"

"I have an engagement," she says.

"In that case, enjoy your engagement," I say.

"Oh, I absolutely will," she says. But why couldn't she leave it at that? She doesn't. Instead, she holds my gaze well beyond the point of any reasonable, rational person. Where most would feel uncomfortable, self-conscious, compelled even to turn or leave. But instead of leaving, she wraps her arms around my waist, drawing me in, offering a kiss against a turned cheek. Next she's beaming off through the squeak of rubber soles down the hallway. "I'll leave you two suburbanites," she says, "to bask in the joys of Mommy A and Mommy B."

And as the door seals, I shift my attention back to, well, fleur-de-lis. Why does everything in this house involve fleur-de-lis? But the sun's angling just so, and I'm thinking, you can't beat that hour before sunset. It smells of evening, too, the damp freshness in the air, as I follow along until French doors part into a garden courtyard where Rebecca shoves a bottle of wine into ice, taking a seat, crossing a leg, dangling the bowl of her glass like so.

As the rim of it touches her mouth, now stained with the color of a sweet patchouli sunset, earthy and warm. "Tami is not confrontational," she's saying. "That's the actual word she used to describe me, confrontational. I am apparently confrontational in her mind, choosing to bring my betrothed to family gatherings." As I try to focus on something other than myself. Other than Madisen, which is not an easy feat.

"You're so beyond betrothed," I say. And she makes the same first move with her pawn. The wine, by the way, is good—dry and, well, wine-like. I glance up. "I can't say I've ever taken you as confrontational. Opinionated, maybe."

"And that would be why she's up the coast," she says, "as opposed to here."

As I grip the back of my neck. "Lucky you," I say.

But that laugh of hers. "We had plans. Bar Harbor, it's been empty for months."

And if I move my rook like so, it'll give her...nope, that leaves the board wide-open.

"I'm afraid I'm being too needy," she says.

"You're not being needy."

As she bends across the table. "Tell me, though. You're okay with this?"

"With what," I say, "taking your pawn?"

"You know," she says.

"I can't say that I've had enough time to sit down and process it," I say matter-of-factly. "Why don't *you* tell me?" And as much as she tries for that poker face. "Don't hold back."

"She was married, you said."

"As are you," I say. "Marriages can be a mistake." Wondering what does it add, really, when one swirls their wine?

"I'm thinking it's too soon to have family discussions," she says. "I mean, I'm not one to dole out relationship advice," which is a total lie because she is. "But were I you," which is never a good preamble, "I'd have to really think on this. That's not to say—"

"Not to say what?"

"Would you have ever imagined," she says, "the two of us here, like this? Me in a tiff about, of all things, my wife, and you—"

"Contemplating the bitter end of life itself?" I say. "No."

And again, there's that look. Distant, you could say, but plenty focused at the same time. It's the kind of look one might give if they didn't know what to say or how to say it.

Then a breeze shifts a few highlights in her hair that frame that recent facial, her chin raised. She's playing single-handed, balancing that glass in the left. "I wasn't saying you're unqualified," she says.

"As a parent? I would certainly hope not."

"Though I couldn't exactly see myself as one," she says. "And besides, just listen to me for a second. What if this girl decides to go back one day, you know, to her ex. For the sake of the child. Then what? Have you even considered that potential outcome?"

"Yeah, that's not going to happen," I say as I down her knight. Next, she's tossing me that *Don't hate me* look. "It wouldn't happen," I repeat.

"Do what you want," she says.

"I plan to."

"I hope it works out."

"You know I can't leave this girl."

"And when have I ever heard you say that?"

But I'm focused on the board, considering my next move, when... You know that pressure? That pressure after you've sunk into the most uncomfortable subject you could ever imagine and you don't want to go there, but they do. So they're on you, staring, and won't let up. That's the look I'm getting.

"You've fallen in love with her," she says.

"Not quite," I say. Then I head into the kitchen to loop that song again. And by the time I get back, she's downed my rook. I take a seat, contemplate strategy.

"Can I confide?" she says.

"Yeah, whatever," since that move right there will be the end of me.

"Rae," she's saying in this so-Rebecca way. "I mean a really important something."

"All right then," I say.

"As in, I can't have you repeating this to anyone. I'm serious."

Rebecca, never one short on drama. "Why?"

"Because I might be thinking—I don't know," she says, running a palm up her arm. "I might be thinking about some sort of separation. Maybe." Next thing, she's skimming her glass of wine along the length of her neck as if trying to cool herself off. "This is good, isn't it? It's imported. We found it on our wine tour in Tuscany. Tami had four cases of it shipped back home. She was saving it for a special occasion."

"Thanks for sharing that with me after the fact," I say, eying my empty glass.

"The thing is," she says, then drifts off into another one of her ungodly pauses. "Listen, if I share something, you can't think differently of me. You have to promise me that. Because there's so much more behind it."

"Isn't there always?" I say as I try to piece it all, her stare, the hush-hush. "Isn't this the only reason *to* get married," I say, "that scandalous affair on the side?"

"That scandalous affair," she says with a look that tells me everything. "Have you ever had to make the most impossible decision," she's saying, bending across, breasts nearly knocking off her queen, not that I'm looking, "like, the kind with no right or wrong? Just… whatever. So it's you alone wondering, *Where do I go?* That shit you deal with when you're just graduating college, when you're picking a career, a life—not now. What do you do?"

"My advice?" I say. "Don't put anything in writing. Or on a credit card."

"Be serious," she says.

"Why?"

"Because, because. This is hard."

"Then stay miserable," I say.

"And suck it up, as if I could, and for how long? And what if staying means leaving the person I want more than life itself?" she says. "It's…heartbreaking."

"What's heartbreaking?"

"It's heartbreaking when I have to tell her we're not going to do this…because I'm married to a woman whose family won't even acknowledge my existence, and she's perfectly fine with that. Tami won't change. So why do I keep expecting her to? And the next thing, guess who's jumping in to take her place? And she gets me. Who does that, drops everything? And why does she think I'm *everything*? She thinks I'm perfect."

"You are blessed with good genetics."

"Right…she says that now, until it's six a.m. and I drank too much last night. That's how it goes."

"What shallow people you've wasted your precious time with."

"You think?" she says. "Maybe that's the reason. Maybe that's why it's never about what I want. And perhaps that's my own fault."

"Perhaps. But that's certainly not my philosophy," I say. "What I want is the only thing that matters. So maybe that's where I'm going wrong."

"Wrong if you're hoping to end up like me," she says. "I'm not even sure if I love Tami. Who knows? What if I don't? How would I know? Or maybe I'm trying to convince myself. To justify my life. So I'm not so torn, that's all."

That song fades into the next as the sky settles. Next she sparks a candle. "I can't believe you waited so long to tell me about this. You know, I love this stuff," I say. "So, what'd you do, meet at some grocery store as the two of you were squeezing various melons?"

"Something like that," she says. "We were actually having dinner here, the four of us, something Tami concocted. She's had it in her head for a while now that we need to make more *couple* friends."

"So you're saying this woman is married, too?"

"I guess you could say that."

"You guess?" I say.

"But here's the thing. She didn't sit next to her wife. She sat next to me, which was odd. And there I was, shaking the entire time. You know the way you can just tell? You can feel how close someone is, when it's too close and you can't turn or look. So how does that happen? I've never felt so nervous in all my life, watching her. Then she followed me into the kitchen. And I was putting it all away or at least trying to. And they were out there talking, I guess. We could hear them. But she just gives me this look. It's hard to explain. And the next thing, I was slicing cherry pie. And she comes up from behind and reaches around me and kept saying…she kept saying that she couldn't take her eyes off me. It's so wrong to want her this way. But it was an absolute mess, that pie. I don't know how that happened. It just went somewhere before I knew what I was doing."

"Sounds like you have a nice little arrangement."

"So why does it feel so awful?" she says.

Then it dawns on me, she hasn't made a move in how long?

And it's her turn, apparently.

"Checkmate," she says.

The next day I'm at Archipelago's people watching, pigeons clustered around the legs of the table, as Madisen saunters up with that distinct air of Monday—unraveled. Her shirt loosely tucked from a half day at the office. And this is how it goes. Right when I was beginning to find my rational and sensible in any of this, right as I'm beginning to step back, reflect—she fixes that gaze on me, peruses me as she makes her way around a bunch of strangers, trailing fingers along the back of that bench with that look she always has, and I'm an absolute mess again.

Before this reaching sort of kiss that doesn't end even as she draws back to find her seat. And what do you even say to that?

You don't. You just sit back since it's not the kiss per se but where it always takes me. And that's exactly where my mind's going. As that musician's going on with his pathetic love song.

Meanwhile, I follow her gaze to that gathering, a crowd, down the way—then to the waitress, this woman beside her with her bag of tea. Then down to her own nails.

"I'm having an *I need Prozac* day," she tells me, slipping a hand under the table until I feel it along my thigh, and that really doesn't help.

"It becomes you," I say. "By the way," I add, leaning in, "you look so painfully gorgeous right now." And she almost smiles.

"But have you ever felt as if you're the only sane person in the universe?" she says. "I think I've become something of their office therapist. And I'm so far behind. But still, I could not wait to…well, to be right here."

"Do you always work late?" I say.

"I will tonight," she says.

"And that's my fault."

"It's not your fault at all," she says.

"I won't keep you then," I say.

"Keep me as long as you'd like," she says, and we tip our heads. "But I'm sure you have a million things to do."

"Nothing that couldn't wait another hour," I say, weaving fingers between hers.

"And everything's all right?" she says.

"Everything's fine," I say. "Why do you ask?"

"Body language," she says.

"So," I say brushing my lips against hers until I feel the heat of her breath. "Is this better?"

"It is," she says grinning.

"But…?"

"But," she says, "tell me I don't have to go back to work."

"I don't want to either," I say.

"You're so impossible," she says. And I just shrug it off. "So what've you been thinking about?"

"I've been wondering how all of this works," I say.

"However you want it to work."

"And why you didn't feel comfortable telling me something like that."

"I haven't exactly been clear minded," she says. "I wanted to do it right. I wish I could do it right. I screwed up."

"As if you ever could," I say.

"Because I can't imagine how weird this must be," she says.

"It's not weird," I say, "just different."

"Unsettling," she says.

"No."

But her face is calm. "You have a beautiful laugh," she says.

"What," I say, "my nervous laugh?"

"Are you nervous?"

"No," I say, but that's a lie.

"What if I stop by, say, eight, eight thirty?" she says.

"Sure."

"Will you be home?"

"Where else would I be?" I say.

Then she does this *um* thing followed by, "I mentioned this to Aline."

And just that name, Aline, this casual, flippant tone, it does something and not in a good way. Since now it's okay to pass time like this and bring an ex up?

"That's to say, I gave her a heads-up so she knows what to pack. We're still on for this weekend, I hope?"

"And how close are the two of you?"

"How close?" she says. "We talk, not often."

And that's not to say I'm angry or jealous. "Are we talking that one-size-fits-all friendship bucket?"

"No," she says. "I wouldn't exactly put her in any bucket."

"But where would you put her?" I say.

The waitress steps in, gets Madisen's order. "Fritters, chickpea, side salad. Just vinaigrette, please." And for some reason, her interruption centers me—as I listen to Madisen. Watching her. Because it's as if, when you're around her, you're the focus of her universe. The only thing that matters. Even if you just so happen to be a server taking her order.

And once we're alone again, if you can call it that, I slide in, tightening her knee between mine.

And her gaze skims my lips. "Are we going too fast?" she says, and I catch that scent, her hair. "Should I worry?" But I can feel her palm between my thighs and her lips at mine—and I guess I've forgotten the question.

CHAPTER FIFTEEN

Introductions and Otherwise

Madisen

July hits with its bouquet of chrysanthemums, fresh wood chips, and cut grass. Read Zyrtec into that. As I peer at two clean-cut boys who burst past my car, eye us, then bolt off high on hormones.

I'm sinking into the driver's seat while Rae fastens her seat belt and I text Aline. *Leaving now*.

Adding Tidy Cats, coffee beans, and vitamin B12 to my grocery list before I forget.

"I'm so, so sorry," Rae's saying with her not-sorry grin.

"But why?" I say. "That we're late, or that you stole the last drop of coffee?" Hoping I don't come off as nervous as I feel. To be honest, nervous is an understatement.

"That we're late, of course."

"So why not share a shower?" I say.

"It saves time," she says, adding a shrug. "And hey, sorry for taking that last cup."

"Why do I forgive so easily?" I say as the engine turns, and I'm wondering how she can get me so worked up like this and praying to God Aline won't be too bent out of shape over this whole hour-late thing. Hoping she doesn't keep me there, embarrass me, or converse for no apparent reason, dragging it out to no end the way she has been. Since I would just as soon stop in and do what we need to do.

But in any regard, it's not as if I can divulge any of this, you know, talk it out so it might not feel quite so unbearable. Given there's one topic I can't bring up—or at least need to stop bringing up—with Rae, and that's my ex.

"You must love your early weekends," she says.

"I'll love it a lot more once I'm caffeinated," I say as I lower my visor, glance at the mirror, check myself, and I look all right, applying lip balm. While Rae settles on a track and starts singing along inaudibly to whatever this is. And she knows every word. I don't. I don't even know what song this is, which makes me feel so out of it.

But you know, it's one of those moments where Aline would've belted it out, at least on any of our tension-filled road trips to visit Mother, just to amuse me—provoke me is what it did.

Unlike Rae, who's more aloof, more laid back, reserved. She doesn't try to cheer me up or change me.

And let me just pause right here to say, I'm okay with this. I really am. Two women I've been hugely involved with are meeting face-to-face in a matter of minutes. Who wouldn't be okay with it?

Not helping matters is this brooding look Rae's giving me. Because why can't I ever think or reason around her? I can't.

Then I'm back on Aline, the kid, what'll we do for dinner?

And I'm pretty lost in my thoughts when I hear, "I look all right?" Breaking my concentration. But it's not a question, really. It's a statement. Since, glancing over, she's almost gloating, delighting in it, wallowing, professing, "I'm afraid she won't like me." As I pull out into traffic, and I can sense her fingers trickling up the nape of my neck, and *please.*

"Aline?" I say chuckling. "She won't care."

But that sigh of hers, it's so suggestive. She doesn't even mean for it to be, but it is. And next, she's checking her phone, which I crane my neck to see, but who can tell. Still that much carries us for the next however many miles through the loudest part of our silence.

That and another one of my fabricated conversations with Mother because I don't agree with a thing she keeps on about. So why do I even try to gain her approval, her support? And why does she need to be so, I don't know, critical about every insignificant thing I do?

And please don't ever let me do the same to Jordan, criticize.

"I can't believe you brought this book," Rae says as she draws an elbow through bucket seats, and my thoughts swim back. "Not exactly a beach read," she says, flipping.

"And what constitutes a beach read?"

"Something that doesn't require a yellow highlighter pen," she says.

"This doesn't require a highlighter," I say.

"Were you always this way?" she says.

"Always what way?"

"I don't know…studious?"

"A nerd, yes," I say. "I thought you were going to say—"

"What?"

"Nothing," I say. "My mind's somewhere else."

"Did she respond?"

"Aline?" I say, and here come those nerves again. "Maybe. I don't know. Did you bring…whatever *that* is?"

"It's in the back seat," she says.

"I won't read the entire time," I say. "I promise. I'm used to doing this alone, and she wants to run around."

"And you're not the run-around type?" she says.

"Not exactly," I say. And all right, that makes me laugh. "Can I ask you something?"

"Why does this somehow feel like a trick question?"

"It's not, but I'm wondering. Do you find me selfish?" I say.

"Why would you ask me that?"

"I don't know, curious…overall, generally," I say as I line the car up with the curb. "Like not telling you, for example? That sort."

"Not telling me?"

"And other things," I say.

"Why do you ask?"

"No reason," I say.

But what is she doing? She's so close, and I mean, does she plan on kissing me—here in the car? She's not, though.

"I don't think you're selfish at all," she says, but her voice sinks to a whisper. "What could change this?" she says. "I think you have high standards." High standards, but what does that mean? And still, she's not doing anything at all except watching my lips, but how I want her to. Because this is going on until I'm flooded with…I'm not even sure. And why don't I ever know how I feel with her? Just that it's good. Just that I can't help but follow her lead. And perhaps the best part about being here like this is that she gets me out of Aline, out of me, out of this conundrum because how am I supposed to behave as they shake hands? That's to say, will they? Because maybe they won't. And what's my introduction? *This is Rae?* No, *I'd like you to meet Rae.* Or *Aline, Rae. Rae, Aline.* Help me here.

Because after that comes Jordan for the rest of the day.

But, what, she's kissing me and I can feel her gripping my hair and I can't even. Why does she have to be so kind to me? "Here's to an entire day of not even touching you," I hear and all the while, the rush of that mail truck as it passes by, pauses at a box—open, shut, repeat.

It's where I could say any number of things. But unfortunately every one of those options would take this to a completely new level of inappropriate. So instead I simply say, "We have tonight."

"In eight to ten hours?" she says.

"Perhaps," I say. And just the way she's gazing at me as if she can't look away. "This feels so strange. Why does it feel so strange?" I say.

"It's not for me," she says.

"I'm glad," I say.

"Thanks for this," she says.

"You say that now."

"No, really," she says.

"Why?" I say.

"I like this being-on-the-other-side thing."

"Were your parents divorced?"

"Yours weren't?"

"No," I say. "But they should be. They're never together."

"So no awkward introductions, no dinners, no bribes?" she says.

"Tell me about your bribes."

"My bribes, which one? So I can remember this game one time— baseball, I'm sure, since they loaded me up on chili dogs. And I'm in this guy's back seat, mom's boyfriend at the time, and it took forever getting out of that parking lot. We weren't even moving. It must've been a stadium or something, and he was trying to impress me…And there was this putrid smell, which is why I mentioned your car being so clean. You know how, when you get takeout, it lingers? So I pushed this button and the window slid down. And thank God, air. But she turns to me and says *Shut the window*. Apparently the air conditioner was on. *But it smells like fish*, I said. *That's leather*, she says. But it wasn't. I love the smell of leather. I didn't know that at the time. Nice car, though, Mercedes. He was talking it up, too. She would've hit the jackpot were it not for me. Since I hit back with *I didn't know leather smelled like fish*," she says, grinning in this juvenile way, adorable actually. "Embarrassed the shit out of her. But yeah, that's all. Awkward introductions," she says. "Let's go do that."

So when we get out, I'm reminded of that cut grass, the chrysanthemums, and I'm shouting over the hood of the car, "I'll need coffee after this," feeling flighty.

Next she's gripping my hand. It's nice. And we walk like that, and I'm thinking, isn't this where Jordan usually dashes out? But no stomping, no yelling, just those same incessant birds waking up.

In fact, it's not until Aline's front door pulls in that Rae's fingers slip from my grip and she's stepping aside to assume some sort of companionable, neighborly, platonic gap between the two of us.

And I'm not exactly sure about the sequence of events that come after that. In fact, I'm only half aware of her existence. At some point, I'm bending into arms, squeezed, dodging a half-eaten Clif Bar pinched between fingers. A pillow tucks under my elbow, forcibly. I can smell that scent of C.O. Bigelow fabric conditioner through those vents. And every time I hope to glance at Aline, hear what she has to say, she's settled on Rae—and Rae on me. Until I hear, "Eight o'clock sharp." And I nod and turn and the kid starts squeezing my hand pretty hard, then leads me off, oblivious to the countless hours I've put into this moment. Weeks of what-ifs and that's it. All effortlessly behind me.

I just…I don't know. Maybe I wish she hadn't been so quick about it. And shouldn't I feel relieved now that it's over? But I'm not. I mean, Aline didn't even try to do anything. But what's she supposed to do? It's not as if I expected her to make a scene or anything like that. But she didn't even fight in the slightest.

As I flip my key and Rae tugs the pillow out from under my arm. "You didn't tell her about me, did you?" But she's not mad.

I pop the trunk. "I couldn't," I say, adding a shrug, grateful she doesn't ask why, since sure, it almost came up, the topic of Rae. But it didn't. Since we don't talk about that, about others. Nor do I think we should.

And I'm dwelling on this, disappointed, as Jordan squeezes right in between us with, "You're pretty cool."

And Rae says, "Am I?" Chuckling.

And next I hear, "Is she your girlfriend?" over my laugh, which is definitely one of relief.

And soon enough we're racing down the highway, wind tugging at my hair as I eavesdrop on a conversation they're having over the headrest. One that goes on nonstop until we get to the lake, where we trek through coarse sand in bare feet and sandals to my usual spot near the fallen tree and unpack. Straightening my hat. Sunglasses slipping down my nose. And I'm passing Jordan a half-empty tube of SPF before setting my phone on top of this hardback on biophilic design, which I do plan to make some progress on, rubbing my eyes as I ponder why this ordinarily sparse little reading nook feels more along the lines of comfortably crowded right about now. "It's never this packed," I say, apologetic amid the screaming and swarming of children. Plastic shovels meet their parents' Stella Artois.

"It's the Fourth of July," Rae says with a laugh as if I should know this.

"That's not until Monday," I say. Then it clicks, and I crawl to my knees and flip the blanket before full-on collapsing.

"Stay here," she says, then reclines beside me.

"No, I'm coming out there with you." But why am I so exhausted?

"I'll take her out," she says. "You just work on that coffee." As she proceeds to peel her shirt overhead, one that bares her abdomen, that bikini tank, the kind that all but flattens an otherwise shapely size C chest. Before she's tugged by the arm to the shore.

And as for me, I'm still widening and lengthening the blanket. I tent my chair, glide sunscreen up an arm and down the next, gazing at Rae as she ducks beneath a low wave only to resurface, sopped, strands flipping over and back like a pompadour. And that laugh, I could hear it a mile away. Before she's leaning in to hear some sort of long and lengthy dialogue with Jordan about who knows what, though I'd like to. Accompanied by the rhythmic symphony of all that is summer. Creasing open my book.

Reading.

And every so often pausing, marking the page with a thumb, shading my brow. Gazing at heads bobbing along waves. That scent of coconut like a gentle breeze up my leg. The taste of root beer lip balm. The monotonous squawk of gulls. Grill-scented everything. Garbled calls and warnings from dads who'd rather be anywhere but here. Boys and girls and belly laughs, that bottomless kind, squeals and shouts to *Do it again...do it again.* As they bury that kid in sand, toes exposed, buckets filling.

And I'm two pages short of finishing this passage when they slog back in snapping, sagging suits. Water flings.

Rae collapses beside me, lifting her gaze as I follow along the rising curve of her hip. Drops of water beading along her skin. "How's your book?" she says as she runs a thumb along those damp lips. And I guess I just linger there for a few, studying her gaze, her lips, wishing I could kiss her. I want to, but I can't. Everyone's here.

"It's captivating," I say with this look. Then she turns and tips her head with the most insatiable grin. *Stop.*

As I'm sitting up, straddling my legs around the Coleman to pull up its lid, distributing lunches. Baguettes wrapped tight in white deli paper. Jordan's bag of Kettle chips.

And another hour at least fades into nothing before the two run back to the water. Which is when I finally meet up for a rather cold dip, though you do get used to it after some time, or at least that's what I'm telling myself as Rae swims over, bouncing, sluggish, slipping a hand lax around my waist before it drifts everywhere it shouldn't. Me, guiding her palm back to the waterline. "You're a hit," I say, admiring lean muscles along her arm.

"You bribe a kid with chocolate," she says.

"It's much more than that."

"I really like this suit," she says.

"Stop...you're making me—"

"What?"

"Blush, and it's so cold," I say.

"I've got you," she says, and she does.

"Who thought up that pink doughnut float you gave her?"

"You think it's a little over the top?"

"I don't. But tell me," I say, "what were the two of you talking about a while back?"

"*You* stuff mostly. Secrets," she says in this cagey way. "That sort."

"I'm curious what sort of secrets my daughter might be sharing."

"Oh, it was nothing important," she says with that laugh. "Look, we made a pact." Uh-huh. "I promised her."

And I leave it at that because, to be honest, I don't think I want to know.

I'm outvoted in favor of pizza at the end of the day, and Rae calls it in, and we swing by and I pick it up. Then along the drive, we're lectured on the trials and tribulations of third grade, on fifth period, on the history of the Fourth of July, on the awesomeness of *Charlotte's Web*, and on Lindsay and Lauren, the kid's BFFs—and this continues nonstop from Haskell Road onto South Willard.

And by ten o'clock, we're drawing knees to our chests on the couch as Jordan crashes, lit blue by the glow of Netflix. Until we slip off and I'm led by fingers gripping loosely along the banister, thinking, who knows. It's late and, well, those hips treading water, those drops of water along bare skin. But the last thing I hear out of Rae is, "About that suit you wore today," before she drifts off.

The following day after drinks, sparklers, fireflies and those fireworks and their smoke lingering through our *Ohhs* and *Ooos*, that gaze resting languid beside me on the pillow with an arm heavy across my hip, and yeah, that's that. And by that, I mean I'm planning to get her a bit more coffee'd up so she can keep up with this.

❖

My workweek is short and drags me into a less eventful weekend, given it happens to fall on Mother's less than spectacular sixty-seventh birthday complete with two invitees: her and me. Because steel, I keep telling myself. That's what I'm made of. So why after one brief overnight in her presence do I feel more like a crushed ball of foil in her fist?

She being my trusted, constant source of criticism.

And thus would explain this brief yet essential sanity break upstairs to call Andi in this sun-filled room complete with that so-not-me floral duvet on my twin-sized adolescent bed where not even a shadow on the wall has changed since the day I turned sixteen. Even that desk I left behind, that poster—now framed as if my youth was something to hold on to or cherish. And the exact same view outside my window.

"Just think of it this way," Andi's saying, ever so hopeful. "You might enjoy yourself this time."

"You act as if I could ever let my guard down low enough," I say, gazing down at this chemical lawn. "You're so fortunate not to know her the way I do."

"Take her out for lunch, have a few drinks, loosen her up."

"She's fourteen years sober," I say. "And not an alcoholic. Seriously, how do you not remember that?"

"I remember that you both love Brooks Brothers." And this is when it hits, that too much of Mother creeping up in me, my shopping for therapy, my reason enough for an occasional visit if only to remind myself how not to be. "Why didn't you bring Rae?" she says.

"Because that would only make matters worse," I say.

"So just a mother-daughter day?"

"Hold out," I say, "she might be screaming."

"Screaming?"

"Lord, make that crying," I say. "I've got to go."

"So full report when you're home?" she says as I dash along the hall toward those sharp jarring echoes rising from the kitchen before taking a seat at my end of the island where Mother is bleary eyed, her trusty phone by her side.

"They're bringing it?"

"No," she says. "They hung up on me." Quietly angered. "They told me to call back when I calm down."

"Jesus Christ, it's not a big deal," I say. "It's just the Sunday paper. Perhaps the carrier's sick."

"It's called doing your goddamned job," she says. "That's what it is." Then she's making her way off in a silent huff, setting her mug at the sink, brewing the next pot. "She needs to be fired."

So I check my phone.

Rae: *Morning, beautiful.*

For an instant mood lift.

Dodging from across the room that gaze now simmering on the national news as she orchestrates whatever it is she's heating on the stove—Egg Beaters from a carton. And all the while, political pundits head off, reminding me of all the conversations we won't be having today.

"Work?" I hear as I study her unrumpled PJ's, the button-up style you'd see on some old man, only feminized in navy with pipe trim in white, fashionable as always with hair once blond now gray, in a style that's never been long like mine. Her glasses so thick they magnify her age as she eyes my phone.

So I apologize. "Just Rae," I say. As I set it aside for whatever conversation it is she's thinking about having.

"Ah," she says in that tone, dismissive. "I thought we'd go downtown," she adds, "shopping."

I shrug.

As she taps along the side of that frying pan. "How is she?"

"Who, Rae?" I say. "Fine."

"What does your *friend* do?"

"I told you that last night. We had a long conversation about this."

"Ah," she says. "That's right, the artistic type."

"Not quite," I say, "more like catalogs—that sort. She does catalogs. She *only* does catalogs, like the kind you get in the mail, websites, that sort." Before adopting a less defensive stance. "She has her own business."

"And that would be why she couldn't make it?"

But I shake my head, change the subject, go on about my unremarkable client, as she's spooning faux eggs onto everyday plates. "I don't normally eat this much," I say.

"You look fine," she tells me, but it's not that. I'm not trying to lose weight. I just don't like eggs. As she piles on more. And I go back to my phone.

Me: *High protein*

Rae: *Caffeine*

Me: *Rescue me.*

Rae: *Swoops in.*

"Is that such a good idea?" I hear.

But I'm already smitten when I say, "Is what a good idea?" To the point that I'm grinning shamelessly, which all but riles her more—which might be my intent.

"You seem to be moving fast," she says, only to mumble something else under her breath, but all I hear is, "Aline," which is her way of reminding me that I have a rather astute ability to epically fail at every relationship, at everything, but let's not consider the nine years that were reasonably good. "I just wouldn't have—"

"What?"

"I wouldn't have done that to you."

"Done what?"

"Divorce, it's rough on the kids, you know. I worry about my granddaughter. How is she?"

You could call once in a while is my unspoken response. But I take a sip of coffee as opposed to taking her bait.

"You've always been like this," she prods. "You've never listened to me. You do your own thing."

Funny, I thought that was my right.

So as the afternoon drags on, I find myself reminiscing about the good old days when she might've cut the edge after lunch with a freshly brewed cup of coffee and Kahlúa.

❖

For the last weekend in July, I'm agreeing to the best friend date out here against the green river, Rae's hand squeezing mine as we steady our way along bobbing boards with the kid just ahead, tottering in her two-piece suit now stretched to cover the entirety of her torso, hair twisted back in French braids.

A not-so-modest powerboat is parked at the end of the dock right past her shoulder, where Andi's lifting a knee, extending a hand, pulling Jordan in, then me, as the deck dips with my weight, or maybe it's just a swell.

Next I gaze at Rae, now gripping Andi's hand. "So you've never been out on the lake?" Andi says before pulling her in. "Nice to finally meet you."

And their eyes meet. "Mutual," I hear and they shake and she brushes past and we slide along a padded seat, her thigh pressed warm against mine. Adding to that is her top, snug, with sleeves up high along her bicep. High and taut across her chest. As I imagine how it might feel to run a finger along those gathers now bunched against her torso. Red creases. Racing stripes bent where it curves. As I lean in to press indebted lips against hers while the boat swims onward.

"Could I convince you to come back," I say, "alone?" Still tasting a trace of that kiss, her skin so warm from the heat of the sun. "I'd like to," I say as the wind lifts our hair, "when it's starlit," as I slip my fingers between hers. A hand resting heavy on my thigh, sundrenched and stuck to this padding as spray glistens across her lips. I can feel it cool against mine.

I'm gazing overhead at the last few darkening clouds, gulls, when my mind shifts to Jordan, now balancing, boney kneed, her small grip tight around a slick white pole.

And after that, a flash of that time with Aline. Her renting that sleeper out there, because what was she thinking? A roar so loud I could hear it vibrate for hours after we'd stopped.

It's funny how a sound, a motor, does that. Makes you feel it again. Makes you see it right down to that glossy woodwork—stocking food under lights so dim, recessed, and ducking afterward into the lounge where we ate by folded tabletop that later turned into a bed piled high in down. No sounds. Drifting. Blinded by sunrise. Her dive. Bobbing, limbs like waves beneath, unnaturally swaying. And without any rain, the sand at the shore seemed like islands. Sun muscling clouds into streams of light. Strands of hair floating at the surface. Paddling her way. Lifting up with her palms flat, then resting on her chin.

Until I slid in.

Feeling her hips, her thighs so slick against mine.

Because that was a different kind of wind out there. *I've asked you to marry me*, she said. Nothing to break it with.

"Thinking about diving in?" Rae says. I can feel our skin rub.

"Yeah, I don't know," I say. "What do you think?"

"What about the kid?"

"She's a fish," I say as I tug my shirt overhead.

CHAPTER SIXTEEN

By the Book

Madisen

I'm listening to NPR's *On Point* along my evening commute, thinking about lawsuits and company documents and complaints, when they segue into *What's happening a little later this hour* and there's my phone.

"That may be over," Andi's telling me.

"Are you kidding?" I say. "And why are you again on that treadmill?" But she ignores me, offering little more than the vocal equivalent of a shrug.

"More like, she's been temporarily ghosted."

"And why would you do something like that?"

"Because I may go back, who knows? I need a break."

"A break...after all but one week?" I say. "I read something like this in a book."

And I'm trying to remember which book it was when she cuts me off with some lecture that ends with "Freud the misogynist?"

And sure, maybe I went a little overboard thinking I could save my marriage sans therapy to the tune of some used psychology textbooks I found on eBay after having an epiphany, which Andi did so kindly put up with for months on end. Because isn't that what you do when you're irrationally brokenhearted and desperate for clarity or who knows—you just end up repeating the same tired stories, the same *Why me?* over and over again to everyone around. Or in my case, to the only one around, which was Andi.

"Look, I'm beyond that," I say. "And that wasn't even the point I was trying to make."

"If you think I need a relationship book after a week, she can't possibly be the one."

"It was something about excitement and anxiety or confusing the two. I'm just saying, it was so you right now. Because how do you know someone in seven days?"

"It was seven rather intense days," she says.

"And if I were her, I'd show up at your next game thinking you were still interested and just too busy to reach out. Isn't the schedule online?"

"She won't."

"How can you be so sure?" I say.

"Look, I'm sure. And relationships aren't by the book."

But those books have helped me function in the same biosphere as Mother, which is what I'm trying to explain to her when our conversation segues into, "Why in the world did you tell her?"

"Because I had to," I say. "She's my mother. I was there, remember, and it just sort of, I don't know, came up."

"You brought it up," she says.

"I know, I know," I say. "It's just that, she knows me."

"She knows your buttons," Andi says.

"But what if I *have* been selfish?"

"You can't be serious," she says. "You're happy, so what? I'm not even going to justify that with an answer."

"No," I say. "I mean introducing her to my kid…and so quickly?"

"She's your girlfriend. She should know your kid. I've been saying this for how long? And think about who you're dealing with. And how long have you been with this girl? I really like her, by the way. Don't ever listen to your mother. I mean it, my God, she's doing it again, trying to control you, bring you down. You are living your best life. Everything's looking up, and again she's sabotaging your joy. How would she know the first thing about lesbians, let alone how we do parenting? Or relationships for that matter? It's not the same. And it's definitely not slow."

Which makes me laugh. "You might be on to something."

"I'm not telling you anything you don't already know. This is your life. Not hers. That's what you're always telling me, isn't it?"

What I don't mention next is the fact that I ordered another book just last week, with two lengthy chapters on infidelity, because I'm still trying to wrap my head around that one. The *Why'd she do it?* And that's not to say I'm bargaining. I'm not denying, either. I'm well into acceptance. I just figure, if I could understand *why* it happened, I won't fall into the same situation again. And maybe it won't be about me anymore, my inadequacies. It might be something else that led Aline astray.

Or perhaps it's none of that and neither of us. Perhaps love simply has an expiry date. That's all.

"Guess who's on the other line?" I say.

"Don't take it," Andi says.

"I have to," I say. "It might be the kid."

"Then call her back," she says.

"If I call back, Aline will definitely answer," I say. "Look, I need to take this."

"Then call me the second you get home," she says.

So I pick up, gut-wrenched to hear Aline. "No, it's fine," I say. "I'm on my way home." Which she knows. It's seven.

"So this *is* bad timing."

"No," I say. And in an attempt to sound more natural, somewhat pulled together, I say, "It's fine. I hear banging. What's for dinner?"

"Nothing you would like," she says. "Roasted root vegetables. Sorry it's so loud. She's back in an hour."

"Where is she?" I say.

"At a neighbor's for PlayStation."

"You know, I never did like your cooking," I say.

"Yes, you did."

"Remember the Daily Dozen?"

And she laughs. "I'm pretty sure I know where this is going. *What to Expect When You're Expecting*," she says. "You turned it into some kind of research project."

"I forgot how much you love to exaggerate," I say.

"You were right, though," she says.

"As if eating at the table would solve any of her emotional problems," I say.

"It amazes me how a child so young can be so hormonal," Aline says.

"She obviously takes after you," I say.

"And this is how I get her into vegetables—drowning it all in maple syrup. She wants doughnuts. For dinner. Everything's an argument with her. So of course I have Hostess for dessert, which would explain my gym membership," she says. "I can't have that stuff in the house. It's too easy."

"Whatever, Aline."

"Speaking of," she says, "you wouldn't happen to have that, would you? You know what I'm talking about. I've looked everywhere—"

"I'm pretty sure you left all the books here."

"I actually took a few," she says. And afterward, she's apologizing. But the fact that she sounds genuine, thoughtful, infuriates me.

"Maybe you could get those back to me," I say.

"It's not like I have any interest in your textbooks."

"They're not textbooks," I say, "unless you took my textbooks."

"No," she says.

"I was thinking the other day about what we could do for her birthday," I say. "Perhaps our parents might actually get along this year."

"As if we could be so lucky," she says.

"If they'll show up in the first place," I say.

"It wouldn't matter to Jordan either way," Aline says.

"At least we did one thing right. We've raised a resilient child."

"We did a lot right," Aline says.

"How do you figure?"

"Let's see," she says. "What did I do right?"

"What, Aline?"

"I think you know the answer to that."

"Don't be this way," I say.

"So you're doing this again."

"Doing what again?" I say.

"Never mind," she says. Even still, why did she have to say that? Would she rather I play along? I won't, and besides, I'm just sad, that's all. Then I hear, "Can I ask you something?"

"That depends," I say.

"I was just wondering, you know, how long?"

"How long, what?" I say.

"How long," she says, "you know."

"What?" I say.

"How long have you been with this girl?"

"Is that what this is about?" I say. And the worst thing is that Rae has been out of my mind this entire time, and I hadn't even realized that until this very moment.

"That's not what this is about," she says.

"Then why'd you call?" I say.

"I called about the book," she says. "I couldn't find it."

"It was *that* important," I say, "that you had to call?"

"Sometimes it's easier to pick up the phone," she says. "I had an hour. And besides, you did pick up."

"And what's that supposed to mean?"

"Just that you knew it was me," she says.

"Why are you so full of yourself?" I say, feeling a bit unnerved. So I pull off and find a parking lot.

"If you're still angry with me," she says, "well, you know what they say. Maybe there's something there."

"Maybe there is," I say before I can take it back.

"So does that mean you're ready to hang up?"

"That was your thing," I say.

"Then talk with me," Aline says.

"Talk about what?"

"About my glorious life," she says in her nonglorious way.

"How's your glorious life?"

"Aside from, well, stuff we dare not discuss—"

"Oh, please, don't even call to tell me about your relationship."

"When it's what you've been waiting for?"

"Aline, seriously? Don't tell me…What, are you getting married?"

"No," she says, through this unnecessarily long pause. "We're through. It's been two weeks now."

We're through. Is that what she just said? Because, just don't.

But next, she's changing the subject. She needs to go. She needs to get back to the stove or oven or whatever it is. So we hang up. And I'm left inventing the rest of it, filling in blanks, as I merge back onto the road, heading home. As my mind winds back through our conversation, and I try to make sense of it.

And, why not. Aren't I well into the acceptance phase? Which means I should be able to take the long scenic route without breaking down this time. Past the house with the copper roof—the last one I saw before that turn I never took, because who in their right mind ends their marriage with a phone call, knowing I'm on my way back to our half-empty home? And it still feels as if this road never ends. It didn't. It won't, will it? You just end up in the next town, and even then.

It's easy to get out of yourself if you want to. If you keep going and never stop. But eventually it'll exhaust you. And you have to turn back and go home and face it.

By the time I pull up to my curb, my mind's still on that call and my day and whether or not UPS arrived so I can read tonight. And calling

Andi since I need to. But I find Rae at my steps instead, unannounced, knees high, giving me that melt-me grin. And it does. It melts me. But then her gaze drifts away once I catch it. And I stay there for a while transfixed, watching her through the car window. Unassuming.

Before gathering my phone, my keys. And at some point before reaching the door, her arms draw me in, and it feels as if she's holding me too tight, as we make our way up, glancing across at one another.

"I didn't expect you," I say.

"I know," she says with that spark in her gaze. "We finished early."

I turn the knob, step inside. "I'm sort of a mess."

But she follows. And it's not that I don't want to see her. It's just really, really bad timing, that's all. Really bad timing.

CHAPTER SEVENTEEN

Simon & Schuster Audio

Rae

"Can't I get you anything, Rachel?" says the receptionist who couldn't be more than nineteen. "A cup of coffee...water?" She's partially hidden behind, or I should say beneath, a vintage half-walled cubicle encircling an empty desk.

And a total of two seats make up their waiting area, which is where she directs me, scarcely ten feet from her desk. Each chair is plastic, and both fail in their attempt to pass as retro. To the contrary, they come off as cheap, orange, and breakable. Uncomfortable, as well. I take one near the window, resting my portfolio against its leg as I admire this spider plant stretched to the light—astounded by the fact that it's not plastic like the rest.

Once I do, the switchboard rings, and she's reciting the same greeting I heard when I called. *How may I direct your call?*

Which reminds me, I should mute my own, slipping it back into its pocket. "I'll transfer you," she says, and silence again to the tune of *Top of the Pops* circa before my time. Music that I half tuned out until I hear Robert John announced and then "Sad Eyes" and, I mean, have you ever actually listened to the words to this song?

I am. And how this guy makes such a coldhearted song seem almost heartfelt is beyond me.

Still I'm waiting, waiting for that falsetto to come, when someone in the next room decides it's time for karaoke—leading to one of those cute bonding moments between me and the receptionist, the kind of grin that takes a bit of this edge off.

Which is fine.

Since I keep repeating *You've got this* over and over in my mind, all too eager to get in and out and to put this technicality behind me even though I've pretty much perfected this whole dog and pony show. Even though I keep landing jobs I'm scarcely qualified to do. My saving grace being the fact that I work largely with creatives who are, by and large, a low-key bunch—especially those who claim the title of Creative Director at fledging start-ups like this one.

And I'm still repeating that mantra when I catch sight of her gaze as she's making her way around another half wall to greet me, sporting a cotton oxford button-down and a nineties middle part, polished off by well-fitting men's trousers—making my gaydar spin off the charts. I extend a hand, shake on it, offer my Ogilvy smile paired with a *glad we're on the same team* nod.

And trailing her lead, I'm marveling at this vast and otherwise shapeless warehouse of a space they've somehow molded into the latest open-office concept, complete with stools and laptops and low-shadow lighting. It's rather cool if you're fond of factories, which I am. But how anyone concentrates with no walls, no doors? Write code or whatever it is they're doing, playing solitaire. Not a soul peeks up.

Then our journey ends at a conference room where she shuts the door and begins flipping pages of my portfolio. I take a seat.

"Can you work in this space?" she says without even so much as a passing glance, leaning against a stretching walnut surface of a table. And I get it. Her silence, this lack of anything remotely close to rapport. She's clearly of the defensive lesbian slant to assume that my tad bit of camaraderie a second ago was, I don't know, inappropriate. Unprofessional. Presumptuous.

"This conference room? I could, sure," I say, cautious. Hoping to clarify with "Anywhere you'd like." Only to recoil afterward, thinking she's going to take that wrong. "If that's what you had in mind?"

"What we had in mind is someone on-site for the duration, I'm thinking six, maybe seven days. Could run longer. It all depends. And that's something you could manage?"

"Of course," I say. "How soon would you be looking to start?"

"A week after Labor Day," she tells me, and I have to wonder what in my portfolio has captured her eye. "At this point, we're bumping into October," she says, and I like her voice, commanding but unquestionably feminine. "This being our first year in attendance. It's the industry's biggest show. We need everything just so, you know what I mean? We need to stand out, make a splash," she says glancing over at me momentarily. "We're what you would call a newcomer, if you haven't noticed." But she doesn't laugh. "I'm hoping to get everything to the design team in a few weeks, so we meet our print schedule."

"In that case, I would need to lock this in," I say, "rather quickly," hoping to mask my irritation since, really, couldn't she have set this up months ago without throwing off my entire schedule?

"I love your work," she says, closing the book then handing it over. And could I be catching the start of a smile? "You really do have an incredible eye, and it fits our brand. I'm sure you hear that often." Yes, that's definitely a smile. "I'd like to hire you."

So I'm thinking, contain yourself long enough to get out the door, which takes forever with contracts and introductions and so on and so forth. Until I'm toting too many bags too many miles in business casual—translation: not my trusty Diesels—up an incline in the middle of one o'clock heat in August in the city, which always feels hotter than it does back home. My only reprieve being my phone, which at least has most of its battery left. So I give Madisen a call at work and she answers, "Madisen Mitchell."

"Oh, how I love your office voice," I say, hoping to pull off smooth, urbane, not an easy feat given this hike and that backbeat pounding from a car accompanied by the constant roar of diesel.

Which only underscores the gentleness in her voice. "I thought you were in that meeting?"

"I'm off to my next job," I say, "which could be all day…make that *will be*. That ridiculous pottery shop," I say.

"How'd your first go?"

"A deal was made," I say. "And yours?"

"They signed, which means I'm set for, I don't know, five years," she says, laughing. "All right, that would be a tad exaggerated. But this, I'd say, is a pretty major client. I'll tell you about it later."

"We'll celebrate," I say.

"We're already hitting Franco's after work."

"Franco's?" I say. "Who is?"

"Sebastien, Anni. A few others."

"Not what's her name," I say. "Darcey, was it?"

"How do you remember that?"

As I round a corner, blasted by a gust of wind and thinking, *I remember everything.*

"They've invited our entire office," she says. "Not sure who actually plans to go."

"Have you called yet about Labor Day?" I say, hopping a curb.

"I plan to."

"You plan to? We're getting tight on time," I say. "I should let them know, either way. Just say yes."

"Maybe."

"God, I'm sorry," I say. "Un momento. Could I get a grilled flatbread, please, with feta to go?"

"Shit. That's my weekend."

"Swap," I say. "Add a root beer seltzer. Yes, please."

"That would require—"

"I know, I know," I say. "It would require speaking to Aline."

"Can't this wait?" Madisen says.

"I'm happy to call her for you," I say. "Just tell her we'll take two weekends in a row in exchange for this huge favor she's about to offer. Yes, to go, please."

"I forgot to tell you—," she says.

"I love you, too," I say.

"Not that. I mean, yes that. God, now I can't think. Let me shut the door." And this right here would be why I rarely go for takeout—$17.50 is ludicrous for a sandwich and flavored water. "She called me the other day."

"Who…Aline?" I say. "Then why didn't you ask her?"

"I couldn't exactly work it in," she says. "The thing is, she and her girlfriend, you know, they apparently split up."

"The one she left you for?"

"Yes."

"So what are you telling me?"

"Just that she called, and you know, she's torn up. That's all. I'm trying to be reasonable. Accommodating. Supportive. And no, not what you're thinking. I'm just trying to shelve the obvious for a while. Does that make any sense?"

"Why?"

"You know," she says.

"I can't say that I do."

"Trust me on this, all right? But your meeting went well?"

"I'm charming," I say.

"I already knew that. Let's celebrate when you get home. Just the two of us."

"It's not a big deal," I say. "So what are you afraid of?"

"I shouldn't have brought this up," she says.

"What, that your ex might want you back?" I say. "As if I should care."

"Exactly."

"Should I?"

Laughing. "She doesn't," I hear. "Come by?"

"I'm not back until really late," I say.

"I'll wait up."

"No, you won't."

"I can try," she says.

But she won't. And at some point after our good-bye, after gazing at porcelain and stoneware and kilns and paint-splattered sinks for hours, filling up I don't know how many memory cards with a thousand shots, I merge back onto the highway and dodge sun glare for a few more hours while juggling another overpriced sandwich against the wheel accompanied by my in-progress audiobook, which I've all but saved for this exact commute.

I'll have to postpone this call with Avery for another day, like tomorrow, because I don't have the energy for that level of perk.

Simon & Schuster audio presents—

Skip.

Chapter Two—

Skip.

Chapter Six—

I mean, why would I assume things were good? That we were anything?

And why'd I put on all the pressure to call a clearly interested ex?

Perhaps there was a reason she didn't want to.

Or perhaps, what I should be asking instead is what type of situation have I gotten myself into where *Call your ex* is even a conversation that we have?

And can I just say, it's not *what* she said that bothers me: *Don't think things.* Because what should I be thinking? I wasn't thinking anything until she said that.

Now I'm wondering what they had to talk about. And why they felt the need to talk about any of it. And doesn't Aline have someone else she can call? And why would Madisen care?

And when was this? Today, yesterday, last week? I think that matters. The length of time matters. Because why didn't she tell me?

Just stop, really—she told me. She waited. So what? I would've waited. I'm getting way too strung out about this.

Chapter Seven—
And I've missed this entire chapter over it.
Rewind.
Chapter Six—
It's been an unusual day, that's all. A long-drawn-out and exhausting day, which could be why I'm reading so far between the lines.

Either that or...I don't know. What bothers me the most, I think, is being compartmentalized, separated, removed from her other life, her Jordan. Her Aline. Her everything. The nonweekend part.

It's seedy, don't you think?

This has been a presentation of Simon & Schuster audio.

When I pull back into town, the dash illuminates in its blue and I catch that hint of fertilized farmland. Red traffic lights flare against a blackening skyline.

I'm exhausted, as is she, slow as we make our way up tall stairs and tuck under the duvet. Listening to the sound of crickets. Amid air that settles with its damp chill, it's unusual calm, stillness.

She weaves her fingers into mine, my arm weighing around her waist, then slipping beneath her shirt. And just knowing she's here, feeling her hips at mine, the sound of her breath like this—it's all I've ever really needed to feel okay, centered, as if none of the rest even matters. As she falls asleep.

But I don't.

My mind won't sit. It won't silence. Instead it's everyplace I don't want it to be as I gaze across the room at the clock advancing through another entire hour of her tossing, her turning, her sound asleep. Until I can't even take it anymore. So I roll over to stare at the door instead.

Because why, why can't I let this go?

CHAPTER EIGHTEEN

Unhappy Anniversary

Madisen

After a week that could only be described as professionally fulfilling yet personally problematic, this right here had been out of mind. That is, our no longer relevant wedding anniversary. That's not to say I wasn't reminded of it thirty days back thanks to those automated alerts that sync across my many gadgets—alarms set years ago to help in planning some sort of dreamy indulgence, something not cliché, anything that might somehow one-up what I surprised her with the year before.

And so much good that did. Because happy anniversary.

Still the fact that it's August 16 isn't the reason Aline and I are sitting across from one another small-talking like old friends over a couple of chocolate chip scones that she happened to grab fresh from the drive-through bakery. It's also not the reason Jordan's now upstairs in her room laughing along with her television as she unpacks an overnight bag and fuels herself with the Egg McMuffin she chose instead.

It's simply a favor. Aline was out, and it would be easier and could save me a trip to her place. In other words, it's procedural, practical, routine even. It's what people do. It's how co-parents co-parent. I'm not so arrogant to read into her impromptu call the other night, which might've overlapped my own moment of…well, reminiscing. The thing is, she isn't pining to get me back. Let's be real. Why would she be?

So why do I feel so guarded?

"Four foot four," she's telling me.

"And that's—?"

"Average," she says, "or just slightly taller—according to her doctor's charts."

"So she takes after you," I say.

"Let's hope not," she says. But taking after Aline wouldn't be so bad. Jordan already has that wry sense of humor, doesn't she? Her vocal fry, those middle-class mannerisms. Those lips, full and round but not plump. Sadly I keep catching myself admiring them. But I'm not quite sure why.

"How've you been?" she says as the sun catches her gaze. "Aside from the obvious—work."

"Needing a vacation," I say, "which can take some finagling."

"Time off, as in home or—"

"That all depends. I had my sights set on Labor Day. Who knows? Maybe a trip up the coast," I add, shrugging it off with "I don't know," and I take in her posture, upright, standoffish, a haze of light now harsh across her face, almost blinding, which must be those clouds parting, the glare only making her light-colored eyes that much more transparent. She squints, then it passes. "The kid would love that."

The kid, I think. What do I even say? "The thing is," I add as she breaks off a piece of pastry and pauses. "I don't know. What would you think if we, maybe, swapped next weekend for the one after that?"

"Oh? You'd rather go alone?" she says.

Then I glance up as she gazes away, and I get a better view, that comfort, her ease in this space, her space, that self-assurance in this low button-down, her long legs crossed in a pair of slack-fitting shorts with sneakers, no socks. I glance to where her knee crosses the other and then back up to her lips again, though I'm trying not to. And I sense her doing the same as I glance away, her gaze wandering all over me. Until I hear, "This is so strange. Seeing you today."

"I can't say that it's not...difficult."

"Yeah. But it feels ordinary," she says. "Don't you think? And at the same time—"

As my lungs swell. To be honest, I'm not exactly sure how to take this. But I could finish her sentence in a million different ways. Uneasy, maybe. Final. Sad. Maddening? And I pinch a few crumbs off my finger since I don't really know how I should respond, shifting in my seat instead as I blurt out something foolish. "It's a nice day." A diversion, I guess.

Then she says, "I keep thinking about...things, you know?"

And I'm lifting my mug to hide my reaction. "That can't be good."

"Not like that," she says. And it's just a joke. But it's not as if I meant it *that* way—the way she's taken it. I meant it the *normal* way.

But I'm fine with her interpretation. So I let it slide. "Where to?" she says.

"Just the coast. I'm not sure yet."

And the next time I feel her gaze, it's so heavy. "I've missed you."

But why did she have to say that? Couldn't we go back to pediatricians and small talk? Then it dawns on me—why does this now feel a touch entitled? It didn't before. Or maybe she hasn't a clue what she's doing or saying. She doesn't care, really. She's speaking off-the-cuff.

"Jordan's awfully quiet up there," I say. "I should go check on her."

But she's propped elbows on the table, bending across. I catch another trace of that scent, light citrus or herbal or something like that, summery. And I gaze along and up her forearm to that ringless knuckle now settling against her lips. "I don't know what I was thinking," she says.

"We can't talk about it anymore," I say. Because, what, it's only now that she's alone that she considers me? But even still, it's hard not to feel anything at all. And at the same time, I hate the fact that I'm weak.

Because that's exactly what I am as I catch her, fixed as much on me as I am on her. I'd forgotten this side of her, how she softens. How she moderates our conversation. "I don't know how to apologize," she says.

"I wouldn't know how to accept," I say. Because what if it isn't a coincidence, nostalgia, this certain day on a certain morning like this? What if she really does, I don't know, regret some of it?

Then again, what if I'm wrong?

I hate that I'm entertaining any of it. And next, Rae comes to mind.

As we finish what few bits we have left. I take a drink of coffee, room temperature now, not scalding like it had been when she came. I thank her for bringing it by, for stopping by. She nods, reclining against the chair with that jilted look in her eye. That silent sort of outburst she's always been so good at. The silence that always makes me lean in, agree with her.

Observing how casual she seems about it all. As if this was hers. This place, that boxwood at the fence, me. I slide my empty plate to the edge to get it out of the way, daring to glance up. Afraid to, actually. Afraid of what I might feel if I do. And I'm trying to figure out if my heart's still broken, or is it, instead, now aching for her.

Feeling that as much as she tried to take it all—the kid, our life, my every last tomorrow—the only real thing she took was my heart. Maybe that's the worst part. It's the only thing I couldn't afford to lose. It's the only thing I can't seem to get past. That part of me that feels forever lost. The gap nothing and no one else could ever fill except her.

"Why is this so hard?" she says, extending a hand across the table as I draw back. And just then, I feel her ankle brush against mine. It settles me. I'm half relieved. It's comforting.

"Isn't this how it works?" I say. But this heaviness in my chest. Like I'm trying to breathe, but I'm holding on, holding it in—just so I won't feel it.

But how long has she been looking at me like that?

As I try to read her.

Because maybe it means...who knows? There's nowhere left for us to go. I'm just disappointed, that's all. "Would you rather I leave?" she says, followed by a grin as the glow of sun shifts across her lips. I ponder it for a while, what she said. I think I enjoy having her here. I can't say why. But, no, I don't want her to go.

In time, though, this holding it in begins to crush my chest. I can't want her, but of course I do. I always have. How do I turn it on and off and on again? Over and over. It's not a switch. "I really should clean up," I say. "I have a billion things to do today."

As I get up and she follows me to the door and walks at such a pace that makes it all feel too proper. Proper and citrus and herbal. Ringless. I don't know what I'm supposed to do. I don't know how to be around her and not want to be touched by her.

The birds have resumed their singing now, or maybe they always were, and Jordan's upstairs. I can hear it now. I catch the scent of geraniums, too.

I pause at the door to rest my hand on the knob, with this heaviness at my shoulder. How long has it been there, her hand? Her lips. I can taste the sweetest cream in her words. They're against mine now.

"I'm sorry," she's telling me.

But I wish I could understand.

Because wasn't love supposed to be pure and innocent, the kind that never leaves? The girl who never thinks twice. But what if love is this right here, twisted and flawed and shifting—something so hard to stop and hold on to, something you can't control. It's not a fairy tale but agony and endurance and forgiveness and holding on and never ending, even when life feels bleak.

Loving her was never contingent upon her loving me. It still isn't. Of course I still love something in her too much. I want her, and I want to feel this. And the only way I *won't* cave, the only way I'm able to stop from leaning in, from letting her kiss me again, is with anger. What good would it do to fall apart with her, when I don't even know if I want to try anymore—not for someone who left, let alone that way, not for something else, and certainly not for *someone* else—when I have too much to lose because maybe I still do believe in that fairy tale. And maybe I've already found her.

"This was a mistake," I say. But my words already breathe against her. "Maybe we're not ready for this." And my heart sinks when I hear it, as I catch her gaze fading into something, I guess you would say, raw. At least that's how it feels all over again as she walks out the door, like I've made the worst mistake of my life. Have I?

So I call Rae. It's either this or stew over nothing or, worse, cry again over a few backward feelings that wanted to drag their feet through my foyer.

"I need to get out of here," I say.

And she mumbles a reply, something like, "Okay."

It's nine o'clock. "Please don't tell me you're still in bed." Though now I wouldn't mind being there myself.

"I'm not," she lies. And afterward, she's getting up. "I'm glad you called."

"Would you be glad to see me?" I say. But why am I crying?

"I thought you had Jordan this weekend," she says, "and wanted some time alone."

So I did. So I didn't want my kid thinking Mom's preoccupied, or worse—that I've deserted her or replaced her with some achingly hot absolutely wonderful woman I don't even deserve.

"I take that back. I would really love to be entertained by you for the rest of the day."

"Okay," she says. And when she does, I can feel my shoulders sink. "Should I even ask? Did something…happen this morning?"

"Let's just see a movie," I say, resigned, because not answering is not a lie and because it was a mistake to have her by. And because whatever happened will never, ever happen again. "Jordan's begged and begged," I say, "but I can't possibly endure a theater packed with preteens on my own," which is good enough of a story to get her on board. Besides, that last bit about being the only adult in a kid-filled theater was no exaggeration.

And by the time we arrive, by the time I'm reclined beside her on the sofa, she's still caffeinating, and Jordan's darting recklessly around a few carved partitions before ogling that painting over her stack of pillows, spinning beneath beams that span a tall ceiling—as if she's found her own private studio for ballet.

The rest of our day jazzes by in much the same way, feeling better than a frozen margarita seaside in Cancun. Crammed with fountain wishes and musty bookshops. Add the spin of that new vinyl shop, where music pours onto the sidewalk. It sucks you in. We grab chili dogs from the cart and get through the movie before heading home, our wallets stuffed with charge receipts. And somewhere in the midst of this, I share my news about Labor Day to a rather enthused girlfriend.

More than that, I gain some semblance of clarity around my life—where I'm going, what I'm doing—during our brief few days together. And it's starting to feel right again because Rae does seem to have this way about her—this way of focusing me. That is, until that welcome sense of clarity begins to feel strained or artificial and not good. And long story short, I'm back to dropping Jordan off solo once our weekend ends.

And I leave the office Wednesday unnerved, indecisive in hopes of making that school recital—the one I promised Jordan I'd attend—by seven when it starts. Only to arrive at an empty parking lot.

Because why, I think, would I do that? Why, why, because I set the wrong date. That's why. And now I'm a full week ahead and won't see Aline after all and am fine with that.

So let's become *that* person who sits in the middle of a field contemplating life.

I won't romanticize this, either. It's not the infinite wildflower kind you might find in, say, *Audubon* magazine, pollinized in pastels or dandelion yellows. There are no birds. I'm not resting alongside the Giving Tree baked in rays.

Instead there's a setting sky and end goals and bases, crabgrass, and I don't even know what kind of weed this is. But the lawn is freshly mowed, with the parking lot safely within sight.

And I'm beginning to imagine Jordan on her days on end following school bells, bumping past mean girls through halls right beyond those double doors, weighed down under a heavy backpack, waving to one of those snobbish sixth graders she hopes to befriend one day.

Because popularity at age eight equals #LifeGoals.

Then it dawns on me. Because sure, I know this logically. But maybe it's just now starting to sink in for some unknown, completely irrational reason. That being, I am an actual parent of a third grader. I'm one of *those* women. She's not a toddler anymore. And how is that? Since I'm far from loosely qualified to take on this role.

Far from loosely qualified to handle any of this.

And it's so like me to fall right back into my same broken patterns, those ruined-me ones, the careless many mistakes. If I could only forgive myself instead of condemning, criticizing, that'd be a start. Step back, think logically for once—as opposed to getting swept up, swept away, swept aside. Still I'm spending far too much of my time and energy on fears and doubts anymore. Questions.

But Andi's right. Pick up and move on. Regret never solved a thing. What's done is done. And just think of it this way: you'll be far better off after this and for this. I'll learn from my mistakes. I'll grow, as they say. Pardon my lack of enthusiasm. This hurts.

So over the next however many minutes, I catalog cons I left behind, to pros for carrying forward.

Page eighty-seven in my book describes this process of letting go. This is how it happens, forgiveness. Now I just need to want to.

Or maybe not. It's not in my best interest to understand, I suppose. We're all trying to do the best we can with the cards we're dealt. Still I've exhausted months trying to get over her, to make sense of her, years to find happy with her. Erase this, correct that—and just blindly accept all the rest? But I can't absolve her.

I'm sure she's now counting the days until she can call again like a landmine. Which means I'll need to figure this out before she does. I suppose.

And until then, I'll just pluck a dandelion, make a wish, and let it go.

Chapter Nineteen

On the Rocks or Frozen

Rae

To celebrate nothing at all on a Wednesday night after working late again, Madisen decides to uncork and pour a glass of her favorite eiswein. Make that two: one for her, one for me. Midweek. No occasion whatsoever.

Meanwhile, I'm sharing a conversation that just ended with Rebecca.

Rebecca: "Maybe I'm just overreacting."

Me: "I don't think you are. But why—what'd Tami say?"

Rebecca: "*We need to work this through.* That's all. So we went away for a weekend in Greenwich Village, the Walker Hotel of all places."

Me: "And you worked it through?"

Rebecca: "We didn't converse, if that's what you're referring to."

Me: "This is almost scandalous. What if she's on to you?"

Rebecca: "If she is, she won't say. Still, how was I supposed to know she wanted a repeat of that classic all over again?"

Me: "Another dinner soirée?"

Rebecca: "I told her no. She didn't ask why. But she's mentioned stuff."

"Now I'm curious," Madisen's saying. "Why do they even carry on with this charade?" She takes a seat at the dining room table, then lifts her laptop.

"There's love," I say. "There's always love—but not always trust. I wouldn't be at all surprised if they, you know, amped up that little dinner party the second time around. They'll do anything to stay together. At the same time, Rebecca's pretty hung up on this girl, so who knows."

"And again, why stay?" she says.

"I guess you'd have to know her. They sort of need this in their own way," I say. "And it's…brazen. Some fuel on that. Me, I'd never get into that sort of thing."

"Staying for good and all?"

"I wouldn't get married…no," I say to that familiar look of cross-examination. "She's just trying to hold on to some semblance of what they might've had in the best way she knows how."

"When flowers would suffice."

"You are kidding," I say.

"I'm not," Madisen says.

"Please don't ever send me FTD if you do something shitty to me," I say.

"Why would you say that? And why not?"

"Well, that's to say, don't do anything shitty to me. But you will. So when you do—"

"First, I won't," she says. "And second, what's your opposition to flowers—and I'm not referring to dye-dipped carnations?"

"I'd rather you just come right out and say *Hey, I really fucked up this time*. It's simple, really—how many of those bouquets do you remember to this day? Because trust me, I won't."

Instead, what I'll remember is this right here—the look she's giving me and the taste of this wine that doesn't taste like wine and this feeling of mild intoxication. I'll remember that simple song that couldn't drown me out when I blurted out *I love you*. The same one I've looped I don't know how many times because what I wouldn't give to relive that again. And the scent in her hair when she's close like this, when she bends across the table, or when she bends to twist a towel around it after a shower as I swipe a palm across a steamed mirror—and those sounds she makes. That's what I'll remember. Those sounds. Not flowers. That's my problem.

And now.

She's taken a seat at the dining room table, feet bare with a heel propped up at the chair's edge, looking that end of day emptied after twelve hours of artificiality and business-formal, now slouched loose, authentic, changed into something more drawstring with that untied tie at the waist.

"I wouldn't call their relationship perfect," I say as I attempt to shift this whole thing back to Rebecca. "But nothing is. Love can be a beautiful kind of ugly sometimes."

"It can be," she says, languid in that after-work sort of way as she peers up over the glow of her laptop, her gaze hanging on my every word.

Before it's back to her screen. And she's doing that thing where you hover over an image to magnify before adding-to-cart.

"I won't expect a bouquet of roses from you anytime soon," she says.

"I'm thinking you might like my kind of apology better," I say.

"And you apologize how?"

"Not with a credit card," I say. "It really wouldn't take much."

"You think?" she says. And this all slips into well, you know, just that slow-going soul-drenching sort of stare down from across the table. Look, it's not a bad thing.

"Help me decide," she says.

"It's your decision," I say.

"I'm just thinking," she says, then crosses her leg intentionally. "What if this becomes one more thing we divvy up one day." Then she laughs.

"Aren't you funny," I say.

"I know," she says. "That shouldn't be my default."

"I hope it's not."

"You're so easy to freak out," she says.

"Well, I'm not about to counsel you on which appliance you should get," I say. "And for the record, I happen to like my place."

As she glides a thumb along the blush of her lip. "I am afraid, though," she says.

"And I'm not?" I say, leaning in.

"But I have more to lose," she says.

"Do you?" I say.

"I do. I mean, say we're still here in a year."

"I hope we are," I say.

"Well, I can't exactly truck my life into a studio loft," she says, "hypothetically."

So I kick back, cross a leg, glance around, listen to that jet pass. "I think you're just trying to get a rise out of me."

"It's just how you do things," she says, clearly intent on me, "once you have a kid. You plan too much." She lifts her glass only to set it aside on the table thoughtlessly. "I happen to think we should talk about the—"

"The hypothetical?" I say.

"Exactly," she says, "the hypothetical," resurfacing the only conversation I don't care to have right now. And, I mean, why is she suddenly pushing this? And it is sudden.

"I'm not exactly the marriage type," I say.

"And, right, I'm almost there with you. I'm almost thinking you're right. Convince me."

"And the other night?" I say.

"I guess I just took it as a rejection," she says in the most beautifully unconvincing way she possibly could.

"It's not," I say.

"Or maybe I just needed a bit more coaxing."

"So not a deal breaker?" I say.

"How did shopping for a blender turn into this?" she says. But I guess I hadn't really thought through the whole kid aspect. "Maybe I was just looking for a suggestion of a plan."

"You know," I say, "the minute you stop planning, you get to the good stuff." Thinking perhaps I should distract her. And I do for a little while—I am. But even this kiss feels like an impasse. And soon enough, she's settled on me in the most complicating way. In the most inflexible way. Even still, it's not as if I could add anything to this conversation, at least nothing she actually wants to hear. "I think you should have a rough sort of idea where your life might go," she says, "even if you never get there. Even if you veer somewhere completely different. That's fine."

"For certain things, sure, I'll give you that. But *this*?" I say, running a thumb against hers. And who knows, maybe this is starting to sink in. Not just the kid thing but…Why are we doing this? Why do we spend so much of our time trying to right some wrong that was done to us by someone else? Blaming, averting, dissuading one another. As if I was Aline. As if I'd ever do something like that. So I'm back to my drink.

And she goes back to her computer. "Can I show you what I've found?" Almost conciliatory.

"Sure," I say. "So tell me again why you need this blender?"

"For that occasional summer evening like this when you just might want a margarita," she says, "and you don't want it leaking all over the counter." But they all seem the same to me, blender after blender, page after page. "This one. Easy to clean, computerized, the works. Five settings—soups, dips, smoothies."

"Listen, it's your money," I say. "Do what you want." And by the time she props her Visa on the keyboard, I'm making my way into the living room to close some windows, the chirping, that constant hum, silenced.

And when I get back, she's still glued to that screen. Me, half tempted to lean in and see what's so fascinating about this blender. But then it dawns on me that it might not be a blender anymore. It might be another email from Aline—but, even still, would it matter? It is what it is. They are what they are.

And let me state for the record that I don't do the jealous thing. But I'm also not okay living in some shadow of a memory. Since there was someone else. A rather serious someone else. And now there's always going to be that somebody else following us around, visiting, emailing her, calling—that sort. Not just those hints you share about someone you knew. Not a distant memory but right here to see, to know, to talk with—to share Madisen with.

Because what'd she tell me the other day? It was the sort of thing you'd never think to say if you were honest-to-God past your past.

"So what should we have for dinner?" Madisen's saying, breaking my train of thought. Next she's shutting her laptop. "And how'd it get so late?"

"You needed a blender," I say.

"But you were enjoying your drink," she says with a grip, this tug at my waistband.

"So did you order it?"

"Of course," she says. "Do you think you might share me with a few strawberries, Jose Cuervo," I hear as she drags a hand across my collar, her mouth so near I can almost taste it.

"I don't like to share," I say.

"You say that now," she says. "You've never tasted my margarita," she says, her mouth teasing before she's slowly edging away. And I follow her along the counter. "So there was this birthday at work," she's saying, "chocolate buttermilk cake. Would you be interested?"

"Do you seriously need to ask me that?" I say.

"Apparently there's a lot I need to ask," she says, "like whether roses might offend you."

"Or how many children you've had," I say.

"I love chocolate buttermilk," she adds tossing me this look and, I mean, come on.

"I'm not easily offended," I say, drawing her in, and this grin, I can't hide it.

But somewhere in the midst of pulling plates and her gesturing for something in the drawer, then "Never mind," after reaching for a server, then slipping that wedge of chocolate along a small enough plate, after all that, something settles. The room settles or we do. And it's as if you could hear a pin drop as I slice a bite of cake with my fork. As I watch her lips glide along the length of hers all too intently, gazing up.

"What you do to me," I say.

"Tell me what I'm doing?" she says.

"You're enjoying this."

"I'm wondering," she says, sucking a dab of frosting off her fingertip, "how they make this so sinful."

You make it sinful. Because she's doing this drop me off my guard thing again, and next, she'll swing right back. It's been this way all night, like that drone of crickets, on and on, only louder after you'd forgotten they were there, once you come back and listen. Every time it does, it's that much harder to ignore. As she sets the plate down on the counter.

"You should have another," I say.

But she shakes her head.

"Why not?" I say.

"I'm thinking," she says in this unraveled way of hers. "It means something, that's all."

"That someday piece of paper?"

"Yes," she says.

"To you," I say, "and everyone else."

"How can you not support something like that? It's not a ring or a piece of paper. And sure, fine, it's not a guarantee. But financially, it's health insurance, joint taxes."

"How romantic," I say, forking that last bite before it slips between her lips as she cups a palm beneath—because sure, I'm hoping to dodge this whole conversation.

"Dessert for our main course," I say. "This is something I could support."

And she gives me that look again. More than that, there's something about this madness that's making her laugh—us, this night, our not adulting. The way her lips slip along the edge of my fork, lifting her gaze to mine, and maybe she is *enjoying* every bit of it.

And I'm thinking this is what I'm going to remember.

"I think you're taking this the wrong way," I say, reaching around, then molding against her hips. But she's still resisting. "I know you are." And that's how we stay—not conceding, not budging, as she lifts her gaze as if to say *Try me*—and I want to. "You know why?"

"Why?" she says.

"Because I couldn't love you more."

"But…?" I hear.

"But I love what we have," I say. "Don't rush the best part. And don't plan something we never thought we'd have in the first place."

And I guess that's just how we leave it. Or at least I do. As we clean up then head upstairs and I shower. And after that, I'm at the edge of the bed, listening to pipes swell then clamp shut, figuring she's had more time to ruminate and reflect, and so have I. So I'm playing it all over in my mind—why not, why we won't, why I can't—expecting some sort of ultimatum to round the corner, when the door to the bathroom makes that sound it always does down the hall, and I'm still tossing pillows across the room, toppling, tipping that stack of linens from their heap on the chair, which reaches that line of wainscoting that edges around the room to the door where she's making her way in, unhurried, a hand stroking the back of her neck in one of those shirts you only sleep in, pinstriped. Undone. Not much else.

Still thinking I should keep on, explain, since she doesn't get me. But what could I say that I haven't already? And besides, she's too inflexible, distracting, seductive in the way she's closing our distance.

So the only thing that comes to mind is, "Do you plan on buttoning this?"

"Did you want me to?"

As if I could say anything except *No. Don't.* As if I could remember what I was doing a minute ago, what I was thinking as I hook a finger over this thin band of elastic around her hips, her cheeks flushed from the heat of that shower, her skin scarcely toweled, flinching as I touch her low along the dip where her thighs stick together. And here, as she makes these sounds, breathy, with hips now molding against mine as I walk back to the edge of the bed, and she's tumbling over, topping me, her hair wet and closing around her face. Then she reaches for something across the mattress, that cotton shirt twisting as she does, draping at her waist, the backs of her thighs still ruddy. My gaze skimming the length of her stretch from a knee that rubs, crawls, to shoulders covered and long strands of hair now tucked beneath its collar, towel-dried, clinging to her skin. That scent of her shampoo. Before the room darkens and all I can feel are the sounds of her words against my mouth. "You'll break my heart."

"I think you maybe want me to," I say, feeling the bend of a knee weighing down on either side of me.

"I think you already have," she says, with despairing lips that search for mine, those hands gripping as she tries to lift my shirt clumsily overhead, straddling me as I reach to find her thighs in the dark, and she's wet, this shirt still open, still riding up her hips. The evening glow pouring in, roving along calm features, sublime as she moves against me, slipping along my hand as I watch her expression fade until she's collapsing against me. Until I flip her around, top her, slip this strip of elastic down lifted hips before parting her knees wide and crawling between, with fingers still damp as they make their way up the center of her thigh. Her breasts flat and full, shapeless on her back.

And as much as she's trying to pull me, show me, or take me—she can't. And eventually she just gives up as tight thighs grip around my hips, her breasts rigid against my tongue. Then a good two, three minutes go by, and she's still arched, her breath so soft but so heavy in this stillness, waiting as I make my way down, easing fingers inside her and *please*, she says.

With those weak sounds she makes as my tongue wets her, and she trembles, she's quivering, sinking into sheets with thighs that squeeze my cheeks before she falls to her side.

Before pulling me up because I can't stop. As I sink against her.

Where her cheek lies flushed against the pillow. The rise and fall of her chest. That sound of the whippoorwill, her breath. That gaze unbroken.

As I trace along the curve of her stomach to the flesh between her legs, and I'm wishing we could do this again.

"In a minute," she's saying, breathless, watching me, studying me or hoping to.

And I'm wondering, how do I stay myself if I stay with her?

As if this right here, tonight, this nobody else, this all of the time was actually me. And it's not.

CHAPTER TWENTY

Our Next 160 Miles

Madisen

I've let the past two weeks slip by under the guise of premature suitcase packing interspersed with near-constant weather checking.

Me: "It'll be unseasonably warm the entire time."

Rae: "As in long sleeves?"

As she dots i's, and as I cross t's, resulting in several later than late nights at the office to wrap things up—complete with a million need-it-nows, none of which ever actually fall off my agenda.

Me: "Try board shorts. And more like ninety degrees."

Until our weekend arrives, Labor Day, having spent our road trip eve doing end-of-week everything apart. And after waking so alert and wishing I could feel this brisk on any normal day at six a.m. at sunrise, dew still shivering along blades of grass. Me sipping coffee as she tugs luggage, shifting one more duffel, if it even fits, over her already weighed down shoulder full of straps that tumble as she leans in to give me this kiss, followed by the most intense stare you could imagine.

"I thought *I* had overpacked," is all I can say as luggage wheels thump down a curb, and she's gazing at me, lids low, with the cutest lift at the corner of her mouth.

And I'm melting. But *ugh*, this phone.

"What now?" I hear as I fumble.

"Nothing," I tell her, shaking my head as I read the screen: *Aline*.

Answering. "Hey, Maddy," I hear, "you wouldn't happen to know that login for the kid's insurance portal, would you?"

"Why?" I say before ducking away.

"Because I cleared my cache, and apparently," she says, "in doing so, I erased every username and login I've ever had."

"And you haven't written this down somewhere?"

"I know, I know. I should," she tells me, slipping all too casually into this right here, comfortable, familiar—or, I should say, *intimate*. "You always took care of that for me."

"It's not as if I have it on me," I say. "I'll give you a call when I'm back at my desk, all right?"

"All right," she says, and just the same, "sure."

As I end the call, I regroup, glancing up at a slow-moving car making its way along the pavement.

"I won't share you," Rae says, startling me with a kiss that backs me against the hood, "with some contractor or whoever that was." And the engine against my palm is still warm. Her hips, tenacious. It's the most challenging way to begin my day.

"We need to go," I say tucking my phone as I collapse over her shoulder and sulking a bit, sure.

"We do," she says.

As she holds me so tight. I can't let go. "Before that traffic backs up," I say.

"I know," she says, "before traffic." I mean, what's this scent she's wearing? It's doing something to me.

But after shoving bags in my deep trunk amid those lenses or whatever else she brought, we're off and onto the highway and into a new playlist, windows down—her elbow at the ledge, hand waving with the wind. Road trips, I think, are the ultimate way to go. No airports, no TSA, no creepy pat downs, no flight cancellations, and nobody to confiscate my nail file.

Still I'm pushing seventy past a string of slow-laners as I scan for patrol cars. And she doesn't seem to mind, unsnapping the glove compartment as she digs for a map. Finding it, giving it a shake, until that beam of sun shines through and down its crease making it appear almost transparent in red and green, with that crooked yellow line that drives east, so past this semi and one more speed sign, which I flat out choose to ignore.

Eight times she's taken this trip. Eight, she's saying as she slips sandals off and bare heels hit the dash. Then I set cruise to sixty-five, change lanes, and she leans in and snaps a selfie with her phone, talking through the best part of this song. "So it's literally on the sea," she's saying. "Their deck, I mean. Back in the day, I guess it was a boat dock. Their place is so old—in a good way. They've renovated."

As I glance sidelong, catching my reflection in those mirrored shades just above that grin, thinking this is nice.

"Sorry," she says, "what were you about to say?" Then she's back on her phone.

And I'm shouting over wind. "I wanted to know what you were doing."

"I'm just sharing this on Facebook. Mind if I tag you?" she says, then tilts her screen to show off our end-of-season tans. ChapStick lips. That smile of hers, my profile caught off guard. Her boyish tank. Both of us hidden beneath shades.

"So what else do they like?" I say.

"Craft beer," she says. "They're all about craft beer. And baseball," two topics I know absolutely nothing about.

"So why don't you do the talking," I say.

Around sixty miles in, we finally do hit that bumper-to-bumper the radio keeps warning us about. Meanwhile she's thumbing, narrating a text: *Heavy traffic. Might be late.* While the guy in the car beside us sings to his dash, windows up, muted, and we inch ahead.

Rae reclines, shades propped atop her head, squinting and shadowed by a hand now cupped to the sun, before she closes her eyes and my gaze lingers down to where fingers clasp at her waist. Her shirt lax at the belt with shorts that tug at the thigh.

And I don't think I catch my second wind until we arrive, shaking hands in a sort of introduction that needs no introduction, given they seem to know too much about me as it is. I get the *How was your drive?* and that sort from two who are unoriginally dressed from head to toe.

And amid their talk of playoffs and whatever else, I just sort of daze off until I'm following their lead to the infamous deck or dock or whatever else you want to call it. Taking it all in, intoxicated by the scents of the Atlantic. Reclined in a low chair, resting feet at planks that quite literally—eventually—drop off to the sea.

Where Rae keeps asking *How are you doing?* and *Can I get you anything?* with a laugh that I can't help but adore.

Near the edge, just before the drop, a simple slab of wood is resting on steel now soldered into some sort of waist-high platform of a table, which is serving more than too many bottles of lagers and ales and odd soda brands, each with trendy labels, the good kind of tortilla chips and not-from-the-jar salsa, squares of cheese and other things.

And that carries us across another four and a half more topics until I'm feeling all too welcome here.

So by evening, we head out for dinner at this place that's dimly lit with the big glass ocean view, and we're served hummus and a basket of crusty bread, then rigatoni marinara, baked cheese. Chianti.

Until a few glasses in after having indulged, we're heading back to the sand and a late setting sun. With two and eventually three getting to work on a bonfire. And sparks begin to fly in no time.

It's really the same kind of conversation everyone has time and again with good people you can't see often enough. The jokes, the confessions, and still the fire grows, pops. As I catch that gaze, too intent on me.

And she leans in with a simple, "Hey."

And I say, "Hey."

And she's asking to go for a dip.

And I'm thinking, a night like this was made for bad hair and eating too much and drinking freely. Not a dip in the sea. Not bikinis.

Yet she's pleading and I'm wishing she didn't have to be so convincing like this. Gripping, tugging me through a salty breeze as it whips hair across my face. And next we're ankle deep at a tide that keeps rolling in and over and out. Her arms bound around my waist, her breasts crushed at my back as one more wave licks and tickles in its slow descent. Trickling as it drips. But she's steadying me, even with that constant tug out as it hopes to yank me everywhere else but right here.

As seaweed slips and curls around an ankle. Under the sky and its vast vibrance. And it hits me in a good way—a helpless but whole way. How I wish I could pause us and this, and nerves, and all of its apprehension and uncertainty, its doubts and misgivings. If I could hold this just a little longer, it might finally make sense.

And I'm hoping to say something profound like that, or maybe something prettier, but I can't really. Instead, I'm feeling a finger tug at a tight strand of hair now resting between my lips and stuck like taffy. Feeling unstable as sand sinks and shifts the earth beneath us.

Even as she's wading deeper, tugging me out, gazing back. Pleading and stretching to my bending as another tide collides up my thighs. And she's amused by this. She's amused. Radiant in light from the sun as it sinks deeper into the sea. With my shirt weighted heavier the wetter it gets.

But how deep is she planning on taking me?

My shirt drenched already, floating, a stream of foam resting between my breasts. Her cheek wet against mine, that hair dripping, skin shivering. But she's warm…here. I can feel her. And her breath sends a chill down my spine.

As she holds me through its lifting of hips before I settle into its dark. It swells around us.

Her thumb smudging against my lips. I can taste its salt on my tongue as I reach above and tug tight strings off the nape of my neck, and my top just floats right off. My skin chilled, her palm warm, hidden beneath buoyant swells of cloth now clinging and floating with the tide. As she draws me in, warms me, slips down me, wets me.

And I can feel her inside me.

That flicking light on the horizon. The tang of salt along her skin. Until I've lost count of the waves still crashing.

Lost count even as she's tucking straps, retying them, covering me, dressing me. Unbalanced as I catch my breath. Her thighs slipping between mine, rubbing, steadying my swaying.

Before we're hand in hand as we head back to the shore, having been out here too long.

And we make our way over, smitten, guilt-ridden, the sand rough, the fire hot.

Marshmallows roasting to a sweet crisp chestnut. Me, indulging in her lurid stare. How she felt out there. How it feels still.

As we collapse along dry towels before sinking wet feet into seaweed and sand and shells. Amid the scent of salt and fish and roasting wood chips. Our hosts sporting caps now. Me, wishing I could do the same, given this wind, but… "I've never been out that way," I hear as I'm handed a bag of marshmallows, the fire warming my face, when they ask Rae if she remembers, and I turn to her.

"You're heading to San Francisco?" she says with a swig of stout. And how dreamy she looks in this glow as I lick a bit of chocolate off just as it's ready to drip. Gazing down to where grains of sand have stuck to her legs and up a pair of heels before I return to find her studying me in that meaningful way.

As we discuss red tide and Haight-Ashbury and beatniks and revolution and women's lib and odd expressions like *tickled pink*. Then back to something about baseball.

Before our foursome shrinks to our intimate twosome under

the guise of "Our evening stroll," they tell us. Excusing themselves, brushing knees, and struggling yet failing to hide the obvious as they leave us to tend the fire.

And I follow Rae's eye to the sand as she sketches mindlessly alongside my hip.

Then another curious grin. It dips and lingers again a little while longer, resurfacing those nerves. And somewhere along the way the bonfire dims, that ginger glow shifting subtly along her jaw. Hair lifting to the breeze. She has me smitten and shy on this of all nights, her toes tucked shallow, hardly aware of my stare.

As I tip and empty my bottle and wiggle it deep in the sand.

It's warmed me sufficiently—the fire has, too. So I lift my shirt overhead, set it aside, lie back, gliding my fingers along my midriff as she tumbles to an elbow. "Why are you so bad?" she says.

"Is it working?" I say.

But as opposed to answering, she gazes along with me at the haze of a sky for a while and points to a glint of starlight. The low fire crackling, the distant waves. The air crisp. Sensing her gaze on me as I turn, and she weaves fingers into mine.

"Maybe we could, I don't know," she says, "call this a night?"

"But won't they be back?" I say.

"No," she's saying. And she stifles a yawn as she stands and says, "I'll text," with a slow swipe across her screen. "It's low enough," she says as she motions to the fire, and I get up and gather odds and ends and pack it up in this bag. Honey Maid. Hershey. My shirt along with bottles that I grip between knuckles while she scoops handfuls of sand and buries what little flame remains.

And we make our way back to their door. Her arm weighted across my shoulder. We brush what bits of sand still cling to our feet.

Before she heads to the kitchen and I pack what should be put away in this unfamiliar space.

And afterward, "This way," I say because our room's somewhere down this dark hall, but there's a tickle at my neck, a tug at my back, and my top slips down and I feel chilled, a breeze whipping past. She's against me now, a flutter of heat like breath up my neck, which ripples down my spine as her palms warm my skin, and she draws me in and we're fumbling as she slips this down my hips. When all I can do is sink into this kiss, not knowing, just sensing that cold at my back as I'm braced against the tile.

"Yes," she says. "To answer that question a while ago, it's working."

And her palm slips up the center of my thigh. I catch my breath.

But next, she steps away. She's twisting a faucet, lifting her shirt. And I'm wondering things as I follow her into the shower, sand circling the drain, until the only thing I can feel is that bar of soap as it glides up my back.

But still it's all very ordinary. Her ducking, wetting hair, soap lathering then dripping down her skin—then mine, rinsing. So why is my heart still racing as we tuck towels and slip up shorts and crawl into bed? Where she brings me to the brink and leaves me there, aching, wanting. Succumbing. And she's saying we can't, but we can't *not* when she parts my knees. Wondering how I could possibly hope to hold back. But all I can do is gaze along a shadow of a hip in the night's air until I hear the sounds of her breath, and she's there with me—and I'm watching her skin in the glow of the moon, nude, as my mind drifts.

I guess it must be about half past eight in the morning when my phone rings again, waking me in a burst of anxiety that needs to stop. So I lean in to pick it up and skim my screen. Which tells me it's Aline.

CHAPTER TWENTY-ONE

The Pickup Line

Rae

Is it me? Or is that aimless squawk of gulls actually missing overhead as I follow Madisen and she pauses to pull keys from her pocket? And afterward, "It's always hard heading back." I suppose I'm to ignore the fact that she hasn't disconnected all weekend, something easy to excuse for work, but...

Still I shrug it off.

Since it's a perfect day otherwise. The scent of salt, the heavy crash of sea, the sky's clear as can be. But the wind—I might prefer overcast to this if it meant no wind. And even still, that bounty of hair tangled, deliberately unkept, in beach waves, air-dried and unmanageable as she shoves her duffel into the trunk before going on about how "They made such a fuss."

"They always do," I say, reflecting on their crumble toppings and coffees on an early morning deck at sunrise.

"I'd like to get something," she says, "a thank-you of sorts."

But I'm only half listening to the rest as I load bags, wishing I could maybe shelve this for another day when there's more space than a compact car to contain an argument. I'd rather talk than argue. But even still.

"Is something wrong?" she says.

I have stewed all weekend as we fried pancakes and poured syrup all over the top, swam, and laughed with one another. And since this had to wait until our drive home, our first truly alone moment in how many days? It's all going to sound so blown up and out of context. Besides, I wouldn't even know where to begin.

Since where does one seemingly minor irritation morph into this enormous kitchen sink variety of grievances? Why, too, I'm wondering, could I have not opened my mouth and thought to say a word or two before it did—back a month or so ago when she didn't even offer me the time of day when I met Aline, as I introduced myself in their disregard. During *Tylenol was packed* and *homework* and *maybe you can get her to do this*?

After all, I still don't even know if Madisen wanted to come to this.

"You just seem unusually quiet today," she says, "that's all." And I can feel my muscles flex as I rub my neck, shrug it off, gaze mindlessly out the car window.

"Maybe we could just get home," I say.

Or maybe had she offered me a simple *that kid* or *nothing*, accompanied by, I don't know, annoyance over that major disruption of a call, it would've sufficed. But of course she couldn't. Which is why I'm not about to talk, not now at least—after good-byes and hugs and those *bing-bing* warnings your car gives—even miles into our return trip.

"So what'd I say?"

"You didn't say anything," I tell her.

"Then what'd I do?"

Can we not start on this?

"I'm sorry," she says. "Whatever it is, I'm sorry."

"Don't be," I say.

"I don't know what to say."

"Yet you had no qualms coming up with a million things to say to your ex? It's fine, really," I add, "you two ducking away."

"Is that what this is about?" she says.

"Why would I care?" I say. But the kitchen sink. So I guess I go off. "You put off how many calls this weekend—at the table, during that way too fucking long movie. And yet one call from her and you're ducking away?"

"And you couldn't bring this up when it happened?" she says.

"What was it?" I say.

"I literally don't remember. Her random stuff," she says, shaking her head, then laughing in that nervous way. "Nothing."

"What random stuff?" I say. "Because I'd like to know."

"Can we not talk about this? Please. Don't let that ruin our trip. This is how she is." But the fake smile, the sudden amnesia. More laughter, even. *I literally don't remember.*

As if just anyone could get her talking like that.

"I really can't talk about this," she says. "And not for the reason you're thinking. Why are you being like this?"

"Being like what?" I say.

"Jealous," she says, chuckling.

Should I be? I think I should. And besides, what would anyone else do in this situation? "So, what?" I say. "Is the kid hurt or something?"

"Don't you think I'd tell you that?"

"Who knows," I say. "I'm not exactly involved, am I?"

"Did you want to be?"

"Do I?" I say. "I believe we've already determined that we're not quite there yet. I mean, I'm hardly competent to take on that role. I would, however, appreciate knowing why your ex seems to think she can just call, knowing you're off with me."

"So this is our entire drive home?"

Perhaps.

"Great. I cannot believe this," she says. And the whole out-the-window thing flips into a blur of warehouse after warehouse, backyards and mile markers and concrete walls, but even still, I can't look at her. I can't face her. It's as if her smiling like that, her everything just pisses me off. It takes everything I said away or mocks it somehow or simplifies it. Erases it. Minimizes it. Minimizes me.

"Look, I don't know," she says. "I didn't tell her the whole story."

"You didn't tell her *what* story?"

"The part about us being together," she says.

"I think she's well aware."

"No, I mean the part where you came," she says, "here, on this trip."

"You didn't tell her that?"

"Like I said, she's complicated."

"What does that mean exactly, complicated? What, does she think that we're friends or something? Is that what you've told her?"

"I wouldn't know what she thinks."

"Do you want her to?" I say. "Do you want her to think you're... Wait a minute. Do you want her to *want* you still?"

But she's shifting in her seat now, watching the mirror. And who knows what that means. Maybe I've made her uncomfortable. Maybe it's traffic. I glance back. It's all so pointless. And afterward, I get the reluctant, "No. Of course not."

Until more radio silence through a few more cramped and painful miles when we pass a sign that says *Rest Area Next Exit* and I lower my window, drop an arm. "Hey," I say, "let's get off."

"Why?" she says. Then her phone again.

"I need something to eat."

"We're late as it is," she says, but that phone.

"For what? Just pull off," I say. "Aren't you getting that?"

"I'm driving," she says as she veers toward the exit.

But it keeps on. Christ. Glancing at her screen. "Your wife needs you."

As we pull off and she takes it and I get out, slam the car door, eavesdrop.

Madisen: "I'm busy. Can't this—"

And the car's still giving off that heated smell. I lean against it, following her, aloof as she strolls the length of a rutted sidewalk.

Madisen: "Put her on." (*The kid*, she mouths.) "What'd they do?... What about? You know."

Before she's leaning against me. So I pull her in—and the wind...

Madisen: "Health Ed, you mean?...I'm not sure about that."

Amid flags whipping overhead.

Madisen: "Really...let me help. I might next weekend. Just bring it along, or better yet, why don't I call once I'm home? The coast...yeah, super warm. Weird, right? For your birthday? What do you want?...She said she would...I know...I will..."

Until their dangling good-bye that ends with, "Love you, too," and to me, "God, I'm so sorry. I had no idea."

And I motion her down the walk. "Don't be," I say, stifling a grin because, sure, that was sort of cute.

Once we get to the food court, I slip my hand in hers, pull the handle. And isn't this always how it goes, the glares. The craned necks making me appreciate home, where being gay isn't such a spectacle.

As we split, me filing into the line at Cinnabon and her heading clear across the way for Subway. So I text Avery.

Me: *Hey*

Avery: *Where are you*

Me: *Never mind. Busy tonight?*

Avery: *Aren't you on vacay*

Me: *Heading home*

Avery: *How'd it go?*

Me: *Shitty*

Me again: *Well sort of*

Which for some reason I find centering because...well, Avery. I have no desire to top her in the drama department.

Avery: *We need adult beverages*

Me: *That I do*

Me again: ;)

Avery: *Where?*

Me: *You tell me*

Avery: *Elements at seven?*

Me: *Affirmative*

Avery: *You can meet Erin!*

I send off a thumbs-up, a smirking emoji, a hugging face emoji. She blows a kiss emoji. I grin (no emoji) and roll my eyes, glancing up to realize I'm conversing with a screen. And, besides, I've reached the register. So I order—adding a Double Chocolate Mocha Chillatta to my BonBites. Pay. While the next person in line orders multiple CinnaPacks as gifts, and she's struggling to wrangle kids as I contemplate why an order this large couldn't have been phoned in in advance.

Before weaving back through an obstacle course of tables and chairs, a straw at my lips as I take a seat paces back, to pick her up near the pickup line.

And all the while, it's like a levee as I hold everything back, or at least try. This whole day, like a flood. But she doesn't even catch me watching her.

We eat in the car on wrappers, not talking. People watching. Wad trash. Top the tank at the pump. And afterward, converse even less the rest of the drive home.

Which means by seven I'm squeezing into a dimly lit pub where I order a drink at the bar. And I'm checking my phone when I hear, "Waiting long?" from Avery, in her singsong freaking me the hell out way. Then she adds, "Hey, girl."

"Just let me grab my drink," I say.

"I saw you walk up," she says. "They gave us a seat upstairs on the patio." And I'm thinking this is the only girl who could carry off a dress like this and still make it look queer despite its plunging neckline, which is where my eye naturally tends to go. "You like?" she's saying.

"How cute," I say, lifting a necklace, "she bought you jewelry."

"Sexual favors," she says. "They reap magnificent rewards."

"You must be a rather good bottom," I say.

"Wouldn't you love to know?"

I shake my head, grab my drink.

"It's been too long," she's telling me with this gaze that sort of floats up to mine.

"It's been a week," I say.

"A week of having no one to talk to," she says. "Isn't that so awful?"

"But your girlfriend," I say.

"I hate that you're not single."

"As if I've ever *not* been single," I say.

"As if you've ever fallen in love."

"Yeah," I say as we make our way up a flight of stairs, "forget I ever said that."

Which is where I meet Carhartt or firefighter—or Erin, I should say—at a table with a drink, and she stands and I take a seat and Avery jumps in with Château de Fontainebleau (which she mispronounces) and *speaking of* and that conversation spirals into the Panthéon.

Because that's the sort of monotony you get with Avery when she's not brooding but, instead, putting on airs, hoping to impress. It's the safe, undamaged, politically correct side before she forgets and slips into her more characteristic risqué. Before all we're hearing about are her favorite sexual positions and how she does it best and who really knows what else.

So I grab my beer. "It's good to see you," I say, noting sunglasses folded on the table, a couple of quarters piled up, and that braided leather tie around Erin's wrist. She's twisting it.

"Possibly in five years," Avery's telling her. And they talk amongst themselves as I marvel again at how Madisen was able to connive her way out of this. The way she's deflected, sidetracked the issue because, what, I finally called her out on it? Because it bothered me? And shouldn't she already know that?

I'm so done with this.

Because really, she hasn't even so much as offered an ounce of consideration for what I might be going through. Which means, now what? We carry on like this indefinitely? Me being treated like her doormat. When there are fundamental differences we're having. Not the compromising kind—they're essential. Like listen to me. Think about me. Consider what you're putting me through. It's not as if I'm asking for the unreasonable, just that she acknowledge occasionally that yeah, yeah, it's shitty. It's hard. I'm sorry. Step out of yourself. When she won't talk, won't listen.

So what am I to do, get upset every time she gets a call? Every time we have to see Aline? When it didn't so much as faze me a couple of weeks ago—and now, that laugh, that *Don't be ridiculous.*

"What don't you like about it?" Erin's saying.

"What is there to like?" Avery says before going on in that long-winded way until we're so far off-topic that I'll never catch up.

"What about you?" Erin's saying.

"What about me?" I say.

"Did you have a nice weekend?" she says.

"What happened to the Panthéon?"

"Aren't you even listening?" Avery says.

"I do little else but listen with you," I say.

"So where's your better half?" Avery says. "I thought you'd bring her."

"Unpacking," I say.

Then she turns to Erin, "They can't come up for air," chuckling.

"You're so funny," I say.

"Which reminds me, that bookshop, did I tell you about that? Erin and I go up to this clerk and ask about their newest titles, you know, under LGBT, and she leads us down into this corner on sexuality, and I kid you not, they had instruction manuals on how to get off. I guess all we do is—" What'd I say? "And to top it off, they were more akin to guides or sex manuals, and did you know that there are certain foods that can actually improve your orgasm?"

"And you ran off to the grocer?" I say.

"Are we ready to order?" Erin says.

"Please," I say. "This drink is so overrated."

"Give this red a try," Erin says.

"I just might," I say.

"It's what she always gets," Avery says before hitting me with, "So?"

"No," I say. "Not now."

"Why?" she says.

"Look, why do you even care so much?"

"Do I look to you like an uncaring person?" Avery says.

"That's debatable," I say, turning to Erin. "So, has she told you about Bernadette?"

"Stop!" Avery says.

"Who's this?" I hear.

"So, Bernadette was this cat she leash trained."

"This is why I knew," Avery says, "that I shouldn't put the two of you together."

"Bernadette wore pearls and lace."

"She was a gift," Avery says, "that I lost in a tragic breakup. So let's not talk about her."

"You loved Bernadette," I say.

When Erin chimes in with, "What else should I know about you?"

"Oh," I say, "I could tell you a few things." Until Avery gives me this death glare. "Speaking of gifts, there happens to be one I need to get."

"As in?"

"As in a birthday gift," I say, "for this kid."

Chapter Twenty-two

Pink Polish and PJ's

Madisen

The thing about me is, I've never been able to lie.

I can still recall that time in the third grade after taking that pencil out of Olivia's unzipped case, the cool glitter kind with the twist-up lead as opposed to my boring yellow No. 2s. And even with a handful of identical others in that case, she still noticed one was gone. And that I was the one who took it.

All right so, I admit, that wasn't too hard to figure out, given I sat right beside her and now gripped an identical pencil complete with glitter design. But that guilt hit right away along with a rush of panic the moment she caught me red-handed—when she asked if it's hers. And, of course, I said no.

It's the same feeling I have as I break the news to Rae. As I stumble over my words. "I just don't think it's a good idea." The only odd part being, this is not a lie. But she's acting as if it is.

That said, I have officially uninvited my girlfriend.

My reason being, Jordan turns nine this weekend, so I'll be playing mom and faking cheesy grins all afternoon while hanging hot pink balloons and slicing pink cake and piling that on to pink paper plates. Finger-raking all the wrapping that scatters across my otherwise pristine living room floor.

Not to mention, Aline being there. Which is...look, it's not even that. And I'm not saying I don't want my girlfriend playing a role. It's just that I'm not ready for that level of involvement. Something I've tried to explain to her—that birthdays aren't an aspect of parenting I personally enjoy, so why burden her as well?

Besides, let's dig a little deeper. Let's not blindly jump into a situation without first examining how it might pan out. How I'm not only placing my girlfriend within conversing distance of my ex but also her parents, my parents. Cousins, uncles. The general consensus among elders surmised into two simple phrases: *Who's your friend?* and *your lifestyle.*

"So Aline'll be there?" she says, and just the thought of those two conversing, comparing notes. Which is not to say I've done anything wrong. But admittedly I haven't exactly drawn the clearest line, either. Not intentionally. But who knows how Aline might frame that—frame any of my comments, good or bad.

Plus I just figure my kid's birthday party is hardly a suitable occasion for...well, those things.

Like I said, I just don't think it's a good idea.

Besides, I've committed this year to remaining one hundred percent focused on my kid as opposed to Rae or, worse, me, me, me. I don't want this to become that epic disaster it was last year, when I could scarcely manage to hold it together through gifts, cake, you know.

Because this is Jordan's day.

And to that end, she's requested a slumber party, though I guarantee slumber will not be on the agenda. And despite my hopes of raising a skateboard-toting tomboy, guests will be gifted goodie bags complete with little compacts and pink nail polish, pink loofahs, pink sleep masks, pink hairbrushes, and pink nail files. I've even stocked our freezer with her favorite strawberry—or as she calls it, pink—ice cream. And this all-nighter just so happens to fall on my visitation weekend, an experience I'm not exactly enthused about sharing with a woman who weakens my soul, my natural ability to *mom* effectively. I'd just as soon we postpone this episode of Chaperones in the City until, say, next year.

And I'm hoping to explain so much to Rae when I catch her gaze from across the table. "It's just a kids' party," I say, shrugging it off. "You know, the piñata, the Smarties, the snappy cone hats?" Next, I lose her to an awfully friendly seagull who's making its clumsy way toward the legs of her chair. "You won't enjoy this," I say. "She's invited ten friends, and they'll be up all night. It's not as if you and I would have any time together. I'll be cleaning up and losing my mind." I say, sucking the last bit of water through my straw. But she's watching whatever that is now taking place over my shoulder—a small gathering of lunchtime suits, the boisterous kind. "Besides," I add, "she's really not a bad person."

And that's when she looks me straight on with, "I wasn't thinking about Aline."

"I don't think I'm being unreasonable," I say.

"You're not being upfront with me, either. Are you? Why can't you be like everyone else and hate your ex?"

Because, because. "We have a daughter," I say. "It's different. I can't exactly forbid her from coming to her daughter's birthday party."

"Have I asked you to?"

"I'm just trying to make sure everyone is comfortable."

"I'm comfortable," she says.

"I'm not," I say.

"Why?" she says.

"I don't know," I say. "And why do you keep looking at me that way?"

"Because you're not looking at me," she says. "I'm trying to have a conversation here."

"But don't you find that more than distracting?" I say, gesturing at that boisterous table.

"Can I ask you something?" she says in the most incredulous way as our waiter rounds the corner with cake, candles. They're singing. And the crowd's getting rowdier. Then she says, "Are you *over* her?" And it's as if, in that moment, the sun shifts and hits me dead on, and it's got to be 110 degrees out here and I'm not even exaggerating. "You're confusing me. I'm starting to feel like some girl you're just killing time with until the two of you figure it all out. And I don't want to be next in line after everything's happened, everything you wanted."

So what am I supposed to do, just shut her out? I can't, and if holding on means that I somehow have feelings, it's not the same. It's not this right here. But I can't tell her that. "Why couldn't I find you before all of that," I say. "It would've been easier. It's just complicated. And I don't want any of this to be complicated."

"It's not complicated," she says.

"It really is," I say, but it feels as if we're both waiting for the other to say something better, to make it right. But I'm shifting again, fidgeting, fretting instead.

"Seriously, why won't you look at me?" Rae says. "You really haven't all day, have you?"

"It's hard," I say. "It's hard for me."

"What's hard?"

"Choosing," I say.

"What are you choosing?" she says.

"I'm choosing to be a parent," I say, "over a girlfriend."

"So is this what we'll always be up against?" she says. "You choosing, because...what? Because Aline is complicated and you're too afraid to make waves—is that what you're saying? To make her feel uncomfortable?"

"This has nothing to do with Aline," I say. "Do you really think I'd be here, that I'd string you along, if I haven't moved on?"

"But has *she*?" Rae says. "And what if she hasn't? Have you thought about that? What if she called you up right now and wanted you back?"

"Why would that matter?" I say.

"Why would it not matter?"

"It doesn't matter," I say.

"It does," she says. "So here, I'll ask you straight up. Do you... *love* her still?" *Love her still.* Do I *love* her still? But it doesn't matter. "God, why did you have to be everything I've ever wanted?"

"It's a birthday party," I say.

"It's not a birthday party," she's saying, reaching back for her wallet—so what, is she leaving? "You have a child together."

"Please don't. Because what are you saying?"

"I'm not about to make this decision for you."

"What decision?" I say.

"I think maybe you need to figure this out on your own," Rae says, "before bringing me into it, because I'm pretty involved here."

But it's not until she actually gets up that it hits, what she's been trying to tell me. What I couldn't hear or maybe I didn't want to face. What I knew would happen. So maybe I make a scene and maybe somewhere in the middle of that scene I say, "You're making a huge mistake." And I'm fuming, so much that it all comes out like some sort of threat, which I didn't even mean. But I don't have the strength to explain, and besides she's leaving, isn't she?

"If it is," she says sliding a twenty under a plate, "we'll see, right?"

When you're ready, the waiter says.

I bury myself in work for the rest of the day. Deadlines and decisions. I snap a few times then apologize. I close my door. I let every call drop to voicemail and, even then, wish the phone would ring again. But when it does, I'm disappointed. It's never her.

It's just hopeless, that's all, and I'm far from inspired—creatively or analytically or at all.

So the day goes on and on and then it ends. I get home, skip dinner, sob in the shower, go to bed, check my phone, second-guess myself to sleep until it all drains me well into Saturday as I'm stringing a bunch of crepe paper. As Jordan wakes. As I vacuum, set the table. As Jordan fries her eggs. And by the time Aline shows up, grinning, clueless, at my foyer, I'm not ashamed to admit that I'm grateful and oddly comforted by this, by her ease and how natural it is to be around her. Even now at my worst.

And maybe that's all I need to get through the next three and a half hours of drop-offs and cake slicing, giggling and gift giving.

That and ducking into the kitchen, scooping drink mix into a punch bowl, which is what I'm focused on when I feel a breeze along the small of my back. And here I am, preoccupied, startled, expecting Jordan as I turn to give her a *Hey, kid.*

When it's Aline instead, her hair parted in that classic way as she settles beside me, too close and for such a long stretch that I'm starting to feel nervous all over again. As I stir. Or maybe it's not even nerves. Maybe I'm just upset. Maybe I'm blaming her. But then again, maybe it's fine.

"I didn't know they made organic fruit juice in hot pink," she's saying.

"It's Kool-Aid," I say, then turn and smile after she does.

"How'd you make it fizzy like that?"

"It's seltzer."

"How sophisticated," she says.

"Sparkling Kool-Aid," I say, "as sophisticated as it gets."

"She's ready for her piñata."

"I haven't filled it yet," I say.

"Is that it," she says, "over there?"

"Feel free," I say, gesturing.

She begins to rip a bag open. "You must've really wanted that weekend off if you're taking this on."

"Look, I appreciate what you did."

"Anything to witness this total one-eighty. You've gone from no artificial flavors," she's saying, "to Kool-Aid?"

"You pick your battles," I say. "I'm not the one hooking her up with Hostess."

"Like I've said, your rules are fine," she says, "but they're meant to be broken."

"Rules and vows apparently," I say. But then it feels petty.

"It's fine," she says. "I was only teasing. I guess I deserve that." And when I glance up, she's checking her phone. "Your in-laws are running a little late."

"That's good," I say. "So am I."

"I was entertaining your mom out there," she tells me. "She's being unusually polite."

"Give her time," I say.

"She thought we looked good together," she says.

"Leave it to her to be inappropriate."

"I'm sure she meant well."

"What else did she say?"

"The usual," she says. "Like *This is bad for the kid* and how we should *Think hard on that*."

"Think hard," I say, then glance over. "And that's what she told you?"

"I didn't mean to upset you," she says.

"Why would she say that?"

"The implication didn't go unnoticed," she says, in that shirt now dipping well enough to evoke curves I hadn't even noticed a moment ago.

"She's so dismissive," I say. "Did you empty those bags?"

As she steps over. "I did," she says.

"I'm looking forward to this," I say, incapable of masking any sarcasm.

"Then why would you sugar them up?"

"Because it's her day," I say.

"I can stay," she says.

"Of course you can't."

"As if I meant that," she says. "Look, just forget it."

"I'm sorry," I say. "I just thought—"

"What, I can't apologize?" she says. "Because this is about the other day, isn't it? And yet you were so unconvincing."

And saying she's in my personal space is an understatement. Which is to say, how long can I pretend to stir? I can't. "You and I, we have these things," I say, and next I'm filling my lungs. I look away.

Maybe she should stay. Maybe I'm wondering. Maybe I'm about to say…something. Do something.

But a few seconds in and she's back on her phone, that knee bent, barefoot. "Ten minutes away," she says.

Ten minutes, I think. And then *boom!*

"What the fuck?"

"I think someone might've popped a balloon out there," she says, calm, brushing my arm in passing and I follow. "Girls!"

Into the living room where I'm thinking, she's so beautiful, just look at her. And I admit to having not always noticed, not this way. Because isn't that how it is when you lose someone? You start to appreciate them. Since here I am, in retrospect. Though I couldn't outright say. It's just that, she is. And I guess there are times like this when I might almost sort of, but still not quite, begin to trust how she could feel about me. Or maybe it crosses my mind, reminiscing…How it was, how we were, how she did. It's all still somewhere beneath the words we shouldn't have said.

And even as I brush that all aside, it's still between us as we sink to our knees to calm Jordan.

As I glance up and she's doing that thing she always did, to catch my eye, which it does, and yeah. It catches me. Or maybe it just sinks me.

CHAPTER TWENTY-THREE

The Truth Comes Out

Rae

Me, walk? I enjoy the drive. But I didn't this morning because autumn, New England, vibrant (unlike my mood) and glowing with that different-colored sky you only get this time of year—as if you've just upgraded from pixilated CRT right into this brilliant LCD big screen. And pretty soon it'll feel so brittle that I'll wonder why I squandered so many days away with the window shut and the radio turned on.

So if you head downhill, what, two, three blocks past an old warehouse turned posh apartments, you eventually reach what's called old downtown, which is small but lined with mom-and-pops behind their high hazy windows with mossy grass lawns half paved over in broken cobblestone. Paint chipped to the snow line. A tight pet store, a health food co-op, a gentleman's barber, and a creemee stand with take-out window, where I bought a waffle cone mashed with double scoops and ate that three blocks until I hit the city park, which I really never see by car. Not the fountain. Not the clay-tinted path where joggers abut raging roadway with their hair tied back, swaying, shadowless, bouncing in spandex, music pounding through wireless earbuds.

Then, as opposed to taking a bench, shaded yet littered in droppings, I became one more figure reclining on the vast green of people watchers beside those reading Jennifer Weiner or Terry McMillan or a Kindle book with *Girl* in its title as they kept a watchful eye on their offspring, who were dizzying with spins twisted in swings before hobbling off.

Still I can't say what I was expecting to find.

Madisen dropping by, lolling beneath a shade tree? Instead she's stringing a piñata and not spiking punch. So whatever I had hoped to find, I didn't. Not there, at least.

I'm not finding it here, either. And regardless of how much I do or don't do or think about doing or wish I'd done or distract myself from doing, my mind feels like a boomerang. I lean idly against the windowsill, listening in on deep voices through the screen, their random laughter, heavy in amusement as if this was high noon beating down on their grungy baseball caps, as they grip cold cans of Bud Light around some engine or manly grill pit, Barbasol and Old Spice, fist bumps and *This one's on me*—that sort. Until I'm seeing her again, entertaining the crew, that warped shadow and the subtle way she hunches when she laughs. When I make her laugh, which was all the time. And I'm back on that again.

Over and over. It never seems to end.

So I dial Elizabeth, who knows intrinsically what's up. "I'm coming over," she says.

"You're really not," I tell her, as I flick a thumb over the spark wheel on my Zippo. "I'm fine," I say and then dive its flame into the hollow pit of another candle. But even I don't believe myself this time, blaming exhaustion following another night of not enough sleep. And after that doesn't work, I blame this drink, which might be the reason I nearly hit send after typing that *missing you* text and why I'm really on the phone with Elizabeth—for more thumb control, which as per usual, at least when it comes to Madisen, I sadly lack.

And I can hear Elizabeth sigh right into the phone. "Why do this, Rae?"

"What am I doing?" I say.

"Pushing everyone out of your life. You shut down. You always have," she says, and why does everyone say this to me? I don't push people out. They leave on their own accord.

"Just stop," I say. "You're accusing me of something you know little about. And when have I ever questioned your motives?" As I lie on the bed sidelong, a shoulder sloped near the edge. Then tossing a pillow. And when that lands at the foot of the bed, I nudge it off.

"It sounds like you've been sobbing all day," she says.

"It's allergies," I lie, "ragweed."

"I'm watching this show," she tells me, "on party crashers. Why haven't I tried this?"

"Because you're always invited," I say.

"Because I'm always invited," she says. "You're absolutely right. But this might be more...I don't know, interesting, if you ask me.

Finding some ritz of a gala. Getting glossed up as if you know some important someone. I could so manage that."

"I won't be joining you," I say.

"And what if we crashed your little princess's party?"

"You can't be referring to Jordan," I say, gradually making my way up to a slouched yet sitting position, my chest heavy. "Just, no."

"It's not exactly party crashing in that case," I hear. "Because…it would be so romantic. It's gallant, don't you think? In a win-her-over sort of way," she says.

"When did I say I wanted to win her over, or back, or anything like that?"

"I thought you were adventurous," she says as if provoking might convince me otherwise.

"And besides," I say, "you're to gift something pink when you come."

"Well isn't that gender-conforming," she says. "But think about it, Rae. The world is burning up. Those polar bears. Please take a moment to consider the polar bears."

"What on earth do polar bears have to do with any of this?"

"I'm talking climate change. We're all going down with the ship. And what do we have left in the meantime?"

"What kind of question is this?" I say. "We have life, weekends in P-town. Chocolate martinis. Cate Blanchett—not to mention Polo, Ralph Lauren for you."

"Don't be so capitalist," she says. "Love. Love is all we have. And you found that. How lucky you are."

"Right. I found the one and only lesbian on earth making child support payments to her ex-wife," I tell her, as my heart sinks again.

"So the truth comes out," she says.

"This has nothing to do with her kid," I say. "It has everything to do with someone who's still highly interested to the point of infringing on our everything. Really, how long have you known me?"

"I've known you long enough," she says.

"Well let me put it this way, how long have you known Madisen?" I say. "Oh yeah, that's right. You don't. Do you? And whatever happened to that thing called loyalty? To me not having to explain myself?" I add, scribbling on an envelope turned hope-to-do list, given all this time I now have, squeezing *haircut* and *45,000-mile checkup* at the end. "It's not a breakup. I told you. It's space."

"Space," I hear.

"Yes," I say.

"And she knows this?"

I don't know. Look, I'm not contacting her to clarify the particulars as to why I stormed out, since what kind of a lame excuse is that? So I say, "Yes. She knows this."

"Well, that's good. Because I'd take it as a green light to hook up with my ex," she says. "You never get angry when someone's trying to steal your girl. You get sentimental, sweet. Then they come back. God, girls are so easy."

"You know what?" I say. "They can have at it. Why would I care? Really. If she's that weak-willed and persuadable, it was never meant to be in the first place."

But leave it to Elizabeth to fall silent after my tangent. Meanwhile, everything in the room dims in that brilliant blue-twilight sort of way. It accentuates the shifting candlelight now reflecting off a copper lamp, sparkling up a wall, as I finger-rip the envelope at the top of this long ignored stack of mail.

"Party crashers," I hear under the shriek of sirens.

"Yeah, we're not doing that," I say. "But sure, I'll let you swing by if you want." Thinking, I could use the company. Though naturally, she blows this whole sit on the floor while we watch a few movies gig out of context by texting the whole gang. Avery, whose girlfriend is apparently off fighting fires. Add Tami and Rebecca, who can scarcely stand to be around one another.

Which means maybe an hour later, when the air's still brisk, smoky even, as I'm closing windows, I hear that rhythmic knock at the door.

And as I'm drawing Elizabeth in, this messenger bag always getting in our way, I catch that cedarwood-meets-violet Le Labo scent. "I come bearing food substance for the sad girl," she tells me, her gaze shifting to Avery, who, after our despairing kiss—or I should say hers—hands me a magnificent (or so I'm told) bottle of wine.

And soon Rebecca and her wife are making their familial way toward my sink for a lengthy bout of silence paired with the restrained clanging of plates.

"And Saturday evening," Avery says, "is apparently *the* most popular night at the pizzeria. Who knew?"

"I did," says Elizabeth, who is always in need of some sort of a drink in their company. "But who didn't call in advance?" As I pass a pie server, noting her technique leaves much to be desired. "Can you lend me a hand?" Still drawn to their customary, their well-acquainted that somehow morphs into a perfectly orchestrated serving system.

"I could simply live on white pizza," Avery says, "at least paired with a good Sangiovese." And I'm wondering if that underhanded gaze might hint of something of an overture. Next she's studying and subsequently crumpling a receipt that was taped on the box before tossing it in the bin. And bent to pull forks, she searches the drawer for my corkscrew, wearing that wide-necked shirt that slopes enough to bare too much skin, offering a glimpse of lace that's supposed to lift a lot of what's presently falling out. "I bought fudge brownies," she's saying, "store-bought but amazing. I wish I had an affinity for baking. Mine are always so sad, sunken."

"I wish I had an affinity for monogamy," Elizabeth is saying, pouring a glass, make that two, before lifting hers. "A toast to the sad girl."

"Remaining single is not the same as being sad," I say. But still, all eyes are on me for what, a toast? When there's nothing *to* toast aside from that eternal bond of marriage, which apparently remains unbreakable even after one does the unforgivable. "To marriage equality," I say.

"To marriage equality," Avery's saying with a far-off gaze, drawing the rim of her glass to her lips as she gazes back across the room at Elizabeth, who's now making her way toward the television where she balances on the balls of her feet, pinches trousers from just above the knees, and slips a disc into the Blu-ray tray.

"So what are we watching?" I say in an attempt to edge away. And I scan DVDs that line the shelf. "Nothing sappy."

Rebecca, swirling, settles beside me, resting a hand on my shoulder. "*The Way We Were.*"

"How sensitive of you," I say, thinking starry-eyed and sadly ever after. I'd prefer something a bit less Madisen, which I admit eliminates everything right about now. Because even were it not in there, I'd find it. "Why not one of mine?" I say.

"You do have quite the collection," Rebecca says. And even after taking a bite, she's careful not to smudge those ruddy lips, appearing winter-fair in a clinging black top, sleeves just above the elbow, chin raised like the upper-middle-class gentry she hopes to always be. "*Blue Jasmine*? Let me guess, this must be one of your midlife crisis flicks. Middle-aged woman quits her job, leaves her cheating spouse, can't handle the void that is adulthood. So she packs up to make a new start overseas in Italy, or somewhere desolate like a range in Montana, where she meets some devastating twenty-year-old and they laugh, spin, fall madly in love, rose petals descend on their bed as credits roll."

"Because that's clearly the kind of movie I'd watch," I say.

"No, but you clearly have a thing for Cate Blanchett. I only know *Carol*," she says, taking another drink. "And *Elizabeth: The Golden Age*."

"When did that come out," I say, "like two thousand six, two thousand seven?" I tote my plate, my drink, over to the couch. And take a seat beside Avery, who's intent on me.

"Two thousand seven," Avery says, "the year I graduated high school, all too jazzed to study early child development at my local community college until I found out that I would earn poverty wages. So I dropped out."

"And now you're a bingo coordinator," I say. She crosses her leg, half facing me.

"It beats poverty," she says, leaning over her plate as she takes a bite, that diamond necklace swaying in the foreground of...*ahem*. I'm thinking she does this sort of thing to me on purpose.

"And you happen to be very good at bingo coordinating," I say, feeling antagonistic—or something like that.

"I happen to think so."

"Where's your dripping hot firefighter?"

"She had a long day," she says, "and didn't feel up to it."

"So just like that, you let her off the hook?"

"Just like that. She's beat and, well, not much into our last-minute plans."

"I see. This one's a scheduler," I say. "Does this mean you schedule everything?"

Then, as I lean across her lap to grab the remote, perhaps we share some sort of moment there. "Don't insinuate," she says.

"I wasn't insinuating a thing," I say.

Once the movie gets going, Elizabeth heads back to the kitchen. "Please tell her she was gravely missed by all," she says, pausing at the island—the flat box, a stack of napkins, my Italian seasoning left out. "By the way, Rae, what is this thing that you have for Cate Blanchett? Really," Elizabeth adds, "I'm intrigued, or maybe a bit jealous, one or the other."

"More like, who doesn't have a thing for Cate," I say, "or just about any woman in a tailored suit?"

"Is that what you see in…well, dare I bring up the one who shall not be mentioned?"

"Madisen?" I say. "She wears a suit well. As do you."

"Me?" she says, laughing, glancing. "Wait, have you ever complimented me?"

"I don't think I have," I say, "so consider yourself now among the fortunate."

With that, Avery escapes to the fridge.

Elizabeth: "What about you, Avery?"

Avery: "What about me?"

Elizabeth: "What's your thing?"

As she traces a palm along the back of Rebecca's wide chair as if intrigued by their matrimonial charade, their carrying on.

Rebecca, swirling: "Avery only cares if they're a top."

As I follow Avery's petite stride back to the couch.

Elizabeth: "Does this mean you've settled? Or have you now become the top?"

Avery: "I haven't settled. And she's not exactly a bottom. Besides, I like a good challenge. Don't you?"

Elizabeth, taking a seat on a floor pillow: "And how does that work?"

Avery: "How does what work? It's all I find."

Elizabeth: "Tops?"

Avery: "And I happen to be an incredibly good bottom."

Elizabeth: "I'd love to see how good you are."

Me: "Don't you think we should watch this movie at some point tonight?"

Elizabeth: "By the way, Avery, how is cohabiting? Have I congratulated you? I happen to think it's a fabulous turn of events."

Avery: "Of course you don't."

Elizabeth: "Why do you think I'm so awful?"

Avery: "I don't. I adore you. That's all."

Elizabeth: "I have no desire to burst your bubble with realism."

Avery: "I'm glad to hear that."

Elizabeth: "Not tonight at least."

Me: "We're never watching this movie, are we?"

Elizabeth: "When do we ever get to hang out like this?"

Avery: "If you're so pleased with this fabulous turn of events, why so opposed to our buying a house?"

Me: "Wait…you're buying a house?"

Elizabeth: "While you've been on the playground with tots, Avery's hooked herself up with a Realtor and is signing her young life away. But here's my issue, which some have already heard. Scenario one, hypothetically, say she one day marries this firefighter and maybe she grows tired of reminding her to hang the towel on the hook where it belongs, as opposed to the bar where it never dries. Or perhaps Erin—is that her name?—never quite materializes into the top of her dreams. Were they to simply marry, they could split at a moment's notice. At least marriage offers divorce. But Scenario two, this white picket fence. And, well, what I'm trying to say is, too many end up like that. They stay—not for love, but for lifestyle. Think about that mortgage as a thirty-year commitment. Because who really knows how long it might take to sell in this economy."

Rebecca: "Spoken by a true authority."

Elizabeth: "All right, so I don't speak from firsthand experience as do you. But you must admit. Haven't either one of you contemplated leaving after one of those heated arguments the two of you have? And don't tell me you haven't because that would be a flat-out lie. But you can't, can you? You own a house. And if you're like every other red-blooded American, that mortgage is underwater. So you sleep on the couch or run off to the coast to get away...Oh, wait, you have Bar Harbor, don't you? Well, there you go. You've purchased two. So maybe you *can* leave. Look, we all go out of our mind once in our lives, fall in love, myself included. The ridiculous *Romeo and Juliet* moment, which is no reason to throw logic to the wind."

Avery: "I forget sometimes how sentimental you are."

Elizabeth: "What little you know about me. I happen to be enormously sentimental."

Avery: "Do illustrate."

Elizabeth: "Are you finally conceding to come back to my place? Because I'm happy to demonstrate."

Avery: "I'm referring to the never-get-over-it kind—that's love. I can't see that ever happening to you."

Elizabeth: "High school. I carried her picture around in my wallet for years. I still have it. I think I have everything she ever gave me."

But what fascinates me is the way Avery can draw this stuff out of the most reserved of people. Stuff I didn't even know. But she does this all the time. It's intriguing to watch it all unravel.

Elizabeth: "Does anyone besides me need a second glass?... Rebecca?"

Rebecca: "Marriage is not a forever honeymoon. Who would even want that? *That* would be exhausting. And really, one drink in and Elizabeth is claiming to be sentimental. And I love how you think, what, that if you jump out fast enough, they won't get hurt. As if that somehow makes it okay to hop around. As if it's about length of time. Isn't that always your excuse, why you can't commit? It's for them? So you won't hurt them. But you do."

Elizabeth: "I don't think there's anything wrong with averting heartbreak."

Rebecca: "But you don't. Because the best way to avoid heartbreak is to let it run its course. There are no mistakes in love. And who's at fault? We're all at fault. You're clearly not over this one."

Elizabeth: "How do you figure that?"

Rebecca: "Isn't that much obvious? She's ruined you for everyone else."

Elizabeth: "Not ruined, refined."

Followed by the kind of air you just need to fill with conversation, but nobody will.

Until, Avery: "Confession time. Tell me…what's it like, sex I mean—and not in detail, unless of course you care to share—when you both don't know what to do? Your first time. I've always wondered that. Like, is the sex really bad? It's not like I've ever been with a virgin."

Elizabeth: "Your first time—"

Me: "Is what, Elizabeth?"

Elizabeth: "It's perfect. It's the most perfect."

Avery: "I had no first."

Elizabeth: "How is that possible?"

Avery: "No, I mean, my first wasn't love. For either of us. She was, well, I just do what strikes my fancy at any given moment."

Elizabeth: "A promiscuous bottom."

Avery: "A promiscuous top."

Elizabeth: "I happen to love bottoms myself."

Me: "So Elizabeth, this girl, she was your first on both accounts?… And, now, why do I find that super sweet?"

Elizabeth: "When did I become the poster child for super sweet?"

And we don't ever actually get to the movie. I mean we do, if you count talking through the gist of it, which segues into another bottle of wine and of course Avery's fudge brownies.

So the next day, after pizza and too many recent cheats, I hit the gym.

Which would be day one of my new workout regimen, otherwise known as naive exhilaration. More like I am invincible, admiring lean biceps as I step in the shower, convinced I look nine billion times better than Jillian Michaels and Megan Rapinoe all wrapped into one glorious lesbian.

That is until day two, which is sheer agony. But I show up, and sure, I'm famished at this stage. So I stroll down and grab another double scoop, eat at the park with pigeons, justifying every lick as a calories-already-burned sort of thing.

Which leads me to day three, also known as immobility.

So day four is a wash because, look, I got out of bed.

Until tomorrow, which is Friday. And, no kidding, Friday is not the best start-over day. Nor is Saturday or Sunday. So…

On Monday, I make a radical comeback. Because at this point, I truly have no excuse. And this becomes my new thing. My working out thing because it's the only way I can not break down and call Madisen.

CHAPTER TWENTY-FOUR

How to Stop Feeling

Madisen

I'm beginning to realize something. That it doesn't matter how many times Aline calls for fill-in-the-blank, the moment I see her name on the screen, my heart begins to race like *emergency*. The hospital kind of emergency where vending machines drop Doritos and M&M's in waiting rooms filled with patients who are entertained by the latest on CNN. And where scrubs wander halls shoving dangling apparatus on stretchers—never a good thing. So I'm bracing to learn why my daughter's being carted into room 201 as I accept the call.

Naturally expecting...well, not this.

"If you're busy doing nothing," I say, "then where's Jordan?"

"She's at my parents'," Aline says, "all weekend."

Truth be told, I sometimes wonder why I keep this up with her, engaging. Expecting cold and aloof when this is how she is. And she'll continue to be this way indefinitely, drawing me in, until I'm able to respond differently.

And here's another thing she does whenever she's holding something back. Or if she can't come up with a suitable way of expressing whatever it is she's trying to say. She'll leave it all to me. She'll expect me to carry the conversation, which is what I'm doing, sharing things that are completely irrelevant. And only after I'm beginning to second-guess my decision to answer my phone do I hear, "Tell me I'm not a screw-up," which draws me back in.

"And why would you say that?"

"You'll remember," she begins, followed by a long-winded monologue about someone she met through one of Jordan's things, her after-school things, those parenting things. A story I find reasonably amusing since who wouldn't, or maybe it's just the way she tells the story that always seems so captivating to me. And I'm laughing for the first time all day.

So I figure the least I can do is lend an ear because sometimes that's the best way to deal with situations like this—put my issues aside and let her amuse me for a while and then we can get back to whatever it was we were doing before she interrupted, which wasn't extraordinary, was it? Given there are only so many times I can sink into wallowing despair accompanied by the poignant strum of Ron Pope on his guitar.

On the other hand, why am I offering her this courtesy? Sacrificing a highly productive night of wallowing, for what? To play therapist for a woman who left me for someone else? It's not as if we're still married, and besides, I have matters I'd like to deal with on my own. Why I feel I owe her anything is beyond me. I only wish I wasn't adoring this whole sensitive side of her so much. That side I'd long forgotten.

And not only that, I wish I hadn't caught myself sinking back into our old familiar patterns right along with her.

"You always make me feel better," she says.

"I'm glad to hear that," I say, hoping to find some semblance of neutral, unemotional middle ground.

"So what else have you been up to?" she says.

"Do you have all night?" I say. Yet even when I try to sound upbeat, it still comes across as flat, monotonous.

"Sure I do," she says, laughing, and afterward, "Why don't I swing by? Do you have any plans?"

But *um*, I hadn't expected that.

"Never mind," she says, and somehow that snaps me back into reality before I say anything I might live to regret. "I'm sorry," she says. The thing is, I still don't trust myself around her, especially now, not like this. "But then again," I hear, "it would be nice to catch up, you know? I could stay awhile, or not. There's so much and…I've wondered…how you've been."

Wondered? "I don't know, Aline."

Because logically I know she could stay five minutes or five hours and it wouldn't make a difference. It's the seeing her part that's unbearable. I'm still trying to get over *her* getting over *me*. And this phone, right now, is the only willpower I've got.

"Just us," I hear, "without those constant interruptions." And I know, I know, I know. She won't stay long. "All right then?" she says.

All right then. "Sure," I hear myself say. Overwhelmed but a touch excited as well, ashamed as I am to admit that. Curious, maybe. Followed by this odd sense of relief that she's not shutting me out the way she used to, as if we could move past this. As if it could ever not hurt. Soon my lungs just sort of deflate, having been held in, I now realize, for quite some time.

So, I'm wondering, this is what we do?

And has she moved on so far that she's indifferent to it all? Which means we catch up, as she says, like friends who shoot the breeze on a Saturday night?

But how could I ever feel so little for her?

Having realized that if I stop breathing long enough, I can stop feeling whatever this is I'm feeling, shouldn't be feeling, nerves, or *who knows anymore*?

Because look at me, I'm trembling, aren't I?

So what in my bureau says *I didn't dress for the occasion* yet *Look at what you've lost* at the same time? As I settle on jogging shorts with a drawstring that might say hanging out with a touch of late-summer something, for all those times when I take that casual jog at nine o'clock on a Saturday night.

So now, what, I just wait. Pick up, tidy up, and wait for her to arrive, which is something I've never been good at, patience.

I guess I could've lingered on the phone with her, listening while she walked at that pace as if she was eternally late, aggravated by traffic or something during those however many minutes it would take her to get from there to here.

Had I kept her on the line, I would've known when she was *a block away* followed by *I'm just outside* and *I'm at your door*, my heart racing with the sound of her knock.

I could never be sensible or rational because it's never, ever logical with her. I don't know why that is. It's just this huge mistake I'm going to make, isn't it?

Because I know exactly how it'll go.

So let's do things differently this time. Maybe?

Like the day we moved in, when I bought champagne in a can to commemorate. But she crawled into bed instead. We couldn't sleep. We talked for hours about how we couldn't sleep. About how I wanted to make love on our staircase gripping the banister. *Tie me to it*, I said. But she laughed. *I won't.* Eventually, though, she did.

And now she wants friendship—after that?

Give me the easy answer, the sure thing. What do I do? What if…? Maybe, maybe, maybe. I don't know. But there's her knock as my fingers pause at the knob and I'm trembling. So maybe I shouldn't do this. Step back, breathe.

Except it's too late. She's holding me. And I'm wondering why we never talked about this when it was insignificant, when we could still feel our way back.

"Can I get you anything," I say, and I can hear my voice quiver, "like a drink?" Thinking as I do how simple yet how complicated it feels to see her this way.

And it's this thing she does just like that. It's the cream on top.

Next, I'm lifting a knee in a chair, casually, as she's discussing gridlock as if this was any other day. As if this was the reason she'd come by. As if she'd never left. And I'm wondering as she does—as I watch her lips move, as she leans over the edge of her cushion casually, fingers woven down the center of parted knees, flat-footed—if she's as nervous as I am. Before we're filling so much time with so many empty words. Pretending, aren't we? I am again. Listening to all those things I want to hear. I want to say them, too. I'm reading into them.

And I catch her gaze lingering on me as we settle back into more of this small talk. As I scrutinize my every move, my every word as if any reminiscing on my part might be misconstrued. Until she's waiting for my response.

"The coast," she's saying, "I was asking if you enjoyed yourself."

"You know how I love the beach," I say. But it just sinks me back into Rae, and I'm crushed again.

"So, you were with her?"

"Yes," I say. Because Jordan must've told her. That's all I can think. And I'm following along as palms rub down the length of her jeans as if squeezing them, and only afterward do I realize she's watching me as I sink into her simmering gaze.

And she says: "Love becomes you."

As simple as that. And I miss this. Wondering why she has me like this, crumbled into a million bits and pieces, doubting every word. If she even knows I am. As I feign unbroken. As I try to figure out, in which way do I miss her?

Then running a finger along my brow. "What are you doing, Aline?"

"There's so much I wish I could say. But I can't."

"Then maybe you shouldn't."

"I'm just sorry," she says.

"Why?" I say. But what I really mean to say is, let's not talk about this. Let's not do this. "It's only now that I've found someone else," I say, "now that your new is gone."

"I didn't enjoy new," I hear.

But you chose new. You chose her. And afterward, as I stand beside the mantel, as I dust the lack of dust along its surface, I'm tempted to divulge even more. One-up her candor. Forgive her. But instead I just say, "Though maybe *I* did."

"Enjoyed new?"

"I enjoyed *her*," I say. Exerting some effort to add, "She and I, we—I guess—broke things off, you know, right afterward." Aline's gaze narrowing. Mine drifting to her palms now at her lips as if she was praying. "Or I should say, she might've broken it off." Then I apologize. "I'm not much company."

And it's intriguing how, as she steps into the doorframe pondering a reply, the light down the hall seems to blind until all that's left is her silhouette, rigid, shifting. I study the way she moves, the way she's glancing down the hall. It makes me wonder what she's planning to do, if she's planning to leave.

And then she says, "Maybe I'll take you up on that drink?"

But we don't say much after that.

As I follow her into a kitchen absent of dialogue yet rich in debate, where she presses her lips to a glass as if preoccupied, while I twist cork. And still I couldn't say whether her look is one of sincerity or mere empathy, as I pour enough for each of us.

She drags a chair out from under the table and takes a seat. As I join her, I ask, "And how did you convince your parents to take Jordan for more than a few hours?"

"It's some opening," she says. Then she begins to talk with her hands. But it doesn't really matter what she says—I find it interesting. I hope she stays. It feels as if I've said so much, and now I need her to stay if only to tell me it's okay. I'm okay.

"And what'll you do with yourself all weekend?" I say.

"No clue," she says, crossing a leg out from under the table. "Doesn't it feel like we're going through the same, or similar, you and I? And somehow we've found ourselves back here in the same place." Her shoulders lifting.

And through the course of the next few hours, I talk over her. She talks around the truth. Our glasses fill without my knowing. The house settles. And the night begins to peer in. As our small talk melds into her, occasionally opinionated.

As this becomes that, and my mood shifts into something else altogether, which is good, until I hardly notice her lips, her breath, near mine. But she's so close, isn't she? It's like this subtle bit of nothing. But it's not nothing. It's everything. Her gaze, inconsolable. But isn't she the one consoling me? As I manage to shift. Shaken when I say… something, I don't know.

But Aline has complicated this, confused me, making it hard to avoid her, leaving me no time to consider what I'm doing, and besides… "Would you like another glass?" I say pouring. But the only thing she wants is a reason why. As in, why can't we?

Then she sets her glass in the sink, and it makes that sound.

And she turns to me. But I don't know what to say. And next she's pulling keys. But I don't want her to go.

As I contemplate boundaries and where mine have gone, while she edges past my shoulder. And I sense her breath near mine. As if this was my last and only chance.

❖

With a hand covering my eyes to block the morning glare, I can hear Andi half shouting into the phone. "You would *not* believe who I ran into last night."

"Who," I say, groggy, stretching to find the clock.

"Since when do you sleep in?" she says.

"I'm not."

"All I can say is, next time, warn me," she says, garbled, before that white noise you always get when someone's lost their signal.

As I roll and startle the cat, who bolts from my pillow.

"Warn you?" I say.

"Who's calling?" I hear, and it's Aline and she's standing at the doorframe fully dressed when it all floods back.

"Is that who I…?"

"You're breaking up, Andi."

"It's Andi," I say before, "What didn't I warn you about?"

"I'll make us some coffee," Aline says.

"We need to…" Andi says, "because why is *you know who*…and what—?"

Oh my God, this is frustrating. "Who did you see? Rae?"

"Yes!" I finally hear clear as a bell.

"Is she mad? What'd she say?"

"You tell me?" she says.

"I was going to call," I say, "then—"

"I know, I know," she says. "She told me about Aline."

"She told you *what* about Aline?" I say.

But she's talking over me with, "I said *no way*, but—"

"It's not what you think."

"Right," she says.

"Where was this?"

"Where else?" Andi says. "Pool."

"Lovely," I say.

"I shouldn't tell you this."

"Tell me what?"

Dead air.

Holy fuck. "Tell me what?" I say. "Andi, you're breaking up. Where are you?" But she doesn't respond. *Tell me what?* And I'm whispering into an endless hum of white noise. "I'll call you later," I say, "okay?"

When Aline gets back, she hands me a mug and slides into bed. But we're not exactly communicative. Even still, I'm not about to talk her through this silence again. As if there was anything left to say.

"How is she?"

"Who, Andi?" I say. "She's fine." But why do I feel like I've made the biggest mistake of my life? When I haven't. "Look, maybe we shouldn't do this sort of thing."

"What *sort of thing*," she says with air quotes. "We did nothing at all."

"You have such a warped outlook," I say.

"And you exist in a perpetual state of regret."

"I don't regret anything," I say, thinking *I don't regret you, not what we had, not any of this.*

"Then what are you thinking?" she says.

As I tug sheets, feel along the edge of the table, twisting hair. And afterward, she's watching me. "I'm thinking we need to find a clearer line, that's all."

"And where's your line?" she says. "I won't cross it."

"We can't go back," I say.

"Who says we can't go forward?" she says.

"I'm trying to," I say. "Which is why you're here. Which is not working. And I'm not angry. I'm not bitter. I know that's what you're thinking, and I'm not. But seriously, what'd you think last night would even accomplish, after everything you've put me through? That I might swallow my pride and let it go? And please don't act as if your brief bout of reminiscing was anything more than your extended farewell," I say. "Because I can't not see you with her—can't you understand that? And you can't just slip right back into my life as if it never happened. As if what you say right now, what you do, means nothing to me. Because you mean everything to me," I say. "Don't be careless."

As we argue in circles, until I'm wishing I could go back to talking *around* this instead of *about* it. Her convincing me otherwise. Me wondering if there will ever be something in our ending aside from this overwhelming weight of grief. This drained of feeling anything at all. My wanting to find some good in it, in us—in me again.

And as much as this feels like another end, I don't know if there ever will be an end with her. And when I realize this, it's somehow encouraging and disconcerting at the same time.

Later, really as soon as I find myself alone, I call Andi because, "Not *that*," I say. "We just talked, I swear. But you know, that's not why I called."

"Listen, I pulled her aside, Rae, last night. She asked about you." And just with the sound of that, my stomach flips. "Not right off. It was weird. She kept glancing around, asking about me and…Let's just say, this girl knows a thing or two about soccer. Were you aware of this?"

"Go on," I say.

"Well we got around to the whole *How's she been?* thing and this is where I'm like, shouldn't *I* be asking *you*? Seriously, since when?"

"I didn't feel like talking about it," I say.

"I got the sense that she might've, who knows, wanted to run into you."

"She's there all the time," I say.

"She's not, actually."

"Aline and I are trading schedules. She'll have Jordan alternating weekends and I'll have her the rest of the week. She's being, I don't know, cool right now."

"So did you?" Andi says.

"Of course I didn't," I say.

"You did."

"Why would you think that?"

"You're serious," she says.

"Yes, I'm serious. Not that it matters. She slept on the couch."

"Why?" Andi says.

"We had a few drinks. That's all. And I didn't want her driving home like that. Can we not go there?"

"Where would I go?"

"Where you always go. Where I could've gone," I say. "As if this was simple."

"Well, it's where I would've gone," she says.

Chapter Twenty-five

Spanx

Rae

After berating myself over everything I said, everything I did because I'm such an idiot, I just hit the gym. Which is like the most amped up workout I've ever experienced in my life.

Not that Avery's thinking the same.

"They have classes and trainers for that," I tell her.

"How could I possibly spin wrong?"

"You could, I don't know, pull a hamstring at the rate you're going. Who knows?" I say. "Besides, why are you so averse to weights?"

"Because," she says, "they'll make me bulky."

"They won't make you bulky," I say, taking in curves only accentuated by this posture. Add that cropped tank. "We need to work twenty times harder than a man," I say, "just to get anything remotely close to muscle," thinking *We need to work twenty times harder than a man to get anything at all in this world.* And I'm tucking a towel behind my neck when she gives me her best contemptuous-can-be-evocative look while slipping off the seat. "It's biologically impossible," I say.

"Yet look at those two," she says. "I can't even."

"What are you talking about?" I say.

"I'll never fit the mold," she says.

"There is no mold, and they'll never have what you have."

"And what's that?"

"Cleavage," I say.

"Stop, they wouldn't want it," she says. "It gets in the way."

"Or me." I grin.

"I don't have you," she says.

"You'll always have me," I say. "And think about it this way—I don't know one lesbian who doesn't love a woman who trains."

"When I'd rather just shop," she says, twisting weights as if dangling a handbag, limp. "It's such a gorgeous day. It's dripping in sunshine."

"Try a squat," I say. "Humor me. But do it, c'mon, for real." Admiring her form.

"If you're trying to coach me—to save me from entering Spanx territory, which is where I'm heading—might I suggest you keep your day job?"

"What would motivate you?" I say.

"Sitting over here on the bench, watching you," she says. And soon we're back on bungalow vs. condo vs. that two-story cape she found on Realtor.com. That is, until I finish a few more sets. "And will we indulge in one of those cute little faux energy drinks I saw at the café?" she says.

"Why don't I buy you lunch, instead."

"So is this a date?" she says.

"If that's what you'd like to call it."

"And to what do I owe this honor?" she says.

"To your one squat," I say. "And that top."

"Lunch," she says, "then shopping?"

"Sure, anything you want," I say.

"Anything?" she says.

So by two, we're enjoying precisely that along with a few tall glasses of iced coffee, unsweetened for me, on a glimmering patio under the wooden trellis at Archipelago which, draped in white string lights, is feeling almost festive.

Albeit, I'm not.

But from here, from underneath their canopy, you can just sense the enthusiasm all around, those crowds. Shops for blocks now shoulder-to-shoulder. And I'm thinking it must have something to do with that tax-free weekend. Or back to school. Who knows? Something like that.

But the next thing I know, Avery's doing this thing where she swirls a tall drink spoon in her glass for no apparent reason. In other words, she's hoping to get my attention. And I know why. It's not as if I've been exactly tolerable since we left the gym.

Maybe I've run out of upbeat things to share—or more precisely, maybe she's more interested in her life and I'm more interested in mine.

And we can't seem to find common ground. So this day has evolved into a long string of one-sided conversations, her too consumed with real estate and me, well, isn't that a given?

"I was only trying to help," she says before taking her first bite.

"Only trying to help," I say, "by playing matchmaker? *My friend's newly out of a relationship* as she lifts her bra is not the locker room talk I was expecting."

"She seemed your type."

I shrug. *My type.*

"And she was so into you," she says.

But there's something about this vibe. That truck backing up, its persistent beep. Brake lights. And cold, like that blast we had last spring, almost coat weather, when rosebushes are fighting to hold their bloom. The ground dry, yet covered in leaves that are wet and stuck to this, that. As I picture Madisen peeling out of her day with that fall to your knees sort of effect she had on me. I should've known she'd avoid this place.

"So elusive," Avery says.

"Who, me?" I say, leaning across the table.

"Why do I feel as if you're keeping something from me," she says.

"I don't know. You tell me."

"What's making you smile like that?" she says.

Was I smiling?

"What were you thinking about?" she says.

"Nothing."

"Right. You never share the good stuff."

"If you must know, I was thinking," I say, "how so few people know what they want."

"Yourself included?"

"Oh, I know what I want."

"Then go after it," she says.

"And I was considering all the bad advice you've given."

"You're too prideful," she says.

"Maybe you could not lecture me," I say. "There's more to it."

"Such as?" she says.

"Why would I want anyone I had to chase?"

"You could never win me over," she says. "Because that's always what gets me."

"Right, we all know how you operate. This was, plain and simple, bad timing," I say. "So let's drop it, all right?" And why is it every time

I'm beginning to feel like a semifunctional human being, like after that workout, something reels me back in to feeling like this?

"Let's stop in there," she says, preoccupied.

"Stop in where?" I say.

"That new shop across the way."

Admittedly, her on and on does have a *Get Madisen off my mind* quality to it.

So, later, she's tucking under an arm and we're bracing the breeze of passing traffic, making our way in stride through a crosswalk, zigzagging behind parked cars. "I cannot believe you're considering a lifelong mortgage with some girl you randomly met at Panera."

"I know, a sleazy sandwich shop," Avery says. "And why can't you use her name?"

"Erin. But what else do you really know?"

"More than you," she says giggling.

"Like?" I say.

"Like her favorite color is khaki."

"That's not a color," I say.

"And I make her nervous. She tells me that all the time."

"Such an old line," I say.

"So the other night, there was some woman by herself in the back of a car waiting. And Erin made up this long story about her. Was she lonely? Exhausted after a long day of who knows what? Who was she waiting for, and why the back seat? It wasn't Uber."

"How deep," I say.

"She's creative like that," Avery says, gazing into the storefront at a mannequin, its black wig. Avery's reflection layered in glass over faded pink and black and cursive script.

"So where does this girl stand on, say, politics?"

"Why does it matter?" she says.

"Because it does," I say. "And religion?"

"Never brought it up."

"What if she's using you?" I say.

"You're so jealous."

"Yeah, I'm not," I add, evading some guy before he walks into me. "I just know your type."

"No. You're freaking out because this is the first girl to put up with me for...how long has it been?" she says. "By the way, what's my type?"

"Let's just say they don't like me."

And she somehow finds a way to get closer. "Sure they do," I hear, before, "I think I want that. Let's go inside."

"Must we?" I say. And while this is far from the type of place I'd ever shop, she drags me in, enthused, browsing amid its natural light. "Why do you like this stuff?" I say, perusing.

"I don't know."

Not to mention, it feels unnaturally quiet in here. Maybe it's all the commotion out there. And once the door smacks shut with its string of bells, we're left with little more than that scent of lime and coriander.

"What do you think about this?" she says, lifting a padded hanger.

"Well, I wouldn't exactly call this Spanx territory."

"But is it *me*?"

"It's something," I say. "It's really nice."

"Nice as in something you'd like?"

"Why would you care what I like?"

"So you don't like it?" she says.

"That's not at all what I said. I just don't usually do this thing. I mean, why wear anything if this is what you had in mind?"

"Because," she says, gesturing up a thigh. "It lifts just so."

"I see. So you plan on leaving this little number on the entire time?"

"That's what I had in mind," she says. But not hearing the support she'd wanted, she puts it back on the rack. "We had an argument."

"I'm sorry."

"She thought I was mocking her. I was teasing. I was only messing around."

"Domestic quarrels," I say.

"You couldn't relate."

"Not at the moment," I say, "no."

"What about this? Black," I hear, "or teacup blue?"

"Why not try both?" I say. "Let's get a room."

"I thought you'd never ask," she says.

There's a clerk behind the counter busying herself with everything unimportant. But there's nobody else here. Still, when I draw the curtain, as it makes a quiet clamor, I cringe, ducking in, fumbling, tying ribbons stitched at either side, which is apparently all they have as far as a door. As far as privacy, that is. A curtain. And then I turn, and she's tugging jeans down and along an ankle.

Me, scrolling my phone—wavering. Wondering if Madisen would even care if I sent some random text like this from out of the blue.

"And I don't even know what to make of it," Avery's saying, unclasping her bra. I shake my head, then go back to my phone, scrolling.

The next time I glance up, she's considering the fit and fall of fabric now reflected in three angles of the same mirror. "Does this make my chest look big?"

"Isn't that the point?" I say.

"But is that bad?"

"That's never bad," I say.

"Then adjust this for me?" she says, lifting hair. "I need your advice."

"What kind of advice," I say. Then I get up, set my phone down.

"Do you think I'm making a mistake?"

"I don't think you're making a mistake," I say, fitting arms around hips as she rests against me.

"But I go too fast," she says. "You always tell me that."

"It's part of your charm," I say.

"For a time," she says adjusting this and tugging that. "For a time it is and then…I don't know. I'm frightened all of a sudden," she says, leaning back against my chest, my palm slipping up the front of her. Because I won't lie, I feel as if I'm being skipped over, left behind.

"Fear means you're doing something right," I say. Though I sometimes wonder if I might be advising myself as opposed to her. "What if she's *it*?"

"That frightens me even more," she says.

"Hey," I say, "can we not do this?"

"What are we doing?" she says.

"We're not doing anything. And you need to get out of this," I say, lifting her hem thinking *I can't lose you.* I can't lose this. As I hold and hang and she braces for balance.

"I love you," she says. "And I just don't want anything to come between us. That's all."

"There wasn't a stitch between us a second ago," I say.

"You've lost that chance," she says. "Perhaps."

"Well, I think you should get Spanx."

And this gaze. "Why is that?"

"This is far, far too easy to lift," I say. "And I'm thinking she needs to work for it."

CHAPTER TWENTY-SIX

Replica Jazz Club, 3.4 oz.

Madisen

How many weeks has it been? And still I hadn't touched it. I couldn't. I was content to leave it right where it was on my bureau because Rae might realize one day that she left it—and call or ask for it back or stop by. Where I might say the right thing and she might too and maybe...? Who knows?

What was I thinking?

I wasn't thinking, that's what. I was spraying it on. I was over her, more like hoping to remember her, and that scent only carried me back to everything I couldn't resist about her.

And let me just say one thing which is both on and off topic. And that is, if you happen upon a chance to purchase one of those exorbitant kitchen appliances after your plain version from Bed Bath & Beyond bids adieu, offer yourself that one simple upgrade. Because I've now learned that having the right tool for the job, like bartending, is nothing short of essential.

Which leads me to that perfect pair of jeans, those tempting you from the rack well after you've wandered off—despite their made-for-you fit—because they're still out of your price range regardless of the fact that they've been marked down from, say, $169 to a penny under $70. I mean, how many times in life do you find such perfect suitability? Really. I believe something akin to nirvana occurs when a girl buttons up a well-fitted pair of jeans. It sort of helps her forget, don't you think?

And tonight those jeans and this finely blended margarita are my passport to getting through life, my getting over her, and her, and getting over myself at the same time.

"I'm still marveling at the fact that anyone thought to put you in charge of marketing," Andi's saying as she flattens the rim of her glass against a plate of kosher salt. "And by the way, how'd you accomplish the rest?"

"Let's just say, I finagled it," I say.

"You finagled it," she says. "Why don't you just pass the kid off to me at five? I can make dinner."

"Which would defeat the whole purpose, don't you think? You have no idea how hard Aline was to convince on this."

"And please don't tell me you fell for her noble intentions line in stopping by," Andi says.

"I thought we might be friends," I say.

"Why would you even want to be?" she says.

"I'm not sure. It just feels as if everything's so final, and why? Why does it need to be? And why can't we," I say, "when everyone else does?"

"I don't. Unless of course it literally meant nothing to me, in which case it's just a nicer way to say good-bye, you know, less abrupt. Come to think of it, you might be the only real friend I have."

"As it should be," I say.

"Yeah, and you never even pay attention," she says. "But whatever. How's the kid?"

"She's fast becoming a geek like me," I say, "straight As."

"You're not a geek."

"I am," I say. "Could you hand me that?"

Next, she's reaching across the counter, and as she does, I notice her grip, her hands—they're not as small as mine. Then her hair, that tuck, and not just the color but every shade and how it's lighter here and not there. Those things. So maybe I haven't been paying attention to her. Maybe, too, it's not just her but with everything else, as well.

"Did I tell you Aline had her cleaning the entire house?" I say. "After school. It's like I've landed a new maid service."

"You really can be so naive about certain things," she says, glaring while slicing lime.

"She's not a bad person," I say.

"She's bad for you."

"She blames me," I say.

"Let her," she says. "And for the record, when I said you needed to communicate, I meant more along the lines of a business arrangement." I pour, and I nearly overflow her glass to the point that she needs to lean in to take a sip before lifting it from the counter—licking that taste of salt off her lips. "So this is like, what, six hundred calories, something like that."

"Since when do you care?" I say. "You burn at least a trillion out on the field."

"Well, I finally have abs," she says. And, right, who hasn't noticed, even as she drowns in that threadbare T-shirt.

"Well, I made this healthy for you," I say.

"Don't lie to me."

"It's all fruit. Come on, why am I even engaging you? Let's not care about anything at all for this one incredibly well-deserved evening of debauchery. It's just me and you and Jose."

"To your shot of Cuervo."

"Double," I say. "And to my new jeans."

"Yeah," she says, "to those jeans."

"And your beautiful obsession," I say.

"She's not my obsession," Andi says.

"I think she is."

"I'm not that interested."

"Lies," I say. "Would you look at that smile? *Not interested* means you haven't climbed a balcony to serenade her yet."

"You act as if I do this all the time."

"You don't," I say. "So tell me about this girl."

"I don't have enough energy to analyze what this is or isn't," she says. "It's not that sort of thing. We have a good time."

"A good time could be defined in so many ways," I say. "And for the record, I'm not analyzing you."

"Remember when we did this every weekend?"

"God, through Jordan's terrible twos," I say.

"And through your many arguments," she says.

"That was Aline," I say.

"I seem to recall you started a few."

"And it was that silent type of arguing she did."

"The worst kind," she says.

"But then we made up," I say as she makes her way across the room, catches my gaze, lifts a brow. "What are you afraid of?"

"With this girl?" she says. "Everything. She's out of my league."

"Is she straight?" I say.

"I don't think so. You can tell, you know? She's just young."

"How young?" I say.

"Too young," Andi says.

"You're worrying me."

"No, just twelve years," she says.

"All right, thus explaining your preoccupation with abs all of a sudden."

"Here you go again, analyzing me," she says.

"I'm just observant, that's all. And go ahead and text her already."

"That can wait."

"Why?" I say.

"Because," she says, "I'm with you."

"When has that ever stopped you?" I say.

"Who wants to seem eager?"

"Eager?" I say. "It's just courteous."

"You've spent too many years in the comforts of marriage to think you can dish out dating advice. And at the same time, you don't take my advice when I try to drag you out for a few drinks as opposed to traipsing along with Aline down memory lane," she says.

"Why?" I say. "So I could bump into Rae? How not eager of me."

"And by the way, I happen to know exactly what I'm doing," she says.

"So what movie did you see?"

"It's an A24 film. You wouldn't like it."

"I don't mind those," I say. But then her phone's vibrating again. "I just need to be in the mood, that's all."

Andi, reading her screen, lifting her glass as she does. "You're not bad for an amateur," she says.

"Bartender, you mean?"

"Yes," she says.

"It's a rather expensive blender."

"No, it's you," she says lifting her gaze, slipping her phone across the counter. "So how long do you plan on keeping this up?"

"Keeping what up?"

"Keeping up this charade," she says.

"What charade would that be?"

"Listen, I can tell when you're happy and when it's all just a farce. And this *you* is far from sincere."

"I don't know, Andi. Maybe you just shouldn't bring it up," I say. "That's all."

"What'd I do now?"

"Rae and pool."

"So, what, would you rather I never mentioned her again?"

"I didn't mean that." Sigh. "Long story."

"It sounds like a convoluted mess, if you ask me. Maybe you need to call her out on this," she says while pulling at her sleeves. And only now do I notice that pinkie ring. But I won't ask.

"So she asked about me?" I say.

"Would you like me to give her a message the next time I'm out?"

"With your new girl?" I say.

"If you two would like to go back and forth through me, I'm perfectly fine to play messenger," she says. "And why are we standing here when you have a table?"

"No clue," I say.

"What's so funny?"

"Nothing. I just thought about something, that's all."

"What about?"

"The table. It's nothing."

"So here's our rule for tonight: you have to tell me exactly what you're thinking," she says, "the moment I ask. And I'm asking."

"You are kidding me," I say.

"I'm ruining abs for you tonight," she says.

"Chopin," I say.

"Okay, rule number two," she says, "don't be cryptic."

"Was I? But you're so sick of hearing about her."

"So it's Rae again?" she says. "And what's the absolute worst that could happen?"

"She could say it's over."

"She already did."

"Maybe I'm pretending it's not," I say, "like I have another chance if I wait, if I give her space."

"Wait for what?"

"I don't know. Things are different now. I have the kid every day," I say. "And why should I apologize for that?"

"I never said you should."

"Have you ever kept something," I say, "like, from an ex. I mean, after."

"What," she says, "like some shirt?"

"Yeah," I say. "Like that."

"Sure."

"Do you ever wear it?" I say.

"Do I wear it?"

"Yeah," I say, "like, have you ever worn it afterward?"

"No."

"Then why do you keep it?"

"I don't know," she says, "sentimental reasons. I guess."

As she checks her phone, shakes her head. And that grin is simply devastating. "First thing on your mind," I say.

"Don't," she says.

"Your rule," I say.

"Game over."

"But we tell each other everything," I say. "I tell you everything."

"No, you don't," she says.

"You are so in love with this girl," I say.

"We just met."

"Yeah?" I say.

"Yeah," she says, smitten.

"Oh my God, you're so cute," I say. "I think we need another round."

"If we do," she says, "you'll need to hide my phone from me."

By Monday, Powell's back at the office with his loud voice, carrying plan tubes, when Kristen steps into my office, seals the door behind her back facing me, then makes her way around to my side of the desk. She leans across, pointing at mock-ups on her iPad, and she's asking for advice. Or maybe I'm to make a decision. When all I want is lunch.

"I haven't eaten. Have you?" I say.

And let me pause right here to say, I'm thinking about giving it back just so I'm not tempted to spray it on, again. Because I did again. I just don't know how yet. I've thought about maybe a text. But then I'll see her, and could I handle that? She must know it's missing. She wore it every day. And there must be a reason, too, why she hasn't called to ask for it back.

But we're walking past cyclists now who clip my stride, and I bump some woman's handbag. Then everything is drowned in the squeal of brakes as we dodge accordion doors that open to the city bus.

But I'm less focused on crowds once we hit Archipelago and more on our host, who escorts us, and soon enough, here's that table I had with Rae, and it's empty as he wipes it dry.

"We can wait," I say, standing by as they stack plates, clear silverware, wipe it down. "I'd like this table, if that's okay?"

And once it's clear, she takes a seat and I slide in to review more proofs.

"The Pearson account," she says, "with this overlaid across the entire front side. Something clean, simple. Maybe put one mailer out four times a year." And this leads to budget approval, and she's leaning in, asking, charming in that sorority way. "You know the best part," she says, "is that we're way under budget."

I motion for the waiter, ordering as we carry on with more pleasantries. Her tomatoes. Jordan. And as our plates arrive, I'm still learning the delicacies of aioli vs. mayonnaise and how they're not the same.

But after lunch, as we make our way back to the office, amused, relating, connecting with one another, having forgotten the pains of my day, comes the constant weight of missing Rae.

CHAPTER TWENTY-SEVEN

Spinning

Rae

Avery's singing along to the twang they've piped in overhead, occasionally interrupting herself with more goings on to our *mm-hmms*, and all I can say is, seriously, how much caffeine has this girl had? To the contrary, I'm going for something more along the lines of reserved as I make my way to the cramped ticket counter and hand the guy my stub.

Then, once I get through that line, I say, "God, this is so small town, hay ride, petting zoo."

"How is it you've never even been to a county fair?" Avery's saying, skimming hips through the tight turnstile as she reaches back to take Erin's hand.

"Because I was waiting for you to de-virginize me," I say.

And soon we're filing into a family crowd to the tune of *boom-chick-chick* with the weight of my arm at her shoulder. Enjoying the calm breeze paired with the warmth of mid-autumn as I peruse lights strung above and overhead. Scanning boots and Levi's. Eavesdropping as we tread on the heels of girls, fresh-faced and high-schoolish, in that floral scent of some nondescript body spray they all douse themselves in.

We skirt their grandstand, their sports bar, their string of ATMs before ducking under the cool shade of a canvas awning.

"I love you for coming today," she says, too animated with that mad hair flowing like the wind as she shouts for fried dough.

"You'd love me regardless," I say. Ordering, "Diet Coke, please," as I reach for my back pocket.

And I guess this place does have its airs of corncob Americana—crisp and luminescent in every misty color of the rainbow as if prepping for that season finale we've all been waiting up for.

Waiting while smashed, that is, between some dude's elbow and Avery's gigantic bust when I'm handed a waxed cup that chimes with ice, only to get full-on body slammed. "Jordan?" I say, dumbfounded. "Hey, kid." I can't exactly say *What the fuck?* "You could maybe try to not...suffocate me," I add, squeezing through the line, then shifting her little lovefest out of harm's way. "What on earth are you doing here?"

"What are *you* doing here?" she says.

"Me?" I say, scanning the crowd.

"Yeah, you."

"Food."

"You don't have food," she says.

"No, really, how'd you get here?"

"How else?" she says.

"So you're with those two?" I say, perusing the unfamiliars, the not-Madisens.

She nods, and I'm thinking why am I suddenly getting that heart-skipping *All eyes are on me* vibe? "My friends are over there," she says with that whole adolescent shrug thing.

"Friends," I say, glancing, "as in that one girl plus how many other guys?" Which makes her blush, and that amuses me, so I laugh. Though she does not. "They're cute," I say.

"Look..." she says.

"What?"

"Come talk with Belle-mère."

And *um*. "Why would I do that?"

"Why not?"

"Did she send you over?" I say.

"No."

Okay then, "Listen, we sort of..." *Had a falling out*, I begin to say.

But as opposed to hanging out and maybe continuing our little heart-to-heart, the kid opts to drag me clear across the fairgrounds between beers in clear cups and mom jeans and carnies until I'm face-to-face with...

Mercy.

And not just Madisen but, holy shit, who's shoving me so hard into her, and I'm sorry, where was I going with this?

I was going to blurt out something I shouldn't, that's what. But instead, I'm apologizing and, I guess, wondering what she's thinking. Wondering what I'm thinking. But it all hits with such a rush that I can't think aside from *God, she looks incredible*. Not that I say that, of course, I don't. But she does.

And soon enough, my lips are finding my straw, and I'm glancing up at sunlit features. Catching her flashing glance.

Until Aline bends into view to fix, I don't know, something. And I guess I hadn't noticed her there.

So taking a step back, I give her some sort of *Sorry to intrude* thing and maybe something's said between the two of us. I don't know. But I'm realizing gradually that perhaps I maybe shouldn't be here.

Maybe, but the kid's going on about something, this shirt, her oversized hoping-to-be-grunge attempt at owning the legacy of Kurt Cobain.

"Since when did you start listening to Nirvana?" I say.

"Since someone else did," Madisen's saying, gesturing—and just her voice takes me someplace else, takes me back, since I guess I'd forgotten it. Since maybe I had to. Since maybe that's easier.

So I'm watching her. Flustered, slipping a hand down the back of my neck. As she settles on me—blank, I guess.

No, not blank. What is it?

But Aline decides to break in to our little moment again with, "Right over there, who she's hoping to impress," as if I could pin some unknown someone out of a crowd of hundreds.

And since I can't, I settle back, hoping I don't look like a fool, though I know I do. But at any rate, "It's great seeing you again," I say, resigned, "and really, really sorry about this."

Amid our clenched and forced conversations as those two exchange glances and I catch myself, transfixed. The whole time I'm hoping to find a suitable way of saying nothing at all. As I gaze down at her hands talking, stroking an arm as if she was cold, but it's not cold. How those fingers brush her lips while she leans in—close, in an all too familiar way.

"Please stay," I hear her say.

But they step away. And I take a drink. I study her walk. Their miles apart and that Ferris wheel, their nudge, a nod, their low-key, my view pinched between pedestrians. My heart racing. My stomach sinking. Thinking why am I here?

And wouldn't it be easier, safer, to vanish unnoticed.

Slip away. Find an exit. Find my car.

But before this clicks, they're parting ways. And Madisen's making her way back—at her pace—unrushed, slow, rhythmic.

Until we're somehow alone. Alone.

And I'm wishing I could set this place aside, the busyness, our requisite social graces, my trepidation. When I catch her peeking at me.

"I hadn't expected to see you," I say with a smile, then ducking glare as a casual strand of hair crosses her lips and I want to fix it.

"You almost didn't," she says. And you would think that after all this time I'd have something better to say. But I don't. "It's just half day for me. It's her weekend, not mine."

"Then why are you here?" I say.

"Long story," she says.

"No, tell me."

"This isn't exactly your thing," she says. "Is it?"

Leaning in, glancing at me and those eyes. And what if I am reading into this? I could be. I do that. I have. But something is telling me I'm not. Reading into it, that is. "So what are you saying?" And I'm thinking *I've missed you.*

"I'm just surprised," she says, "that's all."

"To see me?" I say.

"Yes," she says.

"So that door's closed?" I say with a nod to Aline.

"Do you want it to be?" she says.

"I do," I say.

And she laughs.

"What?"

"Don't be silly," she says.

"No?"

"Yes," she says, "it's closed."

"Then I have to ask…"

"What?" she says.

"Is this one?"

"Closed?" she says.

"Yeah," I say.

"What would you like me to say?"

"That you're glad to see me," I say.

And glancing everywhere but here, she says, "I'm glad to see you."

"Are you?" I say.

"Yes," she says.

"You realize rain was in the forecast," I say. "You would've been drenched in that."

"I brought my umbrella," she says.

"That's unfortunate," I say.

Next, she's carrying on about, "That's the name of the place. And there's this pretty little beach and margaritas and sixty degrees—"

So I cut her off with, "Madisen," as her eyes search mine—for what? "What are you doing? Because you didn't keep me here for a weather report, I hope."

And that smile, it's all I need. So we walk.

"Could I buy you lunch?" I say.

And she says, "Sure," as we settle into some sort of what-do-I-say-next thing. Her sliding that straw through the lid of her cup, and it squeaks but not in an obvious way, just unexpected. Playful. When all I can do is focus on that *D* drawn on it in grease pencil. Her lips sucking more of its air than anything else.

And then she starts in about some boy.

"With who?" I say, "Jordan? So she's straight?"

"Officially," she says. "She just came out."

"She came out?" I say with a laugh thinking *missing you* is an understatement.

"I believe *Bell-mère, I'm sorry...I like pink and don't like girls* were her exact words." Before she's gazing off, and when she does, I'm just lost in this. I'm lost in her.

"The first of many disappointments," I say. As she glances at me as if to say...I don't know. Before leaning to toss her cup. "Would you like another?" I say.

But she shakes her head, settles in, brushes against my arm. And that's when I remember—Avery. Who's waiting.

Thumbing my phone, fretting, sensing Madisen watching as I do, as if I was a puzzle she was trying to piece together. And that's flooding me with another rush of nerves.

And then, "You do this thing," she's saying as I step to the edge of foot traffic.

And I glance up. "What thing?"

"That thing," I hear. Texting back: *Give me ten.* Her gaze still fixed on me. I can sense it. "When you're thinking...not always."

"About what?" I ask.

"I wouldn't know," she says.

"Wouldn't you?"

"I like it," she mouths and her gaze sinks to my lips and mine to hers.

Interrupted by...

Avery: *I won a teddy bear.*

Me, amused: *Congratulations.*

And I blurt out, "I almost called you." And this is so hard, the saying of it. The stalling and stalling, since how can I put any of this into words when they have no meaning. When they're not enough. "God, you look incredible."

And she says, "So do you." And when her hand brushes mine, I catch it, hold it. As I mirror her cheesy grin and we stroll again in our silence.

Until my phone goes off.

And she says: "Avery?"

And I say, "Yes." Thumbing.

"What'd she say?"

And I shrug. "Nothing."

"Something," I hear.

"And you really want to know?" As my gaze lingers a little while. And even still. She's doing that thing with her lips again. "She told me," I say, "to kiss you."

"And you said?"

"That I'd love to."

But it's one of those things just beyond reach. Like the way you taste sugar from that puff of cotton candy still hopeful it won't melt, won't liquefy, like that. It's sweet and you try and she's everything and exhausting. But you're the one who melts. Regardless.

"And when do you figure this out?" she says, after *that* kind of a kiss.

"And what's that?" I say as my palm's finding its way down the curve of her back.

"That you're the absolute end for me."

"You think?" I say.

And it dawns on me that there's no sound to hear—no cords no beats no pulse outside my own, in all of the song's upheaval. In all of her honeyed and candied and sublime. With this dusted turquoise sky. The sluggish spin of a wheel. Miles and miles of air-whipped laughter.

Our silence.

As I slip my hand in hers and sink into her gaze and she lingers on mine and I draw her in and say, "Maybe I was hoping for something else."

"What were you hoping for?" she says.

"Well, not to be an end," I say. "Why are you making me want forever?"

CHAPTER TWENTY-EIGHT

Forever

Madisen

While unpacking grocery bags and putting it all away, I'm thinking about those oblong shadows, distorted, now sneaking up my wall—as I contemplate forever. Because what does that even mean, *forever*?

Still it's all she had to say, the only word I heard, after which I remember thinking, she's smiling at me. She's smiling and what do I do? What am I supposed to do now? Say something, that's right. I'm supposed to say…*what*? I didn't know what to say.

So what did I say?

I think I might've said, *I love you*. That's all, because what else could I say? I *love* you. Glancing at her, and she was smiling again. She was smiling and that meant I was okay. And then I felt her lips near mine, and well, it's as if I needed her arms to hold me there so I could find some semblance of stable ground, because stability seemed to have slipped out from under me. My mind slipped out as well.

Because how could she say that, forever. There's some part of me, still, that doesn't believe it. Since all we really have is now. Isn't that what she said? Here, with that imperfect smile, her laughing irrepressibly, her dry voice in the morning because we won't sleep tonight, will we? And her meaningless messages I read on my phone throughout my day. The notes that keep me going. That's all she can give me.

And maybe I like not knowing what's next.

As this unstable song fades into the next, and I hear her keys jingle and turn to open the door in the living room, that tight bolt twisting then closing behind her as she lets herself in. Those creaks down the hall.

And suddenly, it's as if her being here makes everything seem sweet and simple and fine.

Yet unsettling still.

Me, flustered the moment I realize she's here beside me, and closer still, until our arms are touching, and what was I doing?

What am I doing?

I was doing something. Hoping to slice a few last-minute berries, some potatoes in no particular order. But now I feel jumbled. Hurried, unnerved, unraveled, petrified. My heart rushing. As if she and I were back along that trail with the sun on our backs warming my skin, flushed as we reached the peak. As her fingers slipped and weaved through mine, her arms subtle around my waist, holding me back, my toes braced at the ledge of a cliff that felt so high, dizzying. I felt high. It felt unstoppable, rushed. Out of control. I could slip at any moment. Fall. Or maybe I already had fallen. Where were the warning signs? Where were the cautions that whispered to me, *You've gone too far.*

As I scrape ends, stems into the compost bin, then back to the water rushing down my hands at the sink, while she's telling me about someone. I don't know. That tree swaying outside and its kaleidoscope of leaves swirling past, nearly indiscernible now.

And I could shut the blind, but I don't.

I could skip this song, as well. But I don't do that either. I remember she played it the night we met, driving me back to my car as the wind blew in, but I didn't care. She was lip synching. She was breathtaking as her thigh flexed to press the brake, block after block, with headlights shifting along her face.

I like the way she thinks.

Not only that, I like the way she *looks* when she thinks and that air that she has, how she'll gaze off mindfully at—what? I never really know. Just some thoughts, I guess, as if thoughts were tangible objects shifting or splintering off—one into the other, into the next—while she tries to figure it out or piece it all together. She's doing that now.

And I like the way, in the midst of all this, in the midst of her thoughts, her figuring it out, she'll settle on the only thing she can't fix or understand or pin down or wrap her head around. Or let go.

Then glance across the room at me. As if I could.

And how that makes me feel—brilliant and helpless and hopelessly inept at life.

Like this. Rae sitting at the edge of the dining room chair pressing palms against one another before they're squeezed between lean thighs, and she's grinning up past lashes in that way she does.

A gaze that triggers such a rush. Such amnesia.

Wondering if I've ever felt this much, this wanted or heard, needed.

Needed for sex, sure. Or for company. For someone to bring along, to brag about, to show off. To take out or take home. To hold this, while they went over there. To appreciate intermittently. To look at from afar. To kiss before rolling over. To pay the bills.

But not like this. Not for me.

Not this intimately.

"So what would this be?" she's asking. But she's leaning in now, and I'm too nervous.

"Just nothing," I say.

"You're something," she says. "Will I like it?"

"I hope so," I say.

But she's smiling at me. "I know so."

About the Author

C. Spencer grew up in Southern California during the '70s and '80s, where she spent two years as an art major in college only to switch midway to English literature. She's worked as a copywriter and editor since 2001. In 2013, she began writing fiction on the side. She and her wife currently reside in Western Massachusetts.

Books Available From Bold Strokes Books

Brooklyn Summer by Maggie Cummings. When opposites attract, can a summer of passion and adventure lead to a lifetime of love? (978-1-63555-578-3)

City Kitty and Country Mouse by Alyssa Linn Palmer. Pulled in two different directions, can a city kitty and a country mouse fall in love and make it work? (978-1-63555-553-0)

Elimination by Jackie D. When a dangerous homegrown terrorist seeks refuge with the Russian mafia, the team will be put to the ultimate test. (978-1-63555-570-7)

In the Shadow of Darkness by Nicole Stillng. Angeline Vallencourt is a reluctant vampire who must decide what she wants more—obscurity, revenge, or the woman who makes her feel alive. (978-1-63555-624-7)

On Second Thought by C. Spencer. Madisen is falling hard for Rae. Even single life and co-parenting are beginning to click. At least, that is, until her ex-wife begins to have second thoughts. (978-1-63555-415-1)

Out of Practice by Carsen Taite. When attorney Abby Keane discovers the wedding blogger tormenting her client is the woman she had a passionate, anonymous vacation fling with, sparks and subpoenas fly. Legal Affairs: one law firm, three best friends, three chances to fall in love. (978-1-63555-359-8)

Providence by Leigh Hays. With every click of the shutter, photographer Rebekiah Kearns finds it harder and harder to keep Lindsey Blackwell in focus without getting too close. (978-1-63555-620-9)

Taking a Shot at Love by KC Richardson. When academic and athletic worlds collide, will English professor Celeste Bouchard and basketball coach Lisa Tobias ignore their attraction to achieve their professional goals? (978-1-63555-549-3)

Flight to the Horizon by Julie Tizard. Airline captain Kerri Sullivan and flight attendant Janine Case struggle to survive an emergency water landing and overcome dark secrets to give love a chance to fly. (978-1-63555-331-4)

In Helen's Hands by Nanisi Barrett D'Arnuk. As her mistress, Helen pushes Mickey to her sensual limits, delivering the pleasure only a BDSM lifestyle can provide her. (978-1-63555-639-1)

Jamis Bachman, Ghost Hunter by Jen Jensen. In Sage Creek, Utah, a poltergeist stirs to life and past secrets emerge. (978-1-63555-605-6)

Moon Shadow by Suzie Clarke. Add betrayal, season with survival, then serve revenge smokin' hot with a sharp knife. (978-1-63555-584-4)

Spellbound by Jean Copeland and Jackie D. When the supernatural worlds of good and evil face off, love might be what saves them all. (978-1-63555-564-6)

Temptation by Kris Bryant. Can experienced nanny Cassie Miller deny her growing attraction and keep her relationship with her boss professional? Or will they sidestep propriety and give in to temptation? (978-1-63555-508-0)

The Inheritance by Ali Vali. Family ties bring Tucker Delacroix and Willow Vernon together, but they could also tear them, and any chance they have at love, apart. (978-1-63555-303-1)

Thief of the Heart by MJ Williamz. Kit Hanson makes a living seducing rich women in casinos and relieving them of the expensive jewelry most won't even miss. But her streak ends when she meets beautiful FBI agent Savannah Brown. (978-1-63555-572-1)

Face Off by PJ Trebelhorn. Hockey player Savannah Wells rarely spends more than a night with any one woman, but when photographer Madison Scott buys the house next door, she's forced to rethink what she expects out of life. (978-1-63555-480-9)

Hot Ice by Aurora Rey, Elle Spencer, and Erin Zak. Can falling in love melt the hearts of the iciest ice queens? Join Aurora Rey, Elle Spencer, and Erin Zak to find out! A contemporary romance novella collection. (978-1-63555-513-4)

Line of Duty by VK Powell. Dr. Dylan Carlyle's professional and personal life is turned upside down when a tragic event at Fairview Station pits her against ambitious, handsome police officer Finley Masters. ((978-1-63555-486-1)

London Undone by Nan Higgins. London Craft reinvents her life after reading a childhood letter to her future self and, in doing so, finds the love she truly wants. (978-1-63555-562-2)

Lunar Eclipse by Gun Brooke. Moon De Cruz lives alone on an uninhabited planet after being shipwrecked in space. Her life changes forever when Captain Beaux Lestarion's arrival threatens the planet and Moon's freedom. (978-1-63555-460-1)

One Small Step by MA Binfield. In this contemporary romance, Iris and Cam discover the meaning of taking chances and following your heart, even if it means getting hurt. (978-1-63555-596-7)

Shadows of a Dream by Nicole Disney. Rainn has the talent to take her rock band all the way, but falling in love is a powerful distraction, and her new girlfriend's meth addiction might just take them both down. 978-1-63555-598-1)

Someone to Love by Jenny Frame. When Davina Trent is given an unexpected family, can she let nanny Wendy Darling teach her to open her heart to the children and to Wendy? (978-1-63555-468-7)

Uncharted by Robyn Nyx. As Rayne Marcellus and Chase Stinsen track the legendary Golden Trinity, they must learn to put their differences aside and depend on one another to survive. (978-1-63555-325-3)

Where We Are by Annie McDonald. A sensual account of two women who discover a way to walk on the same path together with the help of an Indigenous tale, a Canadian art movement, and the mysterious appearance of dimes. (978-1-63555-581-3)